Dedicated to my two favorite exes in the world—
my ex-husbands—
S. P. Santospirito and Eric Hewitson.

TYNE O'CONNELL

was born in Australia holding a glass of champagne, wearing six-inch heels and reading Nancy Mitford. Educated by Catholic nuns in the arts of deportment, elocution, feminism and charm, she spent several years traveling the world as a professional gambler before trading in her dice for a laptop and settling in the U.K. She has previously written five novels for Headline Review, features for U.K. newspapers and magazines— including *Elle, Vogue* and *Marie Claire*—and she spent two years in L.A. as a sitcom writer. Tyne also writes young-adult fiction.

Having misplaced two husbands, Tyne now prefers to live alone with her laptop, Nancy. When not having heated debates with Nancy in their cramped flat in Mayfair, the two divide their time between New York and Los Angeles.

tyne o'connell

SEX
with the
EX

**RED
DRESS
INK**
™

JUN 21 2006

First edition October 2005

SEX WITH THE EX

A Red Dress Ink novel

ISBN 0-373-89536-4

www.RedDressInk.com

Printed in U.S.A.

ACKNOWLEDGMENTS

Air Kisses to London, the city that never stops talking,
drinking and inspiring. It may piss with rain, the public
transport system may be shambolic, it may cost a
mortgage for an evening out, but it's always worth it
because nowhere else does idiosyncratic eccentricity
flourish with such abandon. London; with your cobbled
streets, your stately architecture and your impeccable
ability to queue orderly and patiently in the rain
for a bus that never comes—You Rock!

And then, of course, there is Home House,
my inspiration for Posh House—a private members' club
within a private members' club where history and charm
seep from every chandelier, floorboard,
portrait, antique and member.

Big Kiss to one specific Londoner, the embodiment of
all that is the best of London, the Charm-Encrusted
Niki de Metz. As a single girl in this city where there are
far too many potential exes, I must pay homage to the
following people who make sure I not only survive but
thrive! People like Malcolm Young and Gaetano Speranza
for being preternaturally bright, handsome and owning
pugs and Robin Dutt, for being from another
century where scandalous women like me
were celebrated rather than chastised.

Last, though far, far, far from least,
low bows to the women who get me
and get the best from me, to Laura Dail,
an agent of genius. Margaret O'Neill Marbury,
Keyren Gerlach and RDI—a publishing house so
teeming with talent it humbles me to be on the list!
And then there's my lovely Nick at Eden PR for being
implausibly handsome as well as brilliant.

EX: Greek ex = out (of), as exodus, exorcism. Used as a freely productive prefix forming nouns from titles of office; status etc., with the sense "formally" as in ex-convict, ex-husband, ex-boyfriend.

X: A diagonal cross, used to mark incorrectness, also used to mark on a map a location that is no longer there.

Passion: *noun.* Old and modern French from Christian Latin *pass* = suffer, as in suffering of martyrs, a painful disorder or affliction, an overwhelming barely controllable emotion, a strong sexual feeling, an aim or object pursued with uncontrollable, frequently irrational enthusiasm.

Posh: *adj.; verb & adverb.* Colloquial, origins unknown: smartly dressed, stylish, genteel; affecting to be socially superior. An upper-class manner of behavior; talking and dressing. Often used ironically.

one

Posche House stood majestically at the very epicenter of late-eighteenth-century aristocratic London life. As a hostess, Lady Posche was unrivaled, the power she wielded is impossible to imagine by today's standards.

She was the hostess extraordinaire.

It would be accurate to say that she set the standard. To be on her guest list was to be fashionable. To be excluded from a ball or an important event at Posche House was to be marked out as unfashionable.

Like moths to a flame the aristocracy of fashionable London was drawn to these parties by the reputation of its notorious hostess, Lady Posche, as much as by the bohemian entertainments provided.

It was not uncommon for ladies of a certain standing to lie about being left off the guest list of Posche

House, declaring later to friends that they had been
unable to attend due to illness. The idea that these
ladies wouldn't have dragged themselves from the
jaws of death to appear at Posche House was
ludicrous, and as a consequence, their lies only left
them open to further ridicule and derision.

Secret Passage to the Past:
A Biography of Lady Henriette Posche
By Michael Carpendum

Epiphanies are funny things in that you never have any warning that one is on the way. I was standing in my sybaritic place of work; the grand, chandeliered, marble-pillared drawing room of London's most desirably elitist private members' club, observing London's young partying aristopack when my epiphany came.

Everything and everyone around me was unremarkable, from the ineffably trendy public-school boys and girls of the day with their loud, drunk, posh drawls, hyphenated surnames and titles, to the incestuous hubs of celebrities with their sense of entitlement and innate mistrust of People Not Like Us. Even the stray gay twentysomething millionaire with the diamond stud in his tooth who was now swaying recklessly into the private party was well within the realm of a normal evening at work.

I spoke into my mouthpiece to alert security regarding our stray. He was a member of the club though not part of this private party, who after a few lines of coke could become obstreperous. But then into every social situation a little drama must fall. My job was to minimize its effect and more importantly ensure no one really important witnessed it.

"Security to Tuscany Room, please."

Security, dressed in their trendy loose-fitting Armani suits and black T-shirts arrived almost immediately, although not in time to prevent our stray grabbing an It Girl's famous D-cups and declaring loudly, "Fuck, these are real!"

The girl concerned, Lady Tarmilla (who was rumored to have had a fling with both William and Harry), thankfully took the grope in good part and laughed as if the invasion of her personal space was a compliment she was delighted to have visited on her. Just the same I would have to write an incident report in the event that she changed her feelings, in the regrets of an alcohol-free morning, about having her D-cups groped and decided to make a complaint. I also made a mental note to check just how many incident reports I'd had to write about our diamond-toothed wannabe pop star recently.

Drugs were strictly forbidden at Posh House, but like any exclusive London club, it was impossible to hermetically seal ourselves from the winds from Colombia *all* the time. Our no-tolerance policy was strongly enforced. For a start there was a total lack of flat surfaces in the loo (everything sloped like an *Alice in Wonderland* set). We'd even recently installed a CCTV camera in the toilet to observe people going into the cubicles together in the event our lavatory attendant was on a break. But the occasional incident was to be expected in a club like Posh House where the members, by nature, felt entitled to misbehave. In fact, a sense of entitlement generally was pretty much a prerequisite for membership here.

I observed the eligible men, and not-so-eligible men, as they laughed their easy rich-person's laughs and sipped their expensive champagne. They were a good-looking crowd, but then they always were here. A few of the celebs I knew relatively well had approached me during the course of the evening; a few of the male celebs had flirted and I had politely flirted back. In my job, flirtation is as essential as organization. For the most part, though, these men were accompanied (in the loosest sense of the word) by the usual girls that go hand in hand with these sort of men and these sorts of events; girls with long blond hair, rake-thin bodies, posh drawls and haw-haw laughter.

I wasn't here for eligible men, though. The only thing I was thinking about was how much longer before I could knock off and join my girlfriends at the Met Bar for a cocktail. The truth is I'm not really looking for an eligible man to make mine because, you see, while boyfriends are nice and I've had my share—I was even married once—finding a man to share my life with is not my raison d'être. In fact, I'd even read an article that day defining a new sort of single girl— "the quirky single," which sounded very me. I ticked all five of the qualifying boxes.

* Fulfilling career—tick.
* Strong rewarding friendships—numerous.
* Varied social life! Well, I work in PR—how varied and social is that?

* Financially independent—perfectly adequate thank
  you.
* Sexually fulfilled serial monogamist—that's me.

Now, if I'd been one of those girls longing for Mr. Right
or even Mr. Good Enough, I'd have been talent spotting at
that moment. I'd have been flirting seriously. I'd have seen
this or any gathering of attractive men as a potential chance
to bag My Man. But I wasn't doing anything as late twenti-
eth century and tragic as that. No, no, no. Actually, I was
perving on couples and trying to ascertain the depth of
their love for one another.

Okay, so I'm a different sort of pathetic.

My mother—she insists I call her Kitty—thinks I'm tragic
because I am happy in my career and even happier to just
let my love life, or occasional lack of a love life, jog along.
And for someone with the romantic soul of Kitty, this is
tantamount to being soulless.

I'm not just happy in my career—as in I don't *mind*
going into work—I actually love what I do. As PR for
London's achingly trendy private members' club Posh
House, I live a life other girls my age (just over thirty)
lust after.

I love the hours (dusk till dawn).

I love the world (glamorous and exciting).

The people (the aristo-pack, the rock/pop-ocracy, the
media-ocracy, the literati, the glitterati, etc).

I love the attitude (party till you drop…or flop).

Most of all, I love the whole chaotic craziness of it all.
It's like being in the eye of the zeitgeist storm.

To Kitty this is a heinous crime she'd like to see me hung
for. She has a different sense of justice than the rest of the
world. She thinks I'm even more tragic for referring to my

job as a "career." In fact, the very word *career* is liable to set her off on one.

"You're tragic, the way you bang on about this wretched job of yours as if it is an elixir." When Kitty says the word *job* she manages to make it sound like something really sordid. "Lola! Where is your passion? Your lust for life? Sometimes I can't believe you're the fruit of my loins. Where is the fire in your heart?"

As she says these things, she'll be draped across her chaise longue, her perfectly blond hair swept in a gravity-defying chignon, her makeup impeccable. She always looks as if she's just stepped out from the pages of *Vogue* circa 1960.

Unlike me, with my long dark brown tresses that take forever to make Jennifer-Aniston-straight, Kitty doesn't have bad-hair days. Her hair obeys the way Kitty wishes the rest of us would. Kitty knows how to set a scene. She used to smoke cocktail cigarettes, but since being diagnosed with "lines" she's given up. Now she uses a Nicorette cigarette holder, alternately sucking and waving it about as Chopin tinkers away in the background, and she opines, "You're like a character from some ghastly Jane Austen novel."

And she doesn't mean the main protagonist either; she means one of the spinsters who have no life apart from needlepoint. The women who have no love interests of their own and spend their time eagerly awaiting gossip about the Girls Who Matter. Girls Who Matter being the ones with a romantic soul—and a man.

"I'm warning you, Lola, you'll end up like your aunt Camilla!"

Aunt Camilla, now ninetysomething, never married and as a result she's always being wheeled out—literally, as she's been confined to a wheelchair since her stroke last year—at family gatherings. Kitty points to her with a blood-red nail and declares in her more-elitist-than-thou made-for-the-West-End-stage tones, "This is how you'll end up, Lola! Passionless! Shriveled! Empty! Unwanted and alone! Is that what you want? Is it?"

I suppose it can't be much fun for Aunt Camilla, given that she's not deaf, but Kitty's not the sort of person you engage in an argument. Aunt Camilla just gives me a wink and I give her one back—as if we are two heroic women fighting a common enemy…love.

I despair of going down to see my parents because that's all we ever talk about. My lack of romantic passion. That is to say, it's all Kitty ever talks about, because I don't get a word in edgeways and my father, Martin, is too busy fussing about with his antique French clock collection. He discovered this latest hobby after his fifth honeymoon with my mother. That's right, they divorced and remarried one another four times, all before my eighteenth birthday. "Now, *that's* passion," as my mother delights in pointing out as she and Martin make goo-goo eyes at one another across the drawing room.

My school counselor referred to their relationship as "dangerously dysfunctional, verging on the mentally deranged," but we don't go there. There are lots of places you don't go with Kitty.

Kitty usually has to have a sherry after she's worked herself up into a lather of despair over my love of being an events manager and how it "breaks the very heart that once held me to her bosom."

Yes, she actually talks like that.

I wear her out so.

"Oh, Lola, you wear me out so," she moans, her hand pressed against her weary brow as she summons my father from a chandelier-three-quarter piece so that he can fetch her a sherry. Being a man of great passion, my father lives to pour Kitty's sherry.

I always feel like screaming when I go to visit them in their vast house outside of Richmond, but I instantly soften at the sight of my father in his tatty cardigan, still dashingly handsome at sixty-eight as he rushes to fulfill each and every whim my mother has. He always pats me on the head affectionately and calls me his "lovely Lola."

I love his smile although it rarely rests on me, even when he says "My lovely Lola." His eyes are always on Kitty. She'll usually be wearing mouse-pink chiffon pajamas with marabou trim. Mouse pink is Kitty's favorite color. Bless her.

Martin truly does worship my mother and even though I know he loves me, I can see he frets when I visit and "wear her out so."

We have been in this stalemate since my divorce from Richard, every time I visit; my mother despairing of me, and Martin trying to placate the love of his life with his constant to-ing and fro-ing as he brings in her thimbles of sherry. Having a proper sherry glass, while far more convenient, just wouldn't suit Kitty. She prefers her sherry in a cut-glass crystal thimble.

It seems that it's just me who wears her out. Her heart knows no bounds when it comes to the rest of the world. Apart from parking inspectors—she loathes them. She was up before a magistrate once for setting upon one with a catapult from the attic window.

I guess Kitty has her charms, because the magistrate found her antics the height of hilarity. So many people find Kitty amusing. Even my counselor at school fell victim to her charms when he finally decided we needed a family session. After all his declarations of my parents being "dangerous dys-functionals" he practically drooled over her when she flounced in, all marabou, chiffon, diamonds and fur.

All my life I have worn my mother out. When I was young I wore her out with tales of school. "Oh, Lola, how can you talk of spelling and sums when your mother's heart has been torn apart? Simply torn apart!" Kitty had no hesitation in embroiling me in all her marital to-ings and fro-ings with my father. Even as a child I found her energy for affairs of the heart exhausting. For a woman who rarely leaves her chaise longue she's incredibly energetic when it comes to love.

Kitty thinks I substitute love (or as she refers to it, "passion") for work. I remind her that loads of people envy my job, that magazines have done features on me and my job. *Vogue* declared me "The Queen Bee of London's Party Scene" and I was even voted one of the top one hundred influential people in London by the *Evening Standard*. Okay, so I didn't actually make the top one hundred personally, but my boss did, and I *was* mentioned. My mother would happily swap all my success for a torrid romance, though— preferably with a lot of high drama.

But my job doesn't really allow for high-drama romance. I have to be CCC (Calm, Cool and Collected) all the time. As events manager and PR for Posh House (named with irony after Lady Posche, who once resided there in the eighteenth century and was by all accounts a woman of great passion) I am a one-woman drama-control SWAT team.

Over the past few decades, Posh House has become the haunt of London's IT-erati. As well as doing PR for the club, I am the senior events organizer, responsible for pulling together parties of a lifetime for fashionistas, aristocracy and the über-hip.

Well, that's what it says in the articles.

Vogue, Harpers and their kind have repeatedly described me as number-one choice for organizing "every detail of the most magnificent parties with intelligence, wit, care, flair and imagination, all in the lavish surroundings of London's most exciting and exclusive venue."

Truth? I run around like a deranged woman, impersonating CCC qualities, acting like I live to please and love everyone whilst trying not to have murderous thoughts about pushing irritating members down the magnificent sweeping marble staircase.

But for all its challenges, there's nothing more satisfying than pulling together the scattered threads of a series of disasters and spinning them into a party to remember (for all the right reasons). As part of my job, I not only have to make sure the right guests are at the right parties but I have to *know* these guests. This means after a hard night's work I have to go out till the small hours and meet the people that matter.

In the winter I rarely see daylight. You have to be seen, to be on the scene, to be in the scene—that's PR talk for don't go to bed. But it is true that you have to go to the right events to throw the right events. From the Star Bar at *Top of the Pops* to the opening of the latest club, I'm there. It's my business to know the rock stars, the DJs, the record-company executives, the stylists, the stars, the scene, not to mention the competition.

Officially I only work three days a week at Posh House, but outside of hours I use my celebrity contacts to develop other professional relationships, like with designer labels or department stores. To be successful as a PR in London you either have to be born wealthy or work your arse off, so it helps that I like what I do. It would just be nice if Kitty could be more supportive.

I remind Kitty that romance isn't everything and that many mothers would be proud of my success, but it's like discussing the joys of Top Shop with an Italian heiress who's never shopped outside of Milan. My mother has not worked since marrying my father the first time around—well, apart from small parts in the local theater group. Thanks to her private income (i.e., enormous inheritance), she never had to work. But even her good fortune is seen by her as a personal achievement.

"Life is too short for work, darling. Work is for the lazy, for those who don't dare to dream!"

Kitty wasn't even impressed by my promotion last month.

Then again, I suppose I wasn't exactly overwhelmed myself.

My boss—London's most desirable bachelor, Charlie (Lord Charles Mannox MacField Orbington as he is to Debrett's and the society pages), called me into his plush oak-paneled office for a cordial (that's what he calls champagne) and told me he was changing my title to senior events manager.

I was very excited at first, right up until the point where he explained that, though my position was going to entail far more work and responsibility, he wasn't going to be paying me more money.

"Right ho," I said, already hearing Kitty's taunts in my head.

Then he coughed in his special awkward way and shoved a big black elaborately ribboned YSL carrier bag at me. I took the bag but restrained my furious curiosity, summoning all my CCC qualities as I placed it demurely at my feet, when actually my bra was practically bursting into flames to know of its contents.

"But, erm, you will get your own office sort of affair, obviously," he added.

"Oh well, that's a step up." I nodded agreeably, and it was. Previously I'd had to rely on a mobile phone and the club reception area, but with my mind now firmly on the YSL carrier bag, an office didn't seem such a big deal. I'm nothing if not an easy bribe. I suppose it comes from all the bribes my parents gave me to pass on messages of love or hate to one another when I was growing up.

Charlie was still gabbling. "Actually, more of a cupboard-type affair, really, but there's a phone line and an, erm, well, sort of a chair, a desk thingamee and some sort of filing-cabinet effect going on, if I remember correctly."

"Right ho," I repeated. I always find myself mimicking the madly posh way Charlie talks when I'm with him. Even my pronunciation of *yeah* seems to turn into *yaah* when I'm with him. It's a bit of a nervous tick, really, and I should get to work on it. Right after I've got to work on the implausibly long list of flaws Kitty's constantly pointing out.

"No window, sadly." He looked embarrassed.

"That's a shame."

"But fear not, dearest Lola, as soon as a window becomes available, well, it will be all yours. Top of the list."

"Yaah, I mean, okay, well, fantastic, that is, thanks…I guess. I mean, I'm looking forward to the window when it comes up and all that."

"And as for the phone business, feel free vis-à-vis your extracurricular." He meant my work outside the club—which suited him as much as me because the better connected I was, the better connected the club was.

"Of course." I stood to leave, taking the liberty of peaking inside the big YSL carrier bag, where I spotted this season's much-coveted white YSL flower bag—bag of the season according to *Tatler*—all tucked up nicely in black tissue paper.

I was really touched. "Oh my God, Charlie, this is so cool, I love it!" I exclaimed, pulling it out of its nesting place. I gave him a big cuddle. Charlie's really rather nice to cuddle. I suppose he's quite fit looking in a rosy-cheeked public-school sort of way, and I do think it's adorable the way he's tried to tone his accent down, although when he gets nervous or slightly pissed he can't hide his aristo roots. All my girlfriends adore him, which is a bit embarrassing. They giggle and simper whenever I bring them to the club, which is very, very rarely. There's nothing more tragic than having your girlfriends hiding behind pillars hissing things like, "Here he comes, quick, quick, here he comes now! Isn't he to die for?" every time he comes around a corner.

"The bag? Oh! Well, I thought it might come in handy for Jean, you know for carting her around. You could sort of smuggle her into places that don't allow rabbits and that sort of thing."

When I first got my little black rabbit, Jean Harlot, three years ago, he told me that I could bring her to work with me rather than leave her at home alone.

"No, no, no," he'd insisted. "Can't leave a rabbit home alone, you'll have the EC crawling all over you. Probably breaks a whole legion of animal-rights conventions, leaving little rabbits on their tod. No, bring her in. She'll be company for Cinders." Cinders is Charlie's old black Labrador. She is about six thousand years old in dog years or something.

I jumped at the chance to bring Jean in to work even though I'm fairly sure rabbits get by quite nicely at home alone all over the country, although, actually, Jean is very, well…tactile. Tactile in the sense that she is always trying to hump things. Mortifying, really. The first time she humped Cinders, I almost threw myself down the staircase, although as Charlie pointed out, Cinders didn't seem to mind. She was really lovely about it and just licked Jean's ears—I think she thinks Jean's one of her lost puppies.

Actually, Jean tries to hump everything and everybody. She's got sexual-identity issues according to Kitty, who claims it's because she spends so much time with me. I take this as a not very veiled reference to my own sex life.

No, I'd certainly landed on my feet with Charlie. Lots of bosses can be quite sniffy about bringing pets to work—especially rabbits that hump the furniture and do poohs ("droppings" as we refer to them when the patrons complain). "Droppings make them sound like they just fell from the sky rather than from a bunny's bum," according to Charlie.

"No, she can hop about and you can let her flop around the courtyard in the summer too. I mean, if there aren't too many people out there. Oh, bugger it, actually, just let her have the run of the place."

And run of the place she has had; causing havoc wherever she goes. Often when magazines do photo shoots on Charlie or Posh House, he'll even pose with Jean. He's declared her the club mascot, which is really sweet given her predisposition for humping his arm.

So anyway, my promotion may not have been all it could but I was pleased—especially about the bag. I popped little Jean Harlot into it right away and she nestled down as if she'd been longing for it all her life—well, I clipped it shut actually and gushed about how she loved it. That's the great thing about rabbits, they can't speak for themselves. I think she did like it though, because her little nose popped out, wiggling happily, and I gave it a kiss.

Next thing I knew, Charlie was thrusting a box of business cards into my hand with my name printed on them in whirly-swirly embossed writing.

Lola Morton
Senior Events Manager &
Public Relations Coordinator
Posh House, Marlowe Gardens,
London W1

I didn't really know what the "senior" stood for because it's not as if there is any one junior below me to boss about. But I appreciated the gesture.

"I hope you like them."

"I *love* them," I gushed.

"I thought perhaps we should have some printed for Jean Harlot, give her a bit of purpose, something along the lines of, junior events manager?"

I gave him a little kiss on the cheek. He smelt all lemony and fresh like he always does. Charlie's one of those guys who's reliable in every way imaginable. I am very lucky.

When I went down to visit my parents I showed off the cards and the bag to Kitty.

"Oh, Martin, bring me a sherry," she cried, as if I'd shown her a severed limb or a horse's head. "What are we going to do with this daughter of ours?"

They often discuss me as if I am not in the same room.

"I don't know, Kitty," Martin sighed heavily as he passed her the sherry. "The thing with our daughter is that she's simply got to focus more on finding herself a fellow. I mean, there must be some chap in London willing to take on a girl as lovely as Lola, don't you think? She's not bad looking. Not a stunner like you, of course, my love." He patted me on the head.

"Oh, Martin," Kitty snapped, knocking back her sherry

in one. "Any chap with an ounce of passion would take one look at that two-piece suit she gads about in, not to mention that sexually incontinent rabbit she's always clutching, and run for the Dales."

"Erm, I am in the room," I reminded them. "As is Jean!" I covered her soft floppy ears so her feelings wouldn't be hurt. "Besides, I don't wear a two-piece suit."

"Bring me another sherry, Martin," Kitty exclaimed piteously, obviously more struck than ever by the ennui of her lot. And that was only the Saturday…we still had the Sunday to go.

No wonder I prefer being in London at work than in the sprawling gothic ghastliness of their Surrey manor house. Love my parents as I do, it's hell being stuck down there with two lovesick geriatrics and their fawning housekeeper.

Kitty is completely unsympathetic when I bring up the way it creeps me out to see them slobbering all over each other, although obviously I don't use the term *lovesick geriatrics* or *slobbering* when I have this conversation.

"Biologically you're stuck with parents who love each other. See a therapist," is Kitty's riposte.

It was on the tip of my tongue to mention the school counselor who got me through their four divorces and five marriages.

Martin told me I should celebrate their love for one another and patted me on the head again. I was beginning to feel like Cinders must when Charlie pats her on the head whenever she barks at members who vex her. She occasionally takes to the odd one for no apparent reason. I sometimes feel like giving Kitty a bit of a nip.

But maybe my father's right. God knows none of my friends' parents show any sign of affection for one another…actually, they are all divorced or near enough to it;

sleeping in separate bedrooms or turning a blind eye to affairs. My two closest friends, Elizabeth and Clemmie (short for Clementine), think it's quite sweet that my parents are still so in love—even if they are sickenly demonstrative about it.

It's quite an achievement, so my best friend, Elizabeth, claims that after thirty-eight years and, okay, four divorces and remarriages later, they're still as smitten as the day they first married each other (and then remarried, remarried and remarried…).

See, this is my dilemma. Even though the two of them drive me utterly bonkers, it is hard not to be awed by Kitty and Martin and the passion they still have in their relationship. Even while I'm overseeing my events and parties, I can't help myself, it's almost an obsessive compulsion…I watch the couples. I watch the chemistry between them, the body language and, all right, yes, I watch the passion. It's like watching an engrossing, gory film—impossible to resist.

The party I was currently overseeing was to celebrate the birthday of one of London's biggest property moguls—sorry, landowners, as they refer to it at the top.

Originally from Peru, he'd shipped in crates of a lethal spirit from his homeland and, as far as I could tell, this Machu Picchu stuff was equivalent to a bottle of Bollinger in a shot glass.

"Rudyard Kipling used to drink it," the ridiculously young Machu Picchu PR girl assured me. Initially I was concerned about her being under the drinking age, but after one, she was right, I was already feeling a little poetic. She pressed another on me as I fished the mobile phone of a famous supermodel out of a Picchu Sour.

"Gosh, that's interesting," I gushed. I always gush with my guests when they annoy me, it's part of the role-play—

sometimes my friends say I even gush with them when I'm bored or don't like what they are saying.

"Rudyard Kipling," I added, trying to tone down my gush as I dried off the supermodel's mobile on my new Dolce & Gabbana chiffon sleeve and spoke into my mouthpiece—requesting downstairs to come and fetch it so that it could be locked in the safe. Security had already "assisted" the—by then—rather liquid supermodel into a limo earlier in the evening.

I'd been told to expect all sorts of super thises and super thats. Security arrangements had been made and the necessary special requests filed. For all their glamour, celebrity and prestige, though, they were just a roomful of wealthy men in suits with their cosmetically enhanced harems—sorry entourages. Not an ounce of romance or passion between any of them, I decided.

Coming to the conclusion that my work for the evening was done, when it happened…my epiphany.

One minute I was all CCC (and, okay, slightly gushing) and the next minute I looked up and there they were.

The exes.

My exes.

Well, three of them anyway. Richard, Hamish and Jeremy. Talk about *ex* marking the spot.

In my shock, I dropped poor Jean to the floor.

two

Lady Posche, 1789–1827. Known as Hen to her friends, was born into a grand English family that traced its roots back to William the Conqueror. Henrietta was considered one of the great beauties of her day. She was the daughter of the wealthy maverick, Duke of Bilterten, who was renowned for shooting the eyes out of ancestral portraits he took umbrage to. Apparently he felt that certain eyes were following him about.

For all his eccentricities he was passionately in love with his wife, Caroline, and wrote daily love letters to her, even when they were residing in the same house.

At seventeen, Henrietta fell inexorably in love with the handsome, charismatic youngest son of a marquess, Edward, Lord Edward Haversham.

Evidence suggests that the union was in all likelihood

consummated before a formal proposal of marriage was received, but a proposal was later made and swiftly rejected by Henrietta's father. Realistically, Lord Haversham was not a wealthy man, which may have concerned the duke, but he did not put this forth as his reason for withholding his daughter's hand, however.

In fact, while the reasons he gave seemed spurious at the time, it later proved prescient. "The man was a cad and a bounder."

Secret Passage to the Past:
A Biography of Lady Henrietta Posche
By Michael Carpendum

My first thought was "How dare they!"

Seriously, it was like something out of one of those television setups. To be confronted by the three most major relationships of my life, chatting away happily, knocking back their Machu Picchu sours without a care in the world.

More importantly, without me!

Bastards.

I'd seen them all at Posh House before but not en masse like this, not in a cluster, a pod, right in front of me. This was wrong. It was obscene.

I ducked behind the Machu Picchu drink station to observe them further and as I did so I spotted my boss, Charlie, grabbing Jean—just as she was about to rub herself up and down someone's foot. I watched him as he looked vainly around the room for me.

I whispered in my headset. "I'm hiding behind the Machu Picchu station."

"Ten four, Agent Provocateur," he whispered back into his as he placed Jean on the ground and she hopped on over to me.

I grabbed her and refocused on the exes. It wasn't so much that they looked as if they didn't have a care in the world, or even that all three of them still looked so fit I could scream. The worst of it was they were not with me. Well, actually, let me put that more precisely. One of them in particular was not with me.

Richard.

Up until two years ago, I used to be Mrs. Richard Arbiter Bisque. Yes, I know, what an absurd name. I'd screamed with laughter the first time he'd introduced himself to me; extending one of his well-manicured hands, announcing his name in a muffled, oh-God-is-this-really-my-name sort of way. "Richard Arbiter Bisque."

I quite like that he was ashamed of his name. There's something very endearing about a man who knows when to laugh at himself. Especially when that man has the sexiest, gravelliest laugh. Although, Elizabeth once suggested that if his name embarrassed him that much he could always drop half of it, but I never looked at it like that...not at the time.

From the moment we met, it was all gorgeously romantic and whirlwindish and I'd married him six weeks later. Kitty and Martin had naturally flown to the moon and back with the joy of it all. My friends had pretended to be really excited for me but I knew they weren't by the way they kept saying things like, "Are you sure you're not rushing into this, Lola?"

Meanwhile, Kitty and Martin—imagining themselves to be Surrey's answer to Richard Burton and Elizabeth Taylor, fronted up an obscene amount of money for the wedding reception.

"This is the most marvelous news we could have had!" Kitty had declared when I'd called her from Richard's house in Chelsea with the announcement. All they'd said when I'd called with the news that I had graduated from Bristol with a first, was, "Good, dear, but look we're in the middle of reading the morning papers at the moment, call you back, cheerio." My degree was never mentioned again.

But romance and marriage and passion, well…there was no calming them down over that. "I know it seems really fast," I explained. "I mean, six weeks. Gosh, you're probably thinking we hardly know each other, but—"

"Nonsense. Six weeks is a veritable eternity. Why, Martin knew the first time he caught a glimpse of my shadow that I was the one. Didn't you, darling?" My parents always take phone calls together. There are two phones in every room of the house.

"Oh, Kitty, but what a shadow," Martin extolled. "Even in darkness I could sense the glorious beauty of your soul."

I really wished my parents could have toned it down a bit—especially as I had had them on speakerphone with Richard.

So anyway, I became Mrs. Richard Arbiter Bisque in a civil ceremony at the Chelsea Registry Offices, although I'd actually kept my own name of Morton because, well, Lola Arbiter Bisque just sounded mad. Richard's parents hadn't even bothered to attend, which I found odd, but then they'd moved to the South of France several years before. Still, they didn't even call to congratulate us, although Richard left a message on their phone with the details of our wedding.

The reception was held at Claridges. As parents of the bride, my parents had pushed the boat out so far I was seasick. It doesn't come naturally to me as an events organizer to leave such matters in the hands of someone else—especially if that someone happens to be Kitty. With good cause, as it turned out. For a start there was the food—oysters, lobster and caviar.

"What about the people who don't eat seafood?"

"What rubbish, everyone eats seafood!" Kitty declared. "What could be more simple and humble than the fruits of the sea?"

"Well, there's Jewish people?" I hazarded. "I don't think they—"

"Don't be absurd! Silly girl, of course Jewish people eat oysters, what do you think they lived on during all that parting-of-the-Red-Sea business?"

Kitty isn't really someone you want to go head-to-head with.

Then there were the speeches. "Isn't it marvelous, she's only known him six weeks, you know! Oh, the flourish of love. I could die with pride!" That was how Kitty's speech began, but it picked up a much more floral pace after that, with many an anecdote about herself and my father and their numerous remarriages.

Even Aunt Camilla loved Richard and, okay, I know she was old and kept calling him Oliver, but she was quite tearful with the joy of it and gave us the most beautiful gift a single aunt can give her niece, a week at a spa, although unfortunately it was only for one. But like I said, she was in her nineties.

It was at our wedding reception that Richard met Jeremy and Hamish. In the flush of love, a girl gets all magnanimous and wants to share her happiness. Or in my case, show Jeremy, first love, and Hamish—college sweetheart—what they had so stupidly missed out on.

Me.

But instead of sobbing pathetically over their missed

chance and looking on dolefully as I cut the cake with my husband the way I'd envisioned, they had double-crossed me completely and become friends with the groom, My Husband!

I remember being incensed at the time. "Isn't that like the first rule of ex-etiquette, no becoming friends with your ex-girlfriend's new husband?" I'd complained to my bridesmaids—Elizabeth and Clemmie.

"No, I think that comes after the rule about not inviting ex-lovers to your wedding, Lola," Elizabeth mentioned in her irritatingly pointed way.

It all seemed like yesterday now as I crouched in my little hiding spot behind the Machu Picchu drinks station, clutching Jean to my chest, my heart pounding, my mouth dry as the Gobi.

Seeing the three exes, chatting away like old mates, sent a cocktail of confused emotions coursing through me. Richard was as handsome as ever, tall, lean and, oh fuck…I couldn't bear to look at him, any more than I could bear to look away.

Hamish had put on a little weight, maybe, but even he seemed to look fitter than ever, and he still had that easy laugh and aristocratic bearing that had made me swoon in college. Actually, technically, Hamish and I had never even really broken up, we'd just drifted apart after college. He had his estate to run in Scotland and I had, well, a degree in English literature, which was basically useless, but I had a dream called London.

And then there was Jeremy, still with that adorable little-boy-lost look about him that only a tall, dark, fit millionaire can make seem sexy.

Watching them there in my little hiding spot I couldn't

help but compare them to the men I'd been dating in the two years since my divorce from Richard. And suddenly I was wondering what madness could have possessed me to allow three such lovely guys to exit my life. See, that's the thing about your twenties…you live them without the wisdom you acquire in your thirties!

"So what's our operation, Agent Provocateur?" Charlie asked as he ducked, spylike under the drinks station to join me.

"Operation Ex."

"Will we be requiring backup? Shall I call up our lethal Secret Weapon?"

I raised my eyebrow quizzically.

"Agent Daphne?" Daphne was the gospel-singing cloak-check girl, about as lethal as a nice cup of tea and a short-bread biscuit.

"What's the noun for a gathering of exes, darling?" I inquired, faux casually. "I was thinking ex-cite, what do you think?" My heart was pounding against my rib cage. I really was starting to feel a bit like a covert agent on a dangerous mission.

Charlie, blithely unaware of my trauma, imagined it all to be a game. He'd never seen me flustered, never seen me falling apart, and even when it came to gushing—he agreed with the girls, I only gushed when disinterested. He looked about the room to see where my eyes were fixed. "Depends whose exes we're talking about, old thing. Ex-ocet would be the term if we're talking about a gathering of any of my exes," he mused. "Christ, you haven't spotted any, have you? Not Tamara?"

Charlie had a colorful love life, changing his girlfriends more often than most men changed their sheets. As far as my girlfriends and I were concerned, they all looked alike—

certainly none of them looked like us! They all looked as if he had ordered them from the same catalog. Long, straight, blond hair. Tall. Clear skin, blue eyes, posh-as-all-get-out and skinny as greyhounds.

When I first applied for the job as events coordinator here, I had imagined Charlie to be the son of the owner. It didn't occur to me that someone so young (and good-looking) could be the owner of such a club. I could hardly pay attention to the questions I was being asked, mesmerized as I was by his voice. If a good piece of antique furniture could talk, it would sound like Charlie. Which was probably why, during the interview process, I gave up hope that I'd get the job but decided it would be some sort of achievement if I managed to score a date with one of England's most eligible bachelors out of it.

Since leaving Bristol University, I had worked in several grotty hotels and had grown accustomed to receiving letters from prospective employers at better establishments that began, "Unfortunately…" And those positions were far less prestigious and much more junior PR jobs than the one I was applying for at Posh House, so I was shocked beyond belief when Charlie told me during the interview itself that the job was mine if I wanted it.

I think what I'd actually said was, "Whaaa?"

"Yaah, it's yours if you want it. I can't be shagged interviewing anyone else and you're by far the most attractive and amusing applicant so far."

"Erm, well, that's…"

He ran his hand through his thick thatch of hair. "Fuck, you should have seen the ghastly crew I've had parading in here all day. Veritable march of the cannibals. I was afraid for my life! What is it with PRs? They all have those sinister fixed grins."

I looked as serious as I possibly could. "Oh, yes, don't they! Well, that's lovely."

"Yes, well, not so lovely when Attilina the Hun is eyeing you up for an axe opening."

"No I meant it's lovely that I have the job, not that you had to interview a ghastly crew of axe wielders. Poor you, on that front."

"Right ho, well, I'll push off then, I guess," he'd said, air kissing me and heading toward the door. "Big date."

"Oh," I'd exclaimed, adding, "Does anyone ever go on a small date?" Suddenly shocked by what I'd just said, I thought he might take the job off me for impertinence, but instead he'd laughed.

"No, you're right, dates are always big. Cheerio!" And with that all thoughts of dating Charlie flew out the window and my new career as a PR got properly under way.

I looked at his profile now as he crouched beside me at the drink station, scouring the room. It's funny how can you be attracted to a guy one day and lose all sight of why the next. Self-preservation was partly the case, although watching the way Charlie went through girlfriends I was rather glad I hadn't tested the waters with him myself.

"No, Charlie, you're safe, but don't you think there should be some law against exes becoming friends? Isn't there some statute, some, well, I don't know, social etiquette ruling on that?" I asked, still faux casual.

"Mmm, that's a toughie. I'll have to check my *Ex-etiquette for the Modern Man* to be *absolutely* sure, but no, as far as I'm aware, exes forming friendships with other exes, comes under one of those subclauses of All's Fair in Love and War."

Jean had started to squirm with boredom. I couldn't hold her here forever.

"Jeremy's looking well on it." Jeremy was one of Charlie's personal friends, quite separate to my previous relationship with Posh House. They'd attended the same prep school.

"You think? I thought he was thinning a little on top, actually," I responded bitchily, which was absolute rubbish. Jeremy was looking better than he ever had when I was doing him—clearly working out, big-time.

"So, good night, then? All in all?" Charlie inquired brightly, obviously choosing not to be drawn further on the Jeremy matter.

I had to get out of there.

"I have to get out of here!" I announced abruptly…surprising even myself.

Charlie looked at me, his face one of concern—he really is one of the kindest men I've ever met. "Are you okay, Lola?"

I flicked the switch from romantic fool to businesswoman mode. "Oh, yes, totally. Fantastic party, actually, a really easy crowd, especially considering the kick that Picchu punches." I laughed breezily as if I wasn't on the verge of keeling over with shock.

I hadn't seen Richard for months, and when I had seen him last, we'd had one of those close encounters, only narrowly avoiding that sex-with-the-ex thing.

We'd even snogged. "Come on, Lola, stay the night," Richard had wheedled, his hand running sexily down my spine, but Elizabeth's voice was ringing out in my head, "NO! NO!"

Elizabeth is my most persuasive friend with firsthand experience in these sex-with-the-ex matters, so after a bit of tongue action I was able to resist. I knew from her that *that* way lay disaster. She was living proof of how dangerous sex with the ex could be. She'd broken up with Mike, aka the

Serial Womanizer, a year ago, but every three weeks or so she ended up in bed with him. We all blame her proclivity for sex with the ex for not being able to move on. As she says, they were together for a long time, and for all his faults, he was comfortable (i.e., he knew all about her virtually nonexistent cellulite). She's never, not once, had sex with another guy.

Even she admits that all this sex with the ex has held her back. "Thing is, it's so damn easy. You can call an ex up in the middle of the night and he'll be over like a rocket. Best of all, you can shove him out of bed afterward without looking like a tart. To tell the truth, I can't be shagged doing the whole dating thing and trying to hide the truth about my wobbly bits with someone else. Sex with the ex is like comfort sex, with a little of the thrill of the one-night stand thrown in."

Although lately, even Elizabeth is getting tired of the setup. It's been over two months now and she swears that she's not going to be tempted again, no matter how comfortable and easy it is. She's moved her phone out of the bedroom even, to avoid making any more of her desperate late-night calls.

I was dragged back to the moment as I realized Charlie was asking me more questions about the evening.

"So, did that supermodel girl turn up?"

"Yes, but they carried her out ages ago, so you've missed your chance there. Well, she left her phone in a Picchu sour if you wanted to use that as an excuse…" I passed it over to him.

"No, I was just asking about the evening generally." I noticed that he still pocketed the phone, though. Typical.

"Fine, no problems whatsoever. Apart from when one of the harem girls threw up on a sofa."

"Harem girls?" he asked, raising one of his sand-colored eyebrows questioningly.

That's what I call the cosmetically enhanced entourages of skinny, madly gorgeous girls that tag along to any bash involving London's rich. "I mean, the girls, the younger pretty ones that come with the, erm, older guys."

"Oh, you mean the girls that trail around after the pajama boys?" Charlie remarked.

"Pajama boys?"

This time it was my eyebrows that were raised in confusion.

"As in Hugh Heffner, you know how he always wears…" His sentence melted in the moment though as he finally realized what all my ex angst had been about. "Isn't that your ex-husband over there, talking to Jeremy?"

I nodded.

"Actually, you dated Jeremy once, too, didn't you?"

"Uh-huh."

This city was getting too small for me.

Change the subject, change the subject, my sane side screamed. Change the subject and run. "Yes, and I also dated Hamish," I added insouciantly. "So all in all, three exes all in the same room."

"Blimey!" Charlie responded. "A royal flush."

I was relieved that he didn't make some smart comment then about my dating history. Sometimes I love my boss and his impeccable manners. I breathed a sigh of relief as I squeezed Jean into my chest for a cuddle. "That was very naughty of you crawling along the sofa back and humping that nice lady's hairpiece," I scolded.

Jean looked up into my eyes innocently and blinked as if she didn't know what I was talking about.

"So, let me get this straight. You dated all three of

them? Putting it about a bit around the club, aren't you, old girl?"

Sometimes I truly hate my boss.

"Yes, I dated all three of them but long before I came to work *here!*" I told him pointedly. "Well, apart from Richard. They must be having a little summit or something. Actually, if you don't mind, Charlie, I think I might shoot off. The party's all but over and, well, I have things to do."

"Ex-orcisms?"

"What?"

"Sorry, joke. Not funny. I was referring to the exes. Are you planning on going over to speak to them?"

I blushed. "God no, I'm going to drop Jean off home and go join the girls at the Met Bar," I replied indignantly.

"Okay, well, get going then, seems like we've got everything under control here, Agent Lola," he said, mocking the way I was still whispering into my mouthpiece even though he was only inches away from me. Then he gave me a kiss on the head and Jean a kiss on the nose and left the drinks station.

Jean looked up at me with her big golden eyes and wriggled her nose and I gave her ears a stroke.

Then she started on my arm.

God knows I've tried my best to train her. If only there were rabbit correction schools. Once back at my windowless office I closed the door and pulled myself together, but all I could think of was Richard. And all I could feel was…actually, I didn't know what I felt but it wasn't pleasant.

I gathered up my things, tucking Jean into her large white YSL leather bag and tried to focus on the gentle strains of the grand piano wafting through the wall of my cupboard-cum-office.

I'd just locked the door and was pulling on my coat as Charlie called out to me from the top of the staircase. I waited by the marble pillar outside my office while he took the stairs two at a time in his trademark athletic way.

"I've organized a car to take you home," he explained. See what I mean about him being a sweet boss? "It'll be about five minutes."

I leaned in to air kiss him goodbye and that was when I saw them. Richard and the leggy blonde. I pulled Charlie farther in behind the pillar with me so I could get a better look. The blonde was crying, Richard was looking pissed off. I remembered the look well from our marriage. Richard had always looked pissed off toward the end.

"What's this, another covert op?" Charlie asked.

I dug him in the ribs and shushed him as I watched, frozen with anticipation. Leggy Blonde threw her coat at him. And then Richard did something horrible, something that twisted me up inside so much I wanted to cry out. He took the blonde in his arms and kissed her tenderly on the head the way he used to kiss me when I threw a wobbly. Then he wrapped her up in her coat and put his arms around her and I flashed back to all the times he'd wrapped me in his arms and said, "God, I love you, Lola, I can't live without you."

But clearly he had lived without me. There he was, standing right in front of me, living, breathing and getting on with life without me…and loving someone else.

It was all so horribly wrong. And then I did something I have never done in public, I began to cry.

"I think you might need a drink, old thing," Charlie said, interrupting my hell.

I wiped my errant tears away and pulled myself together. "No, honestly, I'm fine. Just premenstrual something-or-other. It's been a long night," I assured him in my CCC voice.

Charlie put his arm around me and pulled me in for a hug as we watched Richard and the blonde climb into a cab and disappear into the night.

"My car is probably here now, isn't it, Charlie?" I asked crisply, to show I was so over Richard.

I don't know what—if anything—Charlie said, but somehow he must have put me into the car, because the next thing I remember was driving past Selfridges thinking of all the good times Richard and I had shared. Because there were good times. You don't marry a man and agree to share your life, your body, your secrets, your finances without there being good times.

Richard and me, we'd had our good times. I was a fool to throw it away according to Kitty. Memories of the two of us cuddling up in bed on cold winter weekend mornings with the newspapers. Newspapers that were more often than not abandoned in favor of delicious sex—at least far more delicious than the sex I'd been having lately with the stream of "boyfriends" I picked up and dumped like…well, a bit like Charlie dumps his greyhound girlfriends, really.

The familiarity of Richard's body, his touch, his smell, all came flooding back to me as the taxi finally pulled up outside my flat on Grosvenor Street.

Once back in the microscopic confines of my Mayfair flat (only marginally bigger than my cupboard-cum-office affair at work) I tried to shrug off my nostalgia by reminding myself that I was a quirky single, and tried to put all thoughts of Richard from my mind. I deposited Jean in front of the television to watch the news. She's got a thing about keeping up with daily events, Sky News being her favorite.

I set about getting dressed for my evening out with the girls. First choice, Earl jeans, sling-backs and my latest Top Shop tighter-than-tight T-shirt—a girl has to make the most of her C-cups, as Clemmie is forever reminding me.

"Oh bugger!" I cursed, doing a practice Mick Jagger strut in front of the mirror. I turned to Jean for her opinion but she was engrossed in a story about an accident on the M4 motorway. I threw my wardrobe over the bed and changed and rechanged and changed again. I settled on my oldest pair of Levi jeans with the worn holes in the knee and tight T-shirt. This time I wrapped a big green Voyage belt around my hips—the one with the diamante green *V* on the buckle. *V* as in very, very, cool.

By this time I was running late for the girls, so I opted for rock-chick glam hair, which is an exotic way of saying I couldn't be shagged blow-drying it straight. So with my hair tumbling down my back in an unruly cascade of curls, I slapped on some mascara and lip gloss, slipped on my impossibly high Gina sling-backs that Charlie had given me for my last birthday (and which added four and a half inches to my height of five foot five). Finally I grabbed my latest little favorite clutch—the one I bought myself for a tenner at H & M, crammed it with my makeup, slipped my mobile down my cleavage and grabbed my keys.

"Don't worry, Jean, I won't be late tonight," I promised, about to scoop her up for a cuddle, but she hopped away huffily, her focus firmly on the television. Apart from anything else, she knows a lie when she hears one.

three

Henrietta eventually agreed to marry Lord Posche when she was twenty-two after having failed to persuade her father to grant her permission to marry her lover, Lord Haversham. By this stage Lord Haversham was renowned for his gambling and drabbing in Shepherd Market, London. He had lost what money he had through gambling and the general skulduggery that was prevalent in this part of London at the time.

Her marriage to Lord Posche was not a loveless match, but she never completely gave up on her first love, Edward, Lord Haversham.

Secret Passage to the Past:
A Biography of Lady Henrietta Posche
By Michael Carpendum

Within the hour I was at my usual red cozy booth at the Met Bar, a private members' bar on Park Lane. Elizabeth, Clemmie and I usually meet there after work around midnight for a cocktail as it was licensed until three.

Elizabeth and I had met when we studied English literature together at Bristol. Back when we'd both had dreams of running our own PR companies, a dream only Elizabeth had succeeded at making reality. She ran Quantum along with the irrepressible Clemmie. With Elizabeth's brains and Clemmie's connections, they *owned* the teenage-party scene, throwing everything from personal rich-kid parties to major teen balls.

I suppose the reason people become friends is always indefinable, but in our case it had a lot to do with the dusk-to-dawn lifestyles we all shared. Every so often one of us would go off on one and bemoan our shadowy vampire existence, yet none of us has ever done anything to change it.

I love the random madness of London at night and, even more, I adore the quiet stillness of the London dawn too much to miss it.

"My God, Lolly, I love your hair! What have you done to it?" asked Clemmie as she slid into the deep red half-circle booth. "It looks amazing!" she enthused, kissing both my cheeks.

"College-slob hair?" Elizabeth suggested knowingly, referring to our lazy hair days in college when we used to share a blow-dryer between five of us.

"Got it in one," I admitted, leaning over to kiss her as I called over one of our favorite gorgeous waiters. I didn't mention the sighting of exes at first (although I was completely dying to!). Instead, I listened intently as Clemmie and Elizabeth explained how they had decided to spread their teen-scene wings into Europe.

It took two watermelon daiquiris for my resolve to abandon me, and I finally told them of the scene I'd spied from behind the drinks station, taking care to conceal how seeing Richard again had churned me up. Soon we were coming up with a thousand more names for a gathering of exes and gradually I began to unwind. In fact, I must have unwound more than I planned, judging by the muddle of dark curls on the head on the pillow beside me the next morning.

His body had that sweet sweaty post-sex smell that is so delicious on a man you've been loved up with for an age, but somehow is never the same on For One Night Only Guy. It just smells…well…sweaty.

I watched his eyes as they began to flicker awake and tried to understand what force of nature or destiny had brought us together—apart from the tequila shots he was doing off my body at Soho House.

We'd both dozed off about an hour ago after what can only be described as capital-letter SEX. We'd made love in every position in every nook and cranny of his Fulham terrace, which was decked out a bit like an expensively decorated squat—you know, all those boy's toys everywhere?

Giant plasma screen television with surround sound.

Bang & Olufson sound system.

Vintage pinball machines.

Expensive black leather and chrome everything.

Mess and chaos everywhere.

All of it scrupulously dust free, though. Further evidence of the Ultimate London Bachelor Pad accessory—the daily! In his case, a gay couple. He had described them to me the night before as if they were another of his expensive boy's-own status toys.

The sex had been a bit athletic for my taste—at various points of our passion, we broke a speaker, burst a beanbag, tore down a blind and broke the leg off a coffee table. But what the hell, it was his house and I must have burned off, like, I don't know, a gazillion calories in the process. My tummy already felt miles flatter.

"That was amazing, Lisa," he sighed afterward, looking faux lovingly into my eyes and removing a lock of hair from my face as if he truly cared whether I was capable of seeing or not.

Lisa!

Who the hell was Lisa? My name was Lola, Lolly to my mates. Still, as a girl of the world, I knew it wasn't worth correcting him at this late stage of the game. As lovely as he was, with his Caravaggio locks and his olive complexion, he was lovely in an I-don't-expect-this-to-last sort of way. I wasn't even sure, in the cool throb of sobriety, if it should even have begun.

One moment he was introducing himself to me at the bar while I was ordering drinks for the girls, and I remember thinking he was dangerously attractive. Then he had made some corny remark about my name (he had managed at least to get it correct at that stage of the proceedings) and despite not finding it that funny, I laughed and then I thought, well, sometimes a girl just needs an uncomplicated shag.

Hoping no doubt to break the spell of my run-in with the exes, the girls gave me the thumbs-up and that was that. We'd all done some shots and had a chat and a laugh and I'd replied, "What the hell," to his offer to go back to his place.

Maybe that summed up what I hated about my life lately. The "what the hell" attitude I had adopted to love—or rather sex. Suddenly "quirky single" felt more like "irky single."

Three years ago, I would never have slept with a guy like David. I'm pretty sure his name was David?

Three years ago, I thought one-night stands were the preserve of fools setting themselves up for STDs and disappointment. As far as I was concerned, one-night stands were like bad Broadway shows that closed after one night due to lack of interest. But then again, three years ago I was happily married to Richard, enjoying the proceeds and kudos of a play that was never meant to end.

Before that there was Jeremy and before Jeremy there was Christo. Now, he was a keeper (not), rich, polo playing, trust fund. Shame about the cheating. I don't think he could help himself, really. He said it was in his genes. I said, "You mean the fact that you can't stay in them long enough to zip them up?" He just laughed and said I was being "too English about it all." But even Christo had lasted a year and we'd ended happily. I remember Kitty saying, "Every girl needs to know what true love *isn't*." Before Christo, of course, there was Hamish.

I suppose Hamish was the first man to make my heart stop. We'd met in college when Elizabeth was still dating her ex (Mike), only Mike wasn't actually her ex then, he was her boyfriend and Hamish's roommate. We were like a cozy little band of couples; the inseparable four, dating for Bristol. Hamish and I, like most college romances, had drifted apart after finals. We had promised to stay in touch but of course we hadn't. As lovely as it had been, my heart had started again and I just didn't have the enthusiasm for continuing an affair that had run its course.

The thing is though, there had always been *someone.*

My someone.

"Girls called Lola *always* have someone." That was what Clemmie was always telling me during her seemingly perpetual single stages.

I inevitably rolled my eyes whenever she said that and would say something like, "Clemmie, don't be so mad, it's just a name and a really crap one at that."

"Yes, but it's the name of a femme fatale, isn't it?"

I would never have admitted that, of course, but deep down, deep, deep down in my darkest Freudian/Jungian self, I think I actually thought she was right. About me never being single, that is, not the femme fatale thing. I'm about as fatalish as Ben & Jerry's ice cream. At a C-cup and five foot five with hazel eyes, I'm at least six inches and two cup sizes short of being femme fatale material. Also, don't femme fatales have to have dazzling violet eyes with ink-black foot-long eyelashes, rather than hazel eyes with ordinary-length brown lashes?

Richard always said he loved my eyes. He said they changed color with my moods.

Richard.

I flashed back to last night. To the leggy blonde throwing the coat at him, and Richard hugging her, and the way the action had ripped through me like a blade.

He was *my* Richard. I had taken him to be *my* husband. We had taken one another, as in "Do you, Richard Arbiter Bisque, take this woman, Lola Morton, to be your lawfully wedded wife?"

To which he had replied, "Yes, I do" as he looked lovingly into my eyes—and without the slightest bit of hesitation, I might add.

Till death do us part had also been mentioned, and not only by the lady presiding over the civil ceremony, but by Richard—repeatedly. "Don't you love those words," he had said as we went to bed that first night in our suite at Claridges. "Till death do us part!" I'd told him not to be such a soft idiot. He was completely wankered, admittedly, but as they say, *in vino veritas.*

The more I turned our past over in my head the more perfect, the more right, it seemed. And the sex was great, too. I suddenly recalled the day we had gone shopping after our honeymoon and bought our big ebony bed.

Lola loves Richard.

Richard loves Lola.

After it was installed, Richard had carved those words into our bed head. I wonder if he still had that bed? I wonder what Leggy Blonde thought of it if he did. He was the kind of guy that wouldn't have got around to buying a new bed head, so chances were our declaration of eternal love was still there, carved into the ebony wood for all to see.

More importantly, for Leggy Blonde to see.

Since Richard, I hadn't had a proper *someone.* For the past couple of years I'd been unquestionably happy about my quirky singleton existence, but I *had* enjoyed married life. I had enjoyed spooning Richard at night. I had enjoyed staying in and watching DVDs occasionally; snuggled up in our favorite blanket. I always fantasized about having a lovely black Labrador at our feet. Not that Richard and I ever had a Labrador. He was allergic to animal hair—apart from rabbits.

I genuinely thought my marriage to Richard would be like a Broadway smash and just play on and on and on. Richard agreed. He said that the only thing he could be certain of in life was financial success and our marriage.

But as it turned out, he was wrong on both counts.

My Caravaggio look-alike stirred. "There's a Starbucks downstairs, babe, if you want to grab us some coffees," he murmured as he punched a pillow and settled back down under the covers.

Quite apart from the fact that Starbucks was a few hours away from opening, I was outraged by the request. "You want *me* to go get coffee? Should I tidy up a bit while I'm at it? Flick the duster around, wash your socks and do a spot of hoovering?" I asked—well, obviously I didn't actually ask, not out loud. I just looked at him and my whole fed up–ness with him and all the others like him. All the men I'd slept with since splitting with Richard came tumbling down upon me like the bad hangover that would soon be throbbing in my head.

I was sick of the Davids, the Edwards, the Jamies, the Freddies and the dozen other forgettable men I had pulled these past couple of years. And then I started to wonder why I had ever got divorced in the first place? What could possibly have been so bad about my marriage to Richard that had made me trade it in for *this?* Richard used to bring *me* coffee in bed in the morning. Sometimes, he even cooked me breakfast on Sunday and delivered it with all the papers…although, come to think of it, that was only if he was planning on sloping off to work.

David called out. "I'll have a triple-shot latte, babe, and tell the guy to use skim milk."

Dawn was only just struggling with the night, so the chances of finding a Starbucks open were nil. The man was clearly insane. I had just spent the night with a madman. "Sure," I told him as I gathered up my things, pulled on my Earl jeans, slipped on my Gina sling-backs and closed the door on his bachelor squat. It was still dark at five in the morning and I had to trudge to a main road for a cab and it was while I was trudging toward Wandsworth Bridge Road in the thin light of a May dawn that I had my epiphany. I had finally reached the Tipping Point.

When I eventually climbed into a cab on Wandsworth Bridge Road, I wasn't just closing the door on David—or Fulham. I was closing the door on an entire chapter of my life. The chapter entitled The One Night Can't Stand.

Jean was waiting for me as I opened the door of my tiny flat. The morning light had started filtering in through the open blinds. I picked her up and kissed her little nose but she squirmed and wriggled; she wanted her walk.

I shoved her into her bag and skipped on down to Berkeley Square. The uniformed doormen of Annabel's, another of London's private members' clubs, were used to the girl with the rabbit clambering over the railings and watched sentinel-like as I set Jean free for her ritual morning run. I slumped on one of the benches dedicated to some fellow who had once spent many happy moments in this square and began to think about my life. Really think.

Tiredness was beginning to overwhelm me, but as I watched Jean running about, happily humping legs of chairs and trees and anything else she could find and nibbling at the grass, my thoughts turned to Richard. He'd given me Jean on our first-month wedding anniversary. That was when we still had a house and Jean had her own little rabbit hutch—well, more of a rabbit chalet, actually.

What is it about the past? Everything was bigger, brighter and better then...

four

Although considered a great beauty in her day, Henrietta refused to have her portrait painted, declaring that her portrait would be the impressions and memories she left behind. Perhaps her aversion to portraiture came from her father's habit of shooting the eyes out of ancestral portraits he didn't like. She did, however, write a book, *Hold Your Glass Like a Poem,* which was a great success over several "seasons," although it was never reprinted after her death.

By far the most lasting accomplishment of Lady Posche, though, was persuading her husband to build one of the finest private houses then standing in London. Posche House soon became a focus for London society. An invitation to one of her parties was more highly prized than an invitation to the palace. Her parties were known to continue well into the dawn. Sometimes they went for days on end.

Secret Passage to the Past:
A Biography of Lady Henrietta Posche
By Michael Carpendum

Richard and I had met at Posh House a few years after I'd started working here. Only, Richard wasn't a bit posh. He was ordinary, only in a really wealthy sort of way obviously or he wouldn't have been able to afford the £1,500 joining fee and £1,500 annual fee and the general mintedness that was part and parcel of being a Posh House member. I was merely the events coordinator—as opposed to the senior events manager—back in those days.

Richard owned a media dot.com company that was doing really well, and after an especially long line of coke in the loo six weeks after we met, he proposed. I didn't tell that bit to my parents—about the line of coke, I mean. My dad would have always been making jokey references to it, like "Off to powder your nose, are we, Richard?" in a mad knowing sort of way.

Martin and Kitty both like to think they're hip to these things.

Hip and liberal, that's my parents.

Martin really took to Richard. Kitty adored him, too, although I don't think she would have been as chilled about his cocaine usage. "Drugs dampen the passions," and all that. I suppose I wasn't that chilled about it either, to tell the truth, but we were a perfect fit in every other way. Besides, I'd rather have a husband coked to the eyeballs on Colombian marching powder than boring me senseless reading the *Financial Times* out loud to me at breakfast—and he only did that a few times.

No, the more I thought about it, the less reason I could find as to why Richard and I had allowed our love for one another to end up in divorce. He was really kind and generous, and who doesn't appreciate expensive gifts—I'm joking (well, partly). No, seriously, I don't actually go for rich guys, because their sense of entitlement irritates me. Dating a guy with Entitlement Syndrome is like going to an awards ceremony for Biggest Ego. You can hear the drumroll from the moment your date begins, while a montage of their lifetime of achievements rolls on throughout the evening.

I go for men who are easy to talk to, make me laugh and don't count the cost of every little kindness. I also like them to be quite fit and have a full head of hair. Richard scored top marks on all those points—especially the laughter thing. He exuded enthusiasm and had this energy for life and capacity for fun that sort of grabbed you and dragged you along. He lived every moment as if he was making history, and I loved that. "You've got to make it count, Lolly!" he'd always say. He loved making every moment count whether it was reading me poetry at breakfast, or turning up with cereal, a bowl, milk, sugar and spoon one night after I'd done a double shift and I was pretty certain nothing could make me laugh. Richard made me believe that things really would turn out okay, that tomorrow really would be better and the mundane really could be fabulous.

Not that he was too shabby in the bedroom! He may not have been as athletic as David, but we had chemistry together that I had never experienced before or since. For a dot.com boy he was really quite passionate when it came to the ways of the Kama Sutra.

And that's the funny thing—or the not-so-funny thing. I told everyone—including Richard—that I wanted a divorce a year after our wedding because the passion was gone. I know that probably sounded shallow to everyone other than my parents. It definitely sounds shallow to me now, but at the time I suppose I did put a lot of store in passion.

Kitty and Martin have a lot to answer for.

Besides, it wasn't just the passion that had gone. We were fighting all the time, partly because his dot.com had bombed and he'd lost everything—and I mean everything. We'd had to sell our beautiful house in Chelsea, including Jean's rabbit chalet. And we had to trade our cars in for tube passes and I had to go back to work at Posh House and chuck the interior-design course Richard had begged me to take so that we could turn our home into a dot.com meeting place for his business colleagues. I didn't mind about chucking the interior-design course, which was crappier than crap anyway, but I did miss the house and the cars.

But here's the thing, I could have put up with the arguments, the poverty, the strap-hanging journey to work on the tube and even the cocaine, if I truly believed Richard still loved me. If I was sure I came first, I could have borne it all, but the passion was gone and there seemed to be no getting it back. The truth was, after his business went belly up, it seemed *everything* was more important to Richard than me. That's why when people asked why Richard and I split,

I would say the "passion died." As shallow as it sounds, at least it seemed real. Well, it used to seem real at least.

Now I wasn't so sure.

Having spent two years on the London dating circuit, I was less certain. I would have much rather bumped into Richard and had a night in watching television with a curry than a night of athletic sex with my latest One Night Can't Stand. The London dating circuit is a bit like the London tube—the Circle Line. No matter how horrendous it is, you sally forth, day in day out. You dream of a seat but settle for a strap. It's grim, and I was coming to the conclusion that, quirkily single as I was, I wanted more. I wanted what Richard and I had, in the beginning, back.

So that was where the full realization of my epiphany took place. In Berkeley Square as dawn lit up the sky and Jean nibbled on some grass. It had been ages since Richard and I had spoken, and as I watched Jean, I started to imagine excuses for giving him a call. I could tell him about her new white carry bag and how they'd promoted me at work or how Kitty had bought Martin a Napoleonic watch fob for his birthday. Richard had always feigned a genuine interest in my father's hobby…at least I hoped it was feigned. It would be a bit tragic for a thirtysomething man to have an obsessive interest in antique french clocks.

The more I thought about giving him a call the more sensible it seemed; in fact, it suddenly seemed implausible that I *not* call him. I wouldn't mention that I'd seen him last night, though. No, I'd be all breezy and casual, all CCC.

Not that I needed to be breezy.

Not that I needed an excuse.

He was my ex-husband after all. The supposed Love of My Life!

We'd taken vows; my name was carved into his bedpost.

It's only now that I can see I was beginning to think like Kitty.

So I decided a girl doesn't need an excuse to call her ex-husband. I scooped Jean up and popped her back in her bag and climbed over the railings. The moment I arrived back at our flat on Grosvenor Street—great address, but believe me, it breaks all human rights regulations in terms of space— I picked up the phone and speed-dialed Richard's mobile. He's still number 1. Sad, I suppose.

Jean was on my lap, cheerfully nibbling at my jeans. I knew half six in the morning was kind of early, but Richard was always an early bird, and besides, as an ex-wife I felt I had the right to call him early.

He picked up on the first ring, which I took as an omen.

"Babe?" Oh my God, he knew it was me before I even rang…maybe he'd been dreaming about me? This *was* too propitious for words.

Maybe he had seen me last night at Posh House, as well, but had been too embarrassed to come and say hello?

Maybe the argument I'd witnessed between him and Leggy Blonde was the "it's over" speech?

Maybe the kiss on the forehead was the goodbye kiss— the we'll-always-be-friends-but-I-am-still-not-over-my-ex kiss?

"Richard," I replied, in my piss-take of a sultry voice that he'd always found hilarious.

But then he went, "Excuse me, who is this?" in a really pissed-off sort of way. Even Jean seemed shocked. She hopped off my lap and sat on my foot, looking up miserably at me.

Okay, so this wasn't going as well as I had hoped. "Erm, Richard, it's *me.*"

"Me? Who the fuck is this?" He was sounding angry now.

Who the fuck is this? Who the fuck did he think it was? I was his wife…well, ex-wife anyway. I used to be Mrs. Richard Arbiter Bisque. To this day I am the only woman he has ever said "I do" to and now it was "Who the fuck is this?"

But I wasn't going to give up. We were talking lifetime commitment and happiness here, so I gathered myself together. "Erm, it's Lola," I explained humbly.

His tone changed immediately. "Lolly? Shit! Sorry. Are you okay? Is something wrong?"

Why is it when you call an ex, they always presume you are having a disaster? I mean, okay, I confess for the first ten months after we broke up I had him in to change my lightbulbs, remove spiders from my sink and help me move furniture. But hello, we had made vows; sickness, health, better, worse…till death do us part! You don't just walk away from that level of commitment.

"Nothing's the matter," I responded, my voice suffused with exasperation by now. "Can't I call my ex-husband for a chat?" I felt it was about time I reminded him that we were once married.

"Huh? That is, yeah, I guess, but why? Lola are you *sure* you're all right?"

"Of course I'm all right! Why wouldn't I be all right? I'm perfect," I prattled defensively. "I've been working out at the gym. I'm really toned, actually. My career is going stellar, Charlie's just promoted me to senior events manager. I've even got my own office and business cards with swirly-whirly writing on them. Oh, and Jean's got a new bag, you know the latest YSL one with the rose? It's white, which makes it easier to see her poohs—sorry, I mean her droppings."

"It's just that it's six in the fucking morning, Lola!"

Okay, so this early-morning call might not have been the best of ideas. My spirits began to deflate, Jean Harlot hopped off my foot and started sniffing about her litter hutch. She's quite good about doing her business in there. I wandered over to the minifridge (everything in my flat is miniature) and took out a carrot for her, chopped it up with one hand with the phone wedged between my ear and shoulder.

After she finished her business in the hutch, she hopped over to the little pile of carrots and began nibbling happily away. I wish I could be so easily pleased. It's not for everyone, but I had to admit, a carrot, a romp in the park and a hump with a leg of a chair, how easy would that be?

"This was a bad idea," I told Richard.

"No, Lolly, sorry, it's not you, it's me."

"Now, that sounds bad," I told him in my most flirtatious tone. "That's what I said to you before we took our 'break.' You know the one that ended in our divorce?"

He didn't laugh. "Oh, Lolly, I've just had a fuck of a fight with Sally. I think we might have broken up. I thought you were her. I've been calling her mobile but she's switched it off."

I knew from the tone of his voice that he was running his fingers through his hair the way he does when he's frantic. When his company collapsed, I thought he would rub the hair clear off his head.

I didn't like the fact that I was attempting to explore the possibility of rekindling our love and he was running his fingers through his hair over another woman. I kept my tone CCC, though. Breezy is a skill I've learned running events at Posh House. When things fall apart…really badly apart, and they do—all the time—it is more important than ever to act as unfrantic and unruffled as possible. "I didn't know you were still with Sally. I thought you guys already broke up."

Richard's tone was noticeably *not* so breezy. "No, that was the other Sally. Sally Grant. I've been seeing the new Sally for about three months." I'd obviously hit a nerve, because he sounded well pissed off now.

I needed to turn this around, so rather than rise to his mood, I tried some humor. "How many Sallys is that now?"

"What's that supposed to mean?" he snapped. "Her name's got fuck all to do with it. I really like her, Lolly, oh no, oh shit, we were getting on so well. I actually thought this was it. I'm really in love this time. Really, really in love, if you know what I mean."

If I know what you mean? My eyes began to well up.

Jean looked up at me sorrowfully as if sensing my pain. I mean, she might have just wanted more carrot, but I took her look as one of commiseration and solidarity.

I closed my eyes remembering the first time he'd told me that he was in love with me. "Not just love, love," he had explained. "Real love, like in the movies love. Like Bogey and Bacall love." Richard loved old movies, Jean Harlow was his favorite star, which was why we'd called our bunny that, only we had to change it to Jean Harlot on account of her humping.

I didn't say anything. I could feel a tear running down my cheek, and my mouth had gone all dry.

Richard continued to ramble on about his love for Sally. "We just had this stupid row, about nothing, really. Well, about my coke habit, which isn't a habit, you know that. I just did a line with Kev for old time's sake. You know how it is."

Did I mention the arguments we'd had over Richard and his dalliance with cocaine—or as he preferred to call it, Charlie. Charlie made it sound as if it was an old mate or something. When we first met, everyone was doing it—

apart from me. Obviously, CCC and cocaine don't really mix. Anyway, the whole of London was snowing with cocaine when we first met, but times change and in Richard's case, businesses go belly up and you start to grow up and reevaluate.

Richard hadn't ever really reevaluated Charlie, though, and when things were going really badly between the two of us, I started to doubt he ever would.

Then he went, "I thought *you* were Sally, see." He laughed hollowly.

"I'm not surprised when most of the girls you know are called Sally," I teased and then he laughed and told me he missed me. Just like that. "God, I miss you, Lolly," he said.

My heart started to race. "You, too," I told him carefully. "So does Jean."

"Jean?"

"Jean Harlot…our rabbit?"

"Oh yeah, sorry, I forgot."

I was thinking, excuse me, you forgot our rabbit…our first-month-anniversary rabbit? But I didn't say anything.

"So, what did you do to poor Sally that made her run off into the dawn? Apart from have a chat in the loo with 'Charlie,'" I asked, as CCC as you like.

"She asked to move in."

"With you?"

"No, with the postman. Anyway, I freaked and she ran off."

"Why did you freak?" I was intrigued now.

"Well, moving in. It's a bit, well…serious. We've only known one another for three months."

"You asked me to marry you after six weeks," I reminded him, unable to disguise the slight sense of triumph in my voice.

"I know, but you were different."

My mind punched a mental fist in the air.

Yes! I was different. I knew it. He still loved me. He still wanted me. I was right to call. I listened to the sound of his breathing on the other end of the phone. Pictured him lying in bed (naked), talking to me. All thoughts of Sally obliterated from his mind. It was a lovely fantasy but one he brought crashing down with his next words.

"We were young. I was coked to the eyeballs and besides, I've learnt my lesson about jumping into things."

Charming. Loving me was something he now felt he'd *jumped* into under the influence of youth and drugs? So I said, "Better to jump than be pushed, I suppose." The bitterness in my voice was only too clear.

"Sorry, Lolly, but you know what I mean."

"Yeah," I agreed, even though I wasn't sure I did. When we broke up initially it was just meant to be a break. I told him I needed space but the truth was I didn't really know what I needed. I just needed all the fighting to stop. We'd spent the first few months at one another's flats crying and arguing and crying some more. Sometimes we even had sex. Actually, we probably had more sex in that first few months of breakup than in the last three months of marriage. But after a while my friends got to me. When Richard's dot.com dived, it wasn't just his shirt he lost. His debt was my debt, and while I know he did all he could, my friends and family couldn't believe how reckless he had been.

They couldn't cope with the fact that Richard was financially dependent on my earnings while he tried to put his business back together. I didn't mind, though, like I said, as long as I knew he loved me I was happy to trust his dream. Kitty and Martin offered to help but both Richard and I said no. "We'll sink or swim together on our own," we'd assured them.

As it happened we sank.

Ironically, ten months after our split, his company had a breakthrough and he was able to pay me back, but it didn't seem to matter so much then.

The decree nisi, the declaration that our divorce was now six weeks from being final, had come through. We'd both moved on.

Jean hopped over to me and I bundled her into my arms for a cuddle.

"Hey, I've got another call coming in," he said, and I could tell he was obviously hoping it was Sally. "But listen, why don't we get together sometime?"

"Yeah, sounds good," I agreed. "What about tonight?"

But he had already hung up.

five

Reading the letters of Lady Posche, it soon becomes apparent that her marriage to Charles, while successful in many ways (they had three children) did not dampen her ardor for Edward. In fact, she had a secret staircase from her bedroom chamber built into Posche House so that he could visit her in the night after his gambling.

Posche House was built by the eminent architect Sir Richard Ables, a highly respected and honorable man paid by Lord Posche. Yet such was Hen's charm that she was able to convince Sir Richard to omit the secret staircase from his plans.

Edward was so impoverished that for most of her married life he virtually lived at Posche House, and for many years Lord Posche appears to have been accepting of the arrangement, if not thrilled. More interesting is that records and anecdotal evidence suggest London society never guessed at Henrietta's liaison with Edward.

It seems the only person she confided her secret love of Edward to was her sister, Elizabeth.

Secret Passage to the Past:
A Biography of Lady Henrietta Posche
By Michael Carpendum

Having enjoyed life's greatest luxury, a good long sleep, I was sharing a late-afternoon breakfast coffee with Clemmie. Either Clemmie, or Elizabeth and I, always squeezed in a late-afternoon coffee/breakfast before I start work. We'd talk about work, men, fashion and health—the usual. Clemmie is very practical in her approach to life, almost a control freak—only, because she's prone to get overexcited, she doesn't come across as controlling. But just the same, she carefully plans for every contingency in every area. I sometimes think that's why she's never fallen in love. Sometimes you just can't plan for things. Also, the very act of "falling" in love involves a bit of stumbling about. I tell her stuff like that.

She tells me stuff like, "You're such a nut, Lola." Which isn't always what I want to hear.

The reason I wanted to see her today was to discuss the Richard situation. Although out of all my friends I'm closest to Elizabeth, I knew my sudden desire to rekindle things with him were unlikely to get a great reception from her. She never liked Richard…well, nor did Clemmie…but Elizabeth was the most convincing when it came to talking me out of things. And I didn't want to be talked out of this.

"Look, Clemmie, I really need your help, I have this dilemma, see," I explained.

"Oh well, if there's anything I can do. Is it a work thing?"

"No, it's a love thing, actually. I think I want to get back with Richard."

She giggled her little-girl giggle, and even though I normally found her giggle adorable, I told her I didn't see what she found so funny.

"Sorry, I was just thinking of Kitty and Martin, you know, married, divorced, married, divorced and so on. Bit like Henry VIII."

"Without the beheadings," I reminded her. "And Richard and I were only married *once.*"

She stared at me with her big blue eyes. "You're serious, then."

"Yeah, I think I am."

"But where did this come from? I don't understand. You've never spoken about him before then suddenly you see him with his girlfriend and you're having doubts. Why?"

"Yes," I told her as our coffees were delivered to our table by a grumpy girl with a face like a smacked bottom. I gave her my gracious grin—the one that has been perfected on a million graceless patrons at Posh House who live to complain about everything from the ceiling paintings and the brightness of the chandeliers, to the size or number of bubbles in their Cristal champagne. Yes, some people actually measure and count them; it seems to be an increasingly popular pastime—bubble counting. Tiffany's will probably bring out a bubble caliper next Christmas.

I could tell that the smacked-bottom-faced girl still hated us, but I think she was thrown by my grace as she eventually sloped off.

"So, Richard?" Clemmie repeated, twirling one of her ringlets in her fingers, her blue saucer eyes wide with shock.

"Yes, Richard. Why is that so surprising…we were married once, after all."

"Oh, Lolly, you are nuts. Have you told Elizabeth?"

"No. I know what she'll say, but I'm genuinely worried." I lowered my voice to signify the seriousness of the matter. "I mean, what if I did the wrong thing in divorcing him?"

She looked stunned. "But it wasn't just you, was it? It was a mutual thing."

"Mmm. I'm not so sure," I mused as I stirred the froth into my coffee. I hate getting that mustache thing when I drink cappuccinos, only I'd rather have cappuccinos than lattes because they look so luxurious, like clouds you can make go away.

"What do you mean you're not sure? You signed papers, you employed solicitors. We had numerous 'am I doing the right thing divorcing Richard?' dirty martini parties, just so you could be *totally* sure. I thought we were all going to die of liver failure by the time you finally decided it was what you really, really, really wanted." She was mocking me now, not taking it seriously the way I had hoped she would. She was saying all the things I knew Elizabeth would say and it was annoying me deeply.

"But that's just it. Maybe the reason I agonized over my decision so much was because I *wasn't* sure. I'm not sure now because I don't think I was sure then either." Then again maybe I'm never sure about big decisions involving my personal life.

I remember the first time I was given the decision of my new school shoes. "Buckles or laces?" Martin kept asking me—he and Kitty were heading toward their first divorce at the time. I'll never forget the pressure of it all. Would the other girls laugh if I wore buckle shoes? Would they think I was incapable of tying my shoelaces? But then again, the buckles were so pretty, they were lovely.

"Which ones do you feel most passionately about?" he had asked.

Passionately? I was only five, for heaven's sake, but I tried my best to decide where my passions lay, as I could tell he was getting impatient. I mean the buckles were very shiny but I could tie my laces. A skill I was desperate to show off.

Try as I might, I couldn't decide, so Martin decided for me.

Buckles.

Of course, I was a laughingstock for the whole term, not that Kitty or Martin noticed, they were too busy embarking on their first breakup.

Decisions are traumatic. Of course, Kitty puts it down to passion. If you were really passionate about those buckles you wouldn't have minded what the other children thought, she always says if I bring up the subject. I don't mean to bring it up, but weekend visits home take it out of me. By Sunday I'm not fully compos mentis.

Richard and I *did* agree to divorce but I wonder if it was really a decision or merely a resignation to our unhappiness about his company's collapse? Was it the buckle-and-lace issue all over again?

Maybe I could have done more. I mean, is passion everything? Or was I like those middle-aged men who trade their wives in for a younger, more fertile model? Marriage is, after all, meant to be forever, for better or worse. Had we simply fallen at the first hurdle and not bothered to pick one another up and press on into the future?

"I rang him after I went home the other night," I admitted in a whisper.

"You what?" Clemmie shrieked, which caught the attention of the surly waitress.

"Look, Clemmie, I'm worried I might have made the biggest mistake of my life!" I explained quietly, trying to impress on her the gravity of my trauma. As a redhead she was very prone to becoming excitable at the slightest provocation.

But then she seemed to shrug off her shock and calm down. "Creative people worry more because they're more imaginative," she mused as she broke a chunk off her muffin and dunked it into her latte. Clemmie can eat muffins until the cows come home but she never puts on a pound. I watched enviously, feeling peeved that she didn't seem to be taking my dilemma seriously.

So I flung myself into another conversation and that was the end of that. Richard wasn't mentioned by either of us again. We paid our bill and left.

Later that evening over drinks we met up with another friend, Josie, who is blissfully married. We rarely see her now even though she's desperate not to behave like a smug married and is always trying to make light of the fact that being married to the man of her dreams is a bit of a bore. She and Emmanuel had dated during high school, hadn't seen each other for years and then they'd bumped into one another at some art biennial that Clemmie had dragged her to last year and *wham,* suddenly they realized they were made for each other all along. Just like me and Richard, maybe? I thought to myself, sticking my hand in Jean's bag to give her ears a little tickle.

"You make poor Emmanuel sound like your jailer," Clemmie said as she tipped some more champagne into Josie's glass. I was sticking to water as I was still officially working. David Bowie was holding a party at the club and it was my job to make sure things went smoothly. It's weird being an events organizer, people imagine it must be ever so glamorous handling parties for celebrities, but most of the time your head is on the line and you're so worried about something going wrong that you forget you're making Robbie's or Kylie's or Kate's night one to remember.

Also, things do go wrong. Always. The host invites twice as many people as arranged and the venue can't accommodate them. Their assistant does a strop over the guest list and, let's face it, you can't force guests to go to a party. With the best DJ, best goodie bags and best will in the world, guests make their own minds up.

Which wasn't going to be a problem with tonight's party. Quite the opposite. In fact, I had to make sure we were going to be able to close off the garden to members in the event that David's (Bowie) guests decided to spill out. I pulled out my Blackberry wireless organizer and made a note.

Josie was still continuing her marriage-martyr act. "It feels like a prison sometimes. Every night the same man spooning me. Every morning the same man making love to me. Every day the same e-mails reminding me that the same man loves me more than life itself." She was laughing while Clemmie and I mimed violins.

Jean was getting restless and even in the darkness of the bar I was aware that the staff might get suspicious, so I made a move to leave as I spotted Elizabeth coming in.

And then Clemmie, dear sweet serious-minded, scrupulously honest Clemmie blew my cover. "Did you tell Josie about calling Richard?" she asked, licking her swizzle stick.

"You *are* joking?" Josie demanded in a voice that suggested that if I wasn't, she was going to punish me in cruel and unusual ways.

I looked her in the eye. "Look, you got back together with Emmanuel and now you're brilliantly happy. Who's to say the same won't happen with Richard and me?"

"Emmanuel and I dated in high school. It's completely different. You've got history with Richard. You tried marriage and mortgages and all the rest of the deal and you couldn't make that work—not even for a year!"

"But that's my point, maybe I didn't give it time to work."

Elizabeth arrived and asked suspiciously, "Time for what to work?" as she slumped down into the booth beside me.

"I just think I might have made a mistake with Richard."

"Trust me, you didn't. Did you order for me?" she asked as if that should be the end of the discussion.

"That's so unfair. What about you and Mike?"

"Exactly, let me be your example. Sex with the ex ruins you. Do you want to end up like me? One year later and still no rebound guy?"

"I'm not talking about sex," I cried out louder than I meant to. "I'm talking about love. About lifetime commitment, about passion."

Why couldn't anyone understand me? I was thinking at the time.

"Have you been taking Kitty's pills?" Elizabeth asked, looking deeply into my eyes.

"It's true," said Clemmie. "You are sounding a bit mad."

"Look," said Elizabeth, pulling the comb out of her hair

and shaking her long black mane down her back. "You can have sex with the ex but you can't turn the clock back."

"Why not? My parents have."

"Your parents, in case you haven't noticed recently, are bonkers. They tortured each other and you with their marriages and remarriages. It's completely different."

"Why?" I persisted.

"Kitty and Martin have an overdeveloped sense of drama," Clemmie explained sweetly, touching my arm. "You're more or less normal."

Then Elizabeth added, "Normalish," and everyone started to laugh.

I swirled the ice and lemon around my water with the swizzle stick grumpily.

Clemmie and Josie sipped their drinks, neither of them looked that interested in taking the conversation further. Clemmie grabbed a handful of bar snacks from the tray and poured them into her mouth. "Would Jean like a Twiglet?" she offered.

"No, they're really bad for her." I covered Jean's bag protectively with my hand.

Clemmie rolled her eyes. "So is living in a YSL handbag but she seems happy enough with that arrangement. Go on, don't be such a bore, let her have a little treat."

Before I could stop her she'd slipped a Twiglet into Jean's bag and I had to fish it out, she really does get the most awful wind. "Look, can we talk about my second thoughts about Richard properly, please?" I pleaded.

"You're always having second thoughts," Clemmie shrugged.

"You've already said that," I reminded her.

"Usually right at the point that they meet someone else and start moving on," Elizabeth added unhelpfully.

"That is so untrue!" I huffed indignantly.

Elizabeth snorted. "That is as fair as fair can be. Let's go through them, shall we. Macbeth. Dated him for two years at university, dumped him because—"

"His name wasn't Macbeth," Clemmie giggled.

"No, his name was Hamish," I snapped.

"And let's not forget Henry!"

"Who's Henry?" I asked, horrified with myself.

"Poor Henry," teased Elizabeth. "First day at work and you date the boss! That was wrong."

Clemmie shook her head.

"He was not my boss. He was the front-desk manager. I was events organizer. Our paths barely crossed unless I had to ask him to deal with an unruly party that wouldn't leave."

"Also, wasn't he gay?" Clemmie pondered.

"He was *so* not gay!" Sometimes my girlfriends can be really insulting about the men I date. "He asked for anal sex, that's all!"

Elizabeth rolled her eyes. "Same thing. Fine. You dumped him because he was gay. Eight months later he hooks up with another girl and you decided you wanted him back."

"Well, I got it wrong, didn't I? That is not a crime. Besides, at least it proves he wasn't gay," I pointed out.

"So, getting back to Hamish," Clemmie added. "Remind us why you dumped him?"

"He, erm…" Why did I dump Hamish? "He cheated on me," I improvised, although actually I'm pretty sure we just drifted apart—you know, we lacked the X-factor together.

"Is that for sure?"

I suddenly felt ashamed for maligning Hamish's name. "What do you mean 'for sure?' How sure do you want? Forensics?"

"Fine, so why'd you start seeing him again?"

"I wondered if I shouldn't forgive him. Besides, the sex was great!" Well, it was perfectly adequate anyway.

Clemmie shook her head. "Hello? Are you blind? You only started wondering because he started dating another girl."

"She was just a rebound girl. He told me so."

Elizabeth looked me in the eye. "Lola, maybe you can't see the pattern here, but don't you think it's strange that you only start having regrets about the demise of your relationships once the guy has finally moved on? Think about it, Lola," she urged, slurping a sip from Clemmie's glass. "Every single serious relationship you've had since I've known you, you think it's the one. Then you decide it isn't and end it. Then the guy moves on and you have second thoughts. It's a pattern."

All three girls nodded. God, she is right, a voice inside me screamed. But then another voice, a much louder, more strident voice said, "What if they *were* the one, though?"

I put it to them. "What if he *was* the one, though?"

"Which one?"

Talk about missing the point. I rolled my eyes. "Richard, of course."

Clemmie, Josie and Elizabeth looked at one another and shook their heads. Clemmie touched my arm in a patronizing sort of way. "Maybe you just can't cope with the idea of your exes moving on? I mean, that's perfectly natural."

"In a sort of scary bunny boilerish way," Elizabeth retorted.

Then Josie very unhelpfully added, "My advice is move on and find your own Emmanuel." Smug married that she is.

"But that's what I'm saying. What if I found my Emmanuel and let him go because I was afraid because of all, well, the money stuff?"

"And the cocaine stuff," Elizabeth added.

Then Clemmie went, "And don't forget the boring stuff."

I ignored them both and turned to Josie. "How can I be sure it wasn't Richard? You and Emmanuel split up and then found one another again."

"We dated when we were fourteen. We'd never even done it, in fact we hadn't even tongue kissed."

That was when the snotty waitress came over and told me that they didn't allow dogs in the restaurant, and because I was in such a pissy mood because of my friend's unhelpfulness, I went, "Really? But they let *you* in?"

A look passed between the girls that I took to be one of embarrassment.

The waitress said she was going to get the manager and I told her to hurry up.

"Look, Lola, calm down. The girl's just doing her job. Maybe you should let this Richard thing go, hey?" They were stroking me as if I was a mad person they were trying to control before the arrival of the madhouse ambulance.

They'd always hated Richard. Even when I showed them my ring, they'd made a really bad-taste joke about how many grams it was worth. They thought he was a total cokehead.

I spotted the snotty waitress pointing me out to the manager, so I stood to leave. "Look, I have to go anyway and check that everything is going smoothly with preparations for the Bowie party," I told them.

The manager and the snotty waitress arrived as I was struggling out of the booth with all my bags—I always lugged a virtual office around with me. It takes a lot of equipment to be a PR in London.

"Madam, one of our staff has alerted me to the fact that you may be concealing a dog in your bag?"

And even though I'm not usually rude and the manager

was quite cute in a gay way, I went, "Well, one of your staff needs her eyes read! Does this look like a dog to you?" And then I opened Jean's bag and she looked up, her golden eyes blinking at the sudden exposure to light. Her little ears looked so soft and sweet. My heart melted and I think the manager's did, too, because he grinned and stroked her floppy ears and asked her name.

When I told him it was Jean Harlot, he gave me a hug and told me I was adorable and he hoped I'd bring Jean in again sometime.

I gave Miss Snotty Pants a triumphant smile.

I even let the manager take Jean out for a cuddle and within a moment of rabbit/gay-guy bonding, all was well.

As I said my goodbyes, Clemmie jumped up and air kissed me. "Make sure you ask David for his autograph."

Elizabeth went, "And tell him I'm his biggest fan and if Iman ever decides to give him the push, I'll be there to pick up the pieces."

"I'll just make a note of that in my phone," I joked, pulling it out as if to do just that. But then it rang.

"Lola?"

"Yes?"

"It's Richard. I was, well, wondering if you would be free for that drink later?"

six

"'Tis well you have given over your reproaches toward me and relented to come to my bed once more. Possibly it is a weakness in me to aim at the world's esteem as if I could not be happy without it, but there are certain things that custom has made almost of absolute necessity, and reputation I take to be one of those.

Never doubt that I have a particular value for you above any other. It is much easier I am sure to be allowed a good reputation than a good husband, though it will never enter into my head that 'tis possible any man can love where he is not first loved.

For though I love you, I do not see that it puts any value upon women when they marry for love, yet nor do I see that it would give you any advantage to have your wife thought an indiscreet person.

If love is best displayed by discretion, sir, you will see by my discretion that I love you ardently and sincerely above all others."

An extract from a letter written by
Lady Henrietta Posche to her lover,
Edward

I suggested to Richard that we meet at the Star Bar at the *Top of the Pops* show, partly because it was the next day and partly so that he'd see me in my milieu, the CCC Lola he'd fallen in love with in the first place. I frequently dropped in to the show as, along with showcasing live pop acts every week on TV, it also kept its famous guests amused during performance breaks with a behind-scenes bar. An ideal place for me to catch up with people in the music business.

Charlie always has his driver take me and pick me up, which is so sweet, as a lot of the contacts I make there Posh House derives no benefit from. But it's important to know what's happening and to know the people who were making it happen so I was in a position to book top acts.

Richard always said some people live to work, some people work to live, but I do both. When we'd been married, Richard used to come to *Top of the Pops* with me occasionally. At first he pretended not to be impressed by the celebrities I'd introduce him to, and then later, when I realized he was impressed, I stopped bringing him because he'd be embarrassingly grand with everyone. Also I discovered he was doing coke with people in the toilets.

But I put that from my mind now, casting my memory back to the first time he'd come with me when No Doubt was number one. We'd held hands in the cab on the way there and back and necked during the show.

I picked him up at his house in Notting Hill. That is, the house he said was in Notting Hill…the *London A–Z* would suggest it was in Shepherds Bush, but I ignored the niggling irritation of his pretension as I wrote down the address and told him brightly I'd pick him up at six-thirty.

He said right, and put the phone down. I know "right" is only one word, but by the time I'd analyzed and psychoanalyzed it, the word *right* was laden with more romantic promise than any word ever uttered by a man. In fact, he may as well have said, "Right! I want to marry you!" for all the innuendo I read into the word.

I'd planned to spend hours preening myself for our big reunion, but as it was I woke up at two-thirty (afternoon) and being a Friday, Red Door, the Elizabeth Arden salon downstairs from my flat, was fully booked. In a flap, I traumatized Jean and myself about what to wear, finally going for the flesh-colored (mouse pink to Kitty) Jimmy Choo sandals, Voyage jeans and bling-bling, spangly top from Top Shop. Then I threw all my makeup in a tiny little beaded purse and went off to Posh House for a steam, a shower and a chat with Charlie.

"Drink?" he asked as one of the waiters brought Cinders a bowl of water. We were sitting in the courtyard watching Jean have her evening hop around the legs of the members.

"No, I need my wits."

"Darling girl, I hate to be the one to tell you," he said, examining my face, "but you have green eye shadow on one eye and pink on the other. Your wits are not your own this evening. We'll have two cordials," he instructed the waiter.

"Oh, Charlie, it's Richard," I confided when he asked me why I was in such a flap.

"What's the arse done now?" he inquired. "We can cancel his membership. We can ring up the *Mirror* and say he was thrown out for taking drugs in the girls' toilet."

I laughed, even though I cringed at the reference to Richard's drug taking. "I think I might be still in love with him."

"Oh!" Charlie looked slightly unnerved—which wasn't surprising given he'd witnessed Richard with the leggy blonde the other night.

"I don't think the leggy blonde is a serious thing," I reassured him.

"They rarely are," Charlie sighed heavily, as one who would know.

It felt good to finally be open with someone about my re-kindled feelings for Richard, someone who, unlike the girls, wouldn't give me grief. "Oh, Charlie, I can't stop thinking of him. I think I might have made a big mistake in divorcing him."

"I thought it was mutual," Charlie replied mildly, taking a sip of his champagne.

"What's mutual though, really?" I asked for want of anything better to say, but Charlie didn't say anything, which was actually quite nice. Silence, when you are expecting a hectoring lecture, is very comforting. We sat in companionable peace for twenty minutes or more, Charlie staring into the tiny strands of bubbles of his cordial while I redid and redid and redid my makeup.

"You look lovelier without makeup, you know," he told me as I finally proffered my face for his inspection.

I laughed as a girl does when men say crap things like that. "Darling, I'm going to be under the lights of the Star Bar, trying to pull my ex. Believe me, I need all the ammunition I can get."

"Yes, well, the green eye shadow does look pretty dangerous," he teased, scooping Jean up into his lap. He'd kindly agreed to watch her for the evening. I really was very lucky to have such a lovely boss, I thought.

But later when I was all enthusiastic and finally feeling okay about what I was about to do, he kissed me on the head and waved me off, saying, "Be careful, Lola," which pissed me right off.

I turned back and watched him running up the steps two at a time with Jean and hmmphed to myself. Why was everyone telling me to be careful? I wasn't a child. I knew what I was doing. I mean, it wasn't as if I was jumping blindly into a big relationship. I'd already done that when I married him. All I was doing was making sure that I hadn't made a big mistake in divorcing Richard. Actually, when you think about it, I told myself as I buckled myself into the taxi's seat belt, I was being overly cautious, if anything. I was taking a sensible, reasonable approach to my love life for once. Yes, that was it. I was approaching my love life the way I approach the organization of a big event. CCC, that was me, ticking off the boxes and making sure all was in order.

I phoned Richard on my mobile en route, and he made sure he was waiting for me outside his house. My heart did a little fluttering thing when I saw him waiting by the fence, fidgeting with the loose change the way men do when they're nervous. He was looking good, almost gay good; big bright trainers and a pin-striped suit with an open-necked shirt that looked like one I'd once bought him from Gucci.

He kissed me hello rather awkwardly as he climbed into the car—he was going for my cheek and I was going for his lips, so we more or less ended up knocking noses Eskimo style. But it made us giggle and that felt good. Being alone in the taxi with him felt good. We didn't discuss anything meaningful—he asked which acts were on and I told him, but that led to a discussion about our shared love of certain artists and a realization that we'd never had any of those horrible who-gets-what-CD arguments that so many couples had. The bailiff got them.

Once we'd arrived and were sporting our purple access-all-areas artist bands on our wrists, Richard and I ordered vodka and tonics at the bar. They always give double shots at *Top of the Pops,* which in this case I decided was a good thing as Richard clearly needed loosening up. I wanted him to remember how fantastic it was being together, being with me. I needed to work my mojo.

The usual faces were there, it was quite a good lineup that night, with Pink and The Offspring playing, so I steered Richard over toward a group of record executives and artists' managers and introduced him. He became slightly more animated, but still, things weren't going as planned. And I hate that.

I left him with the group and did a whiz round the bar to say a quick hi to everyone. I spotted Catalina, a girl who did PR for a cosmetics company that was always really good at giving me stuff for goodie bags.

"Lolly darling!" she cried, as if I was her oldest and closest friend. As I leaned in for an air kiss she grabbed me and sort of did this swaying-on-the-spot thing with me…a bit like a slow dance. I decided she was drunk. "So, darling, we've got Darna DJ-ing next Thursday night at the new Darna relaunch, you coming?"

Richard sidled up to me and I pulled myself away from Catalina. "I'm just off to the loo. Did you want a line?"

And even though Catalina was drunk, and loads of people (especially in the music world) do coke, I couldn't believe he'd been so unprofessional as to do it at an event I'd taken him to as a guest.

"No," I replied, failing to hide the edge in my voice.

"See you in a bit then," he said, seemingly oblivious to my irritation. I was cringing internally and Cat wasn't so drunk that she didn't notice. I started to feel I was floating outside my body as the evening got progressively worse.

Cocaine was a box I hadn't planned on ticking this evening. My hope for a perfect reunion followed by perfect sex and mutual declarations of everlasting love and "why did we divorce anyway?" was dissipating by the time Richard and I ended up at Nobu, eating sashimi. He hadn't said a thing the whole way back in the car. At one point he'd even put his head in his hands and groaned.

This is not what any girl wants on a date. But I kept it together. I reminded myself I wasn't falling apart and the world was still turning. Maybe I'd been silly about the Richard thing and everyone else had been right. But then at least I'd had the sense to check it out. I was just congratulating myself on my maturity, envisaging telling the girls over coffee later about how much better I felt having sorted out my feelings for Richard once and for all. They'd be awed by my coolness and circumspection and ashamed for having doubted my ability at rationality versus attraction. Reality versus the fantasy of having a man to spoon at night.

I nodded and shrugged my way through dinner while

Richard banged on about the wretched Sally and how much he loved her and pleading with me to help him "sort it out."

"Well, good luck with that," I told him as I stood up impatiently and he signed the bill. Then he ruined everything by looking up at me in the way he'd always looked up at me when he needed me.

"I'm a total shit, aren't I? Going on about me and my problems with Sally. I'm sorry, Lolly." Then he put his hand out and grabbed my wrist.

"I'm sorry, too," I told him, allowing him to pull me onto his lap. And I was sorry. I mean, after all, as far as Richard knew, he was going through a personal crisis and merely sharing it with a friend. He didn't have the slightest inkling of my mad scheme to lure him back to Lola Land. So when he cuddled me I cuddled him back. We were, after all, friends. We might have gone too far to go back but I cared for this man and he cared for me. That was probably how he felt when he cuddled me. I, on the other hand, couldn't help nuzzling his neck and wondering if, like me, he wasn't the tiniest bit turned on. I was fully aware that other diners around looking at us must have seen two people in love.

So my self-delusion kicked in and against sane judgment I invited him to join Elizabeth and Clemmie downstairs at the Met Bar—which wasn't the plan. Well, not my plan. That was Elizabeth's plan. "You can only take him to the Star Bar if you join us at eleven at the Met and promise us this madness is over!" she'd insisted.

"Actually, Lolly, I think I'll take a rain check."

"Fine." I shrugged.

We were at the lifts and he grabbed my shoulders.

"Don't be like that, Lola. We've had a great time."

I smiled up at him and he planted the briefest kiss on my mouth.

Go, just go, I was silently chanting in my head. Go before I wrestle you to the ground and make wild love to you in the lift. He did, in fact, pull me into the lift, but another couple joined us. They were holding hands and smiling up at one another, speaking in that silent couple language that doesn't need actual words.

As the lift doors opened, I pretended I was air kissing a business acquaintance. "What happened to us, Lolly?" he asked, but I left him wondering, because my whole body felt churned up over the events of the evening. Besides, he had Sally. He wanted Sally, not me, and I had to accept that.

The girls were tucked up in their booth by the DJ station.

"Well?" they all asked, desperate for the scoop.

"Well what?"

"What's going on with you and Richard?"

"Absolutely nothing. I just had to be sure that I wasn't still a little bit in love with him," I explained. "And I'm not, so, shall we order?"

Then my mobile vibrated. I recognized the number as I pulled it from my cleavage.

"I'm outside. I need you," he said and then he hung up.

I ignored the faces of my friends as I scrambled out of the booth and chased after him. He was climbing into his cab already. He saw me and held the door open.

"Richard?" I didn't know what I wanted to happen next, but when he said, "Come with me," I dived into the car. He wrapped his arms around me and held me like a drowning person holding on to a piece of broken raft. My phone vibrated again and I turned it off.

Back at his house in Shepherds Bush…I mean Notting Hill…he turned on his CD player and made us tea. For a while nothing was said. I leaned on one of his kitchen benches and watched him move purposefully about his kitchen as the music throbbed away in the living room upstairs. I suddenly regretted my decision to come. I didn't know what I was expecting and now I didn't even know what I wanted.

He passed me the mug and I followed him into the living room. Up until that point, being with Richard again had given me a sense of déjà vu, like I was back in the past, like he was still my husband and I was still his wife. It wasn't really until I walked into the living room and couldn't recognize any of the furniture that it truly hit me.

Richard was living in a parallel world to me now. A world where we didn't choose furnishings together. I don't know why I should have expected to recognize anything, as we'd had to sell everything when Richard's business collapsed, but I suddenly felt awkward and wrong. I definitely wouldn't have allowed him to choose the white-cloth sofa (Jean's droppings), let alone the ghastly abstract canvas dominating the wall. I took one of the white-cloth club chairs as opposed to the sofa but then to my surprise he sat at my feet, the way he always did when we were still married, and leaned his head back so that he was looking up at me. "I've totally fucked up *everything,* Lolly."

There wasn't really much to say. I didn't know if I was the "everything" he was referring to or whether he meant his business or Leggy Blonde, so I just sort of stroked his head and then he started to cry. It was the saddest thing to be sitting with my ex while his tears fell one after another, sadder still that he didn't even wipe them away. It was all very sad and not just because the tears clearly weren't for me.

I put my tea down and sat on the floor beside him, cuddled him and said, "Everything will be okay." And through his wet tears he started to kiss me and I kissed him back and after a while of salty tear kissing he pushed me down on the hardwood floor, his tongue moving familiarly across my lips, his hand struggling with my top. I let him undress me, and I undressed him, and suddenly all the memories of things lost and now found were moving through my body. I think—no, I know it was the same for him. His stare was fixed on my eyes, fixed as in frozen, as if we'd been frozen in time, a time where we belonged to one another. Neither of us spoke as we made slow careful well-rehearsed love on the hard wooden floor while Wyclef Jean and Mary J. Blige sang softly in the background.

Afterward we lay naked and sated and silent on the floor, our fingers and limbs intertwined in a perfect fit. I don't know how long we lay like that, I just know it felt as if time was suspended. The CD player was one of those state-of-the-art ones with a lineup of CDs set up so there was no need to change the music. After some garage and some hip-hop, Wyclef came back on and suddenly we were making mad wild celebratory love and my heart was soaring as the familiar ghetto-passionate lyrics poured out of the stereo about how this was the kind of love that his mother used to warn him about and how he was in trouble.

I almost wanted to laugh because *this* was the sort of love Kitty *wanted* for me. But I didn't laugh because I *was,* in trouble, that is. I was in Real Big Trouble! As Wyclef Jean pleaded for someone to dial 911, I opened my eyes and there she was, the Leggy Blonde standing in the doorway, her face etched with grief.

Richard must have felt me freeze and opened his own eyes, saw where I was looking in time to see Sally's back as she ran from the room. He jumped off me, like I was a hot stove, and sprinted after her.

"Sally! Baby, baby, please," he called and I lay there, naked, alone with no one to call 999 for me.

seven

There is a great deal of evidence that Lady Posche occasionally gave Edward money for his gambling debts.

It seems implausible that her husband could be unaware of this, yet he was by all accounts besotted with his wife, as letters to his family suggest. In one letter he writes to a close friend of the felicity of married life and the pleasure he derives from the beauty and charms of his adored Hen.

In another letter he urges his younger brother to enter the state of matrimony as soon as humanly possible as true happiness without marriage was to his mind impossible. His letters give no indication that his marriage was anything other than a perfect union, which contrasts with Hen's earliest letters to her sister in which she refers to her marriage as "this arrangement."

Secret Passage to the Past:
A Biography of Lady Henrietta Posche
By Michael Carpendum

I arrived in the grandeur of the bedroom as the morning light was slipping through a gap in the heavy purple drapes. "Oh my giddy aunt," I moaned as I climbed into bed and snuggled into the luxury of my goose-down Egyptian-cotton pillow as the events of the past ten hours morphed hideously into events from my marriage and divorce.

God, I was a disaster area. I should be cordoned off with orange police tape, like a crime scene. Sirens should blare at my approach, or better still, I should be alarmed, marked with an X—X for do not approach. The whole thing was so sordid and wrong and poisoned with the memories of my past with Richard. With the help of a makeshift eye mask—I used my knickers—I eventually managed to fall back into a fitful sleep, dreaming I was on a highway without exit ramps. I was so tired but I couldn't afford to fall asleep at the wheel.

I eventually woke up around four in the afternoon, propped myself up on my pillows and turned on my mobile phone to call Charlie. That was when I saw my message box was full.

I rang the service message provider to be told, "You have eight new messages." The first four were from the girls asking where the hell I was. I deleted them all, and then, as I heard the start of a message from Richard, tears sprang to my eyes and I deleted it without listening—along with the three others that followed. There were several text messages, too—again all from Richard, but I deleted them without reading any of them. I was frightened of what they'd say…or more precisely what they wouldn't say.

I'd spent the night at Posh House. After Richard left me naked on the floor, I had scrambled into my clothes while Leggy Blonde sobbed and Richard begged her for forgiveness in an upstairs room. I'd fled the scene and dashed into the dewy dawn, sprinting all the way back to the club in a kind of trance.

Beth, who was manning reception, explained that Charlie had taken Jean home to his place, and then the autopilot, which had got me there, forcing me to put one foot in front of the other, suddenly switched off and I slumped on the gothic church pew in reception and sobbed into my beaded handbag.

Poor Beth.

Trying to comfort a crying Lola. Breezy Lola, never fazed, never flustered. CCC Lola. The world can fall about around me but I am always the consummate professional—according to *London Style* magazine anyway. The girl with the plan.

What a joke. What a bizarre and rather unfunny joke.

Beth did what she could. Herbal tea, offers to talk and eventually the suggestion that I should get some sleep in one of the vacant bedrooms. I'd nodded numbly. I couldn't go home. I couldn't go back to my flat sans Jean and risk Richard *not* coming to find me. At least this way I could almost convince myself that Richard has spent the night worried sick outside my flat in a panic over where I was. As traumatized as I was, in other words.

Thankfully I fell asleep from the emotional exhaustion of the night.

After I showered in the Lady Posche Suite, I rang Charlie and told him what had happened and he said he'd be with me in a jiff, which cheered me up. He was the only person I knew who said things like "in a jiff." He even said "whoops-a-daisy" when someone fell down drunk. He didn't even seem to mind that people found his expressions funny. When I'd take the piss about the expressions he used, he'd say, "What do you mean? Whoops-a-daisy rocks!"

A "jiff" as it turned out was two hours, by which time I'd steadied myself with milky coffee and a croissant and was grabbing the last of the daylight in the courtyard. I didn't ring the girls. I knew what they'd say—especially Elizabeth who had never been one for mincing words—and I felt too raw for her barbed remarks about Richard and how she'd warned me, so I decided to fortify myself with Charlie, who came bounding in with the bunny bag.

I immediately took Jean out and gave her a cuddle.

"So, bit of a fuckup then, Lola old thing?" he remarked, falling into one of the courtyard chairs.

"Just a bit," I agreed. "Oh, Jean, give it up, will you," I scolded as she immediately started up on my arm with her trademark pelvic wiggles.

"Yes, a bit more sensitivity wouldn't go astray, Jean!" Charlie chastised.

I was glad I'd chosen to see Charlie first. With his inimitable love-rat style he wouldn't lecture or criticize. He'd say something like "Heck, so the girlfriend walked in. She must have had kittens!" Then he'd laugh and shake his head of tousled blond hair. That's what I needed. A good laugh. A smile almost spread across my face in anticipation.

But he didn't laugh or say anything amusing at all. Instead he said, "Maybe it's time to get a grip, old girl."

"What do you mean by 'get a grip' exactly?" (I didn't even want to acknowledge the old-girl part!)

"You don't think it's all getting a bit out of hand, this Richard business?"

I felt my hackles rise. "By this Richard business," I replied tartly, "I presume you mean my business?"

He smiled at me in a sad sort of way. "You can tell me I'm speaking out of turn here, but in my experience sex with the ex is like having the same car crash twice."

"You're speaking out of turn," I agreed, brushing an invisible piece of lint off my jeans, not wanting to meet his eyes. "Thank you for looking after Jean," I added in my most businesslike tone. "I'll get out of your hair and see you Tuesday afternoon."

He grabbed my hand. Not my wrist! My hand; interlocking his fingers into mine just as Richard had the night before, and then he pulled me into his lime-scented chest and stroked my hair.

"Oh darling, I'm sorry if I've been insensitive, poor you. First Jean and now me, we're not being very helpful, are we?"

"At least you're not humping me," I joked.

It was so lovely having Charlie to talk to and make me feel better about my absurd behavior that I was actually really disappointed when he announced, "I'm sorry, old thing, but I'm going to have to get going soon. Well, nowish, actually. But if you like, I can call up a car to take you home."

I didn't want to be alone. Being Saturday, Josie would be playing happy house with Emmanuel, and Elizabeth and Clemmie both had dates, so I told him I'd quite like to visit my parents in Richmond, and as I said it I realized it was true. Kitty and Martin were perhaps the only two people in the world who would understand and even sympathize with how I was feeling about Richard.

I arrived to find Kitty watching Kitty's favorite film, *Sunset Boulevard,* on DVD. She didn't find any similarity between herself and the character played by Gloria Swanson; you had to love her. Martin was fiddling with his clocks, but everyone stopped everything when I explained what had been happening that week between Richard and me.

"How obscenely rude, to walk in while you were making love to your own husband!" A typically insane Kitty remark but just the sort of thing I needed to hear.

"Well, technically, he's my ex," I reminded her.

She patted her platinum sweep of hair, and raised one eyebrow from the chaise where she was stretched out like a cat. "There's nothing technical about love, Lola. If you want technical, get a clock." Then she looked darkly at Martin who was fiddling with a clock face on the table. He took the hint and joined us—although still with his clock face—flopping onto a cushion at Kitty's feet.

"Perhaps he gave her a key or something. There had been talk before I saw him of her wanting to move in."

"No doubt she talked him into giving her one, what a sly minx. You must bring her down, Lola! Bring her down, cast her out of his life. Sherry?"

"Thanks, I will actually."

"Martin!"

"My darling?" He smiled up at my mother's beautiful face vaguely. She traced a line along his jaw and blew him a kiss.

"You might offer my daughter a sherry after all she's endured."

I cringed. It was always a bad sign when Kitty started referring to me as "her" daughter. When I was young it usually meant I was about to be shoved off to Aunt Camilla's so they could really get the knives out and go for one another's throats. Martin shuffled about the drinks cabinet while Kitty continued her tirade against Leggy Blonde. It was quite empowering all in all. I found that by the time Kitty finally left me to join Martin in bed, I was feeling quite incensed myself about Leggy Blonde.

As Kitty had so neatly and reasonably put it, "Presumably Richard had already dumped her, called you, realizing what you meant to him, was in the middle of a perfect union with his wife, when she stalked in as if she owned the place. Inevitably he gave the wretch a key to pick her stuff up while he was at work, not while he was in the middle of making love to his wife!"

"Ex-wife!" Elizabeth corrected as I went over Kitty's theory with the girls at Nobu on the Sunday night.

"She sort of has a point, though," I told Elizabeth.

"Sorry, I must have missed that under all the madness," Elizabeth added.

Even Clemmie shrunk at her anger. "I just wish I hadn't deleted his messages now," I sighed, ignoring their opinions.

Elizabeth put her hand on mine. "Darling, not to dredge up the past, but repeat what it was Richard actually said to Sally when he dived off you to pursue her. You were making love, she interrupted, yet he dived off you like you were a hot stove."

"He left you for Sally," Clemmie added unnecessarily.

"Well, yes, but probably to take her to task," I suggested, repeating what I had begun to believe was Kitty's perfectly plausible explanation.

"And what words did he use to take her to task?" Elizabeth asked, her coal-black eyes glinting. I find it really hard lying to Elizabeth.

"Erm…I can't quite remember now. It all happened so fast and then he took her up to the bedroom to sort of have a talk."

"I bet he said, 'I can explain!'" Clemmie suggested mixing her wasabi with her soy sauce. "Men always say that when they haven't got an explanation. They think it will give them time to think up an excuse."

Of course, I remembered the words, but I wasn't going to admit to what he'd said; the memory still hurt and I knew how the girls would react to "Sally baby, please."

"Or, 'It's not what it looks like'?" Elizabeth giggled, spitting her green tea back into the cup with the hilarity of it all.

"The point is," I said stiffly, "he left all those messages and I deleted them and now I don't know what he said."

Elizabeth said something that I missed as I took a mouthful of my tuna sashimi with way too much wasabi and had to gulp down water to curb the explosion in my nose.

Everyone stopped laughing at whatever it was that Elizabeth had said to comfort me. But I didn't want their comfort for a bit of errant wasabi. I wanted them to comfort and reassure me about Richard. After all, even Kitty had been able to do that.

When I got back home to Jean, I cradled her in my arms. Oh Jean, what do I do? She squirmed as I kissed her nose, so I popped her on the ground with some carrot, which she nibbled while watching the news. What would Clemmie and Elizabeth know anyway? Elizabeth just hated Richard for no real reason other than historic evidence. She claimed to care for me, but if that were true, you'd think she'd want me to be happy.

So, in the hopes of nailing the facts down once and for all, I phoned Richard. Jean sat supportively on my lap for the call. I had what I was going to say all mapped out in my brain, but then his phone went to answer, which was surprising because it was already two in the morning, tomorrow was a workday and the phone was by his bed.

I hoped he was okay. Oh no, I thought as I envisaged him wandering the streets morosely, perhaps even tearfully. He probably thought I hated him after refusing to take his calls and then not responding to his messages. Jean blinked up at me and twitched her little nose. "Good idea, Jean, I'll try his mobile."

And then something awful happened. He rejected my call.

I tried again, telling myself not to be paranoid, but then I was rejected again. Buggar. The walls of the flat began to come in on me as reality struck. I did what I always do in times of crisis and started compulsively organizing. I threw a load of washing into the machine, changed Jean's litter box, and by four in the morning I was climbing the walls, having reorganized my entire wardrobe (trying Richard's phone every half hour), lined up all my shoes, taken a Polaroid shot of each pair and glued it to the box. I'd always meant to do that even though I have never managed to put a pair of shoes back in their box in my life, preferring the more traditional strategy of throwing them in a heap in my wardrobe.

Doubts began to grip me as the dawn light started to creep through my blinds, so I took Jean down to Berkeley Square for a run. Sitting on my usual seat, I tried Richard again. Eventually he'd have to get up for work, I told myself as weariness seeped through my bones. Then again, eventually I'd have to go to bed.

eight

"For God's sake, do not complain that you do not see me, Hen. I believe I suffer not less in this matter than you, but 'tis not to be helped. You undo me by dreaming of how happy we might have been. Alas, how can you talk of defying fortune, for nobody lives without it, least of all you, Madam."

A day after Henrietta received this letter from Edward, he arrived in her bedchamber at dawn, penniless, with the stench of dissipation all about his person. He claimed he was a victim of muggery. It is true that his haunts were plagued with skulduggery and dark deeds. Henrietta gave him laudanum for the pain and tended his wounds herself, keeping him in her room while pretending that she was ill so that suspicion would not be aroused by the servants.

She wrote to her sister, Elizabeth: "This madness is part of my love. He is so excellently good when he is injured, Elizabeth, so gentle and obliging. If you could only see the way he looks upon me, 'tis as if he believes me an angel. I fear I may love him all the more at these times…"

Secret Passage to the Past:
A Biography of Lady Henrietta Posche
By Michael Carpendum

Richard finally called me on Monday night as I was fighting my way through the white light of the paparazzi lineup outside the launch party for a new jeweler on Old Bond Street. I'd left two messages on his mobile and one at his home and three at his work. I was covering all bases, so he'd probably worked out by now that there was no escape. I wanted answers…or rather I wanted confirmation of the answers I'd already made up in my head.

"Did you not get my messages?" was his opening gambit.

"Lola…stand between Tamara and Niki!" the paparazzi yelled.

"I'm so sorry," I told him calmly, one finger in my ear, a smile glued to my face. Niki arranged me in the center as the white light of a thousand flashbulbs exploded in my face. "I was upset, and I just deleted them all."

He exhaled. "Yeah, I'm sorry, too."

Niki and Tamara left me just inside the entrance, out of

the glare of the press, told me they'd catch up with me inside while I listened to Richard's long pause. Even above the noise of the throng I could feel the pain in his voice and my heart went out to him. "It's not your fault she pitched up like that," I told him in my most indignant tone, just to reassure him that I understood.

"No, I mean I'm sorry you didn't listen to my messages. I mean, I should have said—"

I cut in, determined to believe the explanation I'd concocted for him, "Waltzing in like that, unannounced. It just frightened the life out of me," I told him. My learner wheels were off now, I was playing the role of supportive wife perfectly. "It wasn't exactly ideal, and given the circumstances, the best thing I could do was leave you to you. Poor you, having to deal with her on your own."

"No, that's what I mean, Lola. Will you give me a chance—"

I made it inside and took a glass of champagne off a tray. "I suppose you gave her a key so she could pick her stuff up, but still she should have given you a time. You could have her for breaking and entering," I half joked, the image of Leggy Blonde cuffed and being led away by a stern police constable was rather soothing. I took a sip of my drink and smiled at the thought.

"No, I gave her the key so she could move in."

I pressed the end button, took a deep breath and threw myself into the launch, the epitome of CCC.

Nicola, the jeweler of the moment (all A-list celebs were buying her exquisite wraps of platinum mesh with diamonds), wrapped me in a warm hug. I hugged her back, seamlessly whisking a caviar canapé off the tray sashaying past. I really don't know how I survived the evening. My head was swimming with a mixture of questions I needed answers to and answers I wished I didn't have. But I wasn't going to get them here and so I threw myself into what I do best, controlling a situation.

After the launch I went on to the private members' club Soho House with Nicola, where her achingly gorgeous friends were gathered for a celebration, and acted as if I was the happiest girl in the world. She showed me her engagement ring—which she'd crafted herself for fun. "No man, just a myth, but fun, don't you think?"

"Adorable," I gushed, remembering my own engagement ring. Richard had bought the diamond in Antwerp from the bourse—more of an investment, he'd told me at the time. He'd set it simply, to show off the stone, he explained. It was nice for a fuck-off huge diamond, but I always felt self-conscious wearing it because, well, it wasn't really me. I felt a bit like a dog dragging its lead.

It was the man I loved, not the ring—but maybe the man I loved, like Nicola's ring, was a myth. Perhaps I loved a man who didn't exist, not in the way I wanted him to exist, at least.

I went to the bathroom, splashed water on my face, reapplied my lip gloss and wished I took cocaine like everyone else so that I could do a line and obliterate the pain, or at least the humiliation.

Our table grew increasingly crowded as others joined us. It was the A-list table at Soho House that night and I needed to be on form. I drew on every resource I had acquired as London's foremost party organizer. These people were my clients as well as my friends, not friends like Clemmie and Elizabeth, maybe, but people I liked, people I wanted to work with, so I laughed, I breezed, and even when Clemmie and Elizabeth joined me, I wore my pain like lip gloss and acted as if I was on top of the world.

At times like this most girls call their mum, but I knew only too well that Kitty would only feed my delusions. The next time I went to the loo, Elizabeth followed me.

"He's screwed you over again, hasn't he?" she said as we were washing our hands.

I smiled at her reflection in the mirror. "You read too much into things, I'm fine, just tired."

"Huh, so you're gushing like a lunatic because…?"

"I'm so not gushing."

"You're gushing like a burst pipe, Lola. Look, darling," she said ever so gently, "I'm your friend. I know this about Richard. You went after him the other night, didn't you?"

My silence said it all.

"Darling, if he's hurt you, I want to kill him."

These were the words that broke me and made me fall into her arms for a much-needed hug. "And then after I've killed him I'm going to come round to your place and wipe every trace of him from your phone, your laptop, your phone book, your mobile. And then I'm going to get you trollied and make you poke every eye out in every photograph you still have intact. Then we'll burn them and hock your engagement ring and spend the proceeds on a we-so-hate-Richard party."

So in the loo of Soho House, the floodgates of reality finally opened and I told her everything that had happened between Richard and me since I'd seen him at Posh House, and how I still couldn't throw off my feelings for him. Elizabeth said I had a family emergency, so I didn't have to go back to the table in the emotionally incontinent state I was in. Elizabeth didn't kill Richard that night but she did follow through on her other promises. By the time I took Jean for her romp around the square at dawn, all traces of Richard had been obliterated from my flat.

Maybe that was long overdue, I'd decided stoically as we'd torn the photographs into tiny mosaic tiles. We couldn't burn them, though, because my flat had no chimney and it was so small we might have burnt the building down. "We can turn them into pulp, though!" Elizabeth had pointed out, so we filled the sink with the tiles of my past with Richard and ran hot water over them.

Perhaps the reason the break with Richard had never seemed real was that we'd never really had the massive Big Breakup arguments and screaming matches. We'd just had "a break" that had drifted into dating other people and finally divorce. We'd gone for a no-claim divorce—by that point there was nothing left to claim, so we hadn't even had a day in court.

I remembered feeling sad on the day my decree nisi came through. By the time the decree absolute arrived, I was involved with my biggest event to date. It arrived the day I appeared in *Vogue* for the first time, and the legal document with its fancy legal wording didn't seem nearly as significant as the glamorous photograph of Charlie, Jean and me. Elizabeth helped me dig up the divorce paper and I fell asleep reading it.

But now the line had finally been drawn and I drifted off to sleep feeling cleansed. It didn't last.

The next afternoon I woke up with a determination to finish the job off. Really finish the job off. By job I meant Richard, by finish off I mean I wanted closure. I wanted to feel that I was over Richard, like it was a decision I was taking, not being forced to take because of him. Like Elizabeth, I suddenly had an overwhelming need to murder him.

I put an ice pack on my eyes to diminish the traces of all my tears of the night before, then I dressed carefully. Dressed to kill, vintage killer Manolo Blahniks, killer skin tight jeans and a Dolce & Gabbana top that screamed cleavage.

"I'm sorry, Jean," I told her as I tucked her into my bag. "I'm going to murder Richard, but I don't want you to get involved, all right, Miss Harlot?" She looked at me in her concerned little way. I hardly ever used her surname, so she must have known something pretty serious was wrong. "It's always the rabbits that suffer," I told her as I patted her bag.

I climbed into a taxi, my body drenched in tuberose, and gave the driver the address of Richard's offices in Hammersmith.

"Off out somewhere special then, are you?" the cabdriver asked sociably.

"Very," I told him. "I'm off to kill my ex-husband."

"Right you are, luv," he replied nervously, slamming the partitioning screen closed.

Richard's offices were housed in a crap seventies building near the tube station, but as I climbed out of my taxi I decided that Richard, being the vain bastard he was, probably called the area Chiswick.

I took a deep breath and rehearsed my lines in my head again. I might have had a close shave with madness and delusion, but I was revived by a large dose of reality by the time the lift doors opened. This man had humiliated me, had played with my emotions, had used me as a Sally Substitute and cast me off. And now I was going to tell him precisely what I thought of him.

It was an open-plan office with about forty employees. I took them all in with a sweeping glance. None of the drones in their little cubicles noticed me as they spoke into telephones, peered at computer screens or tapped away at keyboards.

Richard was on the far left-hand side, one leg casually resting on a chair, chatting to one of his partners. He looked carefree, careless—he didn't look as if he'd witnessed a grenade going off in my life—nor did he look like the guy who'd pulled the pin and thrown it. I strode down the short distance from the lift to the receptionist, who pulled her hand out of a packet of M&M's and physically shrank into her chair at my approach. Looking at her anonymous clothes and home-streaked hair, I doubted that she'd ever dealt with someone dressed like me.

"Tell Mr. Arbiter Bisque that his ex-wife is here to see him," I instructed her in my most authoritative tone.

She scuttled off nervously and I stood there flicking through a back copy of some nerdy computer magazine. I could feel Jean fidgeting in the bag, so I gave her a comforting pat.

"Lola?"

He was only inches away as I spun around on my blade-sharp stilettos to face him.

"Mr. Arbiter Bisque."

He looked stunned by my tone and words. I've never been a vicious person. We'd argued, but I'd always been tearful when I said hurtful things. More than stunned, though, I saw something else in his expression, a mixture of fear and impending embarrassment. He must have been very aware of all his colleagues, who were now all rubbernecking for a better look.

"Are you okay, Lolly, would you like to go out somewhere for a chat?" he suggested in a quiet tone, taking my elbow and leading me toward the lifts as if I was a shoplifter, or a hooker, someone to be ashamed of.

Looking back, I think it was his casual use of my nickname, the name only the people who loved me ever used—that made me lash out. All the things I wanted to say, all the things I needed to say to free myself from the feelings I now knew were as pointless as the care I'd put into my choice of outfit. It was pointless to say those things, too.

So I slapped his face, so hard I thought my hand was broken, turned away and pressed the button for the elevator—which thankfully was still there from my arrival—watched the doors close, nursed my hand and that was that.

It was finally over, I told myself.

I was finally free. There could be no more going back.

I finally had that magical closing-door moment that had eluded me for so long....

nine

"My darling Hen, I hardly know what to say. I cannot begin to fathom the agony of your love for Edward. I thank God that my own marriage is characterized by love and respect for one another, for I have still to find a flaw in dear Bertie. For this reason, I cannot advise you, only assure you that I love you as much as any woman ever loved a sister. Your rapture is your torture and I wonder at your ability to carry yourself in society with the charm and vivacity for which you are so loved and admired. Indeed, you wear your pain like a jewel that becomes you well. Perhaps too well…"

Extract from a letter from Elizabeth to her sister, Lady Henrietta Posche

I rang Elizabeth on my way to work and told her in the briefest terms about my assault on Richard. I made it sound like a boast, the triumph of reason over passion, but the truth was, I was shaken by my bunny-boilerish behavior, which I think Elizabeth picked up on because she didn't try to drag the details out of me the way she normally would.

"That's settled, then, we're all going to the Met afterward to celebrate. See you there around eleven. There's that new DJ on tonight I want to check out. He might be someone you can use, too, there's a lot of heat on him at the moment."

It was important to stay in the loop as far as what was hot and what was up-and-coming, because if you blinked you missed it. I was blinking back tears, though, as I passed Charlie talking to someone in reception. He turned and gave me one of his supergrins, which I returned, determined not to give myself away. I was cuddling Jean, and as he leaned over to stroke her ears, it struck me that Richard hadn't so much as asked about poor little Jean when we'd gone out on the Friday to *Top of the Pops*.

I hid myself in my cupboard-cum-office to do my last checks for the evening's event—a book launch, *Secret Passage to the Past: A Biography of Lady Henrietta Posche* by Michael Carpendum. Michael, a member of Posh House, was one of London's notable personalities, a self-declared dandy; the consummate gentleman. He dressed and behaved with the manners of another age, when men were pretty and women were handsome. He kissed hands, he bowed, he was charm personified. He embodied all the magnificent history of the club, but more importantly he was the sort of patron I could safely count on to give no trouble about guests, champagne, or anything else for that matter. He was just the tonic to take my mind off my afternoon's violence.

I had actually slapped Richard! I still couldn't believe it myself. I still imagined I could feel his cheek on my hand. And that made it worse. No matter how many times I slapped that cheek, I wanted to stroke it. I felt worse, shaken, ashamed—almost everything apart from "better."

"So how is my most gorgeous employee doing today?" Charlie inquired, poking his head around the door as I flicked through the incident reports for the week.

I smiled up at him. "She's perfect."

"As ever," he riposted. "So, all ready for tonight? One hundred and fifty, isn't it?" he asked, referring to the number of guests.

"All is in order, and I even managed to squeeze in a trip to Hammersmith."

Charlie looked nonplussed.

"That's where Richard's office is," I explained. "I slapped

him across the face!" I continued matter-of-factly as I ran
my eyes down the guest list.

"Well, there it is, then," he remarked with equal insouci-
ance, but I could see he was curious because he hung around
the door, obviously keen for more info.

"Did he say anything to provoke this slap?" he inquired
eventually.

"No, we didn't have a conversation. I felt we'd had all the
verbal exchanges we needed. Time for a short sharp slap of
reality," I explained as I drew a line through a guest we'd
banned following a nasty public accusation of theft against
another member the month before. Her handbag was later
found intact in the cloakroom where she had checked it in.
"I simply woke up, realized it was something long overdue
on my to do list, so I dropped in at his office and walloped
him."

"I say. Well…congratulations and all that…I guess."

I looked up at my boss's befuddled face and smiled. It was
hard not to smile when you looked at Charlie. He just had
that sort of face, not because he was good-looking, although
he was, but it was more to do with the warmth he radiated.
He was genuinely kind and thoughtful without being a
saint—which would have been intimidating.

"And you, darling one, how's *your* love life?" I asked him,
suddenly feeling a lot better about everything.

"See, now you're getting me confused with someone else.
My love denies me life!" he announced with a mock-dandy
drama that was pure Michael Carpendum.

"And what cruel wench is this? Is her heart made of
stone?" I gasped breathlessly, carrying on the parody.

"Yes, well, that's what I ask myself sometimes," he sighed,
now kneeling at my feet, staring into my eyes and clasping
my hand. "Sometimes I think she hardly knows I exist!"

"She can't possibly be worthy of you, sir," I told him. "I advise you to sever this inequitable relationship at once!"

"Good God, no! She might wallop me." And with that the phone rang and Charlie left.

"You just slapped dickhead across the face!" Josie squealed with childish delight.

"I decided it was time," I replied, as if we'd discussed it all at length beforehand.

"Anyway, long overdue. We're all meeting up at the Met later."

"I know. Elizabeth told me."

"I'm bringing Emmanuel," she added. "If that's okay?"

"Fabulous. He needs a night out."

"That's what he told me. He's looking forward to everyone being on good form."

"Is that a warning?"

"More of a threat," she teased. "But seriously, Lola…"

"What?"

"Congratulations."

"Erm, thanks. I think."

Clemmie called next. "How do you spell intelligent?"

"Intelligent?"

"Yes, it means really bright, full of smart beans, etc."

"I know what it means."

"Can you spell it?"

"I-N-T-E-L-L-I-G-E-N-T."

"Thanks, I'm just composing a lovely e-mail to you telling you how brilliant you are for slugging old coke chops."

And so my evening continued. My friends, and friends of friends, and people I barely knew calling—falling over themselves to congratulate me for assaulting my ex-husband in his place of work.

By the time I went upstairs to check how the room was

looking for the launch, I'd started to feel a bit bad. All the anger that had drained away when my hand met Richard's cheek was now replaced by a sense that I was somewhat of a fraud.

Yes, I was angry—okay, furious even—and for a moment expressing that anger had felt empowering and liberating, but while Elizabeth and the others had helped me to destroy all vestiges of Richard left in my flat, they couldn't delete or burn the memory of last Friday night when we had made love. It hadn't just been about sex, not totally. I've had plenty of disposable sex since our divorce and that night was like a homecoming, sex without the niggling doubt, sex with the certainty of orgasm from the get-go.

We knew our way around one another's bodies without a compass. We knew the taste, touch and feel of each other, and while there were no big surprises there was plenty of satisfaction.

Much, much, much more satisfaction than could be wiped away with a slap across a cheek.

But I couldn't think about that now, I had the launch to oversee. The author was darting about in full late-eighteenth-century evening dress, spreading his trademark charm amongst his A-list guests. If only all hosts could manage to greet each guest with his Beau Brummel–like panache. Every one was feeling special and loved up. The books were lined against the wall, the champagne flowed, the canapés were being appreciatively devoured, while a piano, played by one of the members, twinkled Chopin elegantly in keeping with the evening.

"Ah, Lola, darling," Michael said, air kissing me with trademark grandeur. "This is for you," he said, passing a copy of the book into my hands. And here's a copy for dear Jean."

"Secret Passage to the Past," I read.

"Fascinating," he declared, grandly closing his hands around my own. "Darling, you must read it. This magical house is a history of gorgeousness!" he declared, kissing the nape of my neck and inhaling me. "Like you, dearest one. Like you."

"Definitely," I assured him, flicking through the pages and scanning the old photographs of Posh House—or rather Posche House, as it was then known. There were hand-written letters composed by the residents, and then a photograph of the secret passage itself. I recognized it immediately as the deep orange passage that led to Charlie's office, and pointed it out to Michael. "So, Lady Posche used to smuggle her lover up these stairs?"

"The very same, darling. And you, my dear, are the Henrietta Posche of contemporary London!" he declared, stroking my cheek seductively.

"I'm definitely reading it, then," I assured him as we kissed goodbye, and for a moment I felt all was right with the world, so I took a break and wandered upstairs to see what Jean was up to.

I'd left her in the care of the drawing-room staff. It was only a Tuesday night and fairly quiet. "Carlos, darling, where's Jean?" I asked one of the staff rushing past with a tray of drinks.

"Jean, she is with that man over there." He pointed to one of the corner sofas where a man and a woman were snuggled with their backs to us.

"Is she okay?" I asked in terror, the image of her humping her way through London's polite society flashing through my mind.

"Oh yes, he ask if he can hold her."

"All right, darling?" asked Faisel, the manager of the drawing room, as he wrapped me in an affectionate hug.

"I'm okay, just worried about Jean getting up to mischief."

"She's fine, sweetheart. She's with what's-his-name, your ex. He's had a few by the look of him." He laughed his trademark dirty laugh as I turned to the sofa and took in the scene more carefully. Dark hair, Richard, sitting beside, blonde hair—Sally!

"Faisel, could you do me a massive favor and bring Jean back over to me?"

"Sure thing, gorgeous," he replied, and then as if grasping my discomfort, he gave me cuddle. "You really okay, babe?"

"Yes, fine, just pissed off that he's here, really." Which was a bit unreasonable as he was a member of the club with every right to be here if he so wanted. Still, after recent events, he had a nerve.

"You wait here, I'll go fetch her."

I watched from the bar area as Faisel spoke to the couple. He picked up Jean, and then Richard turned around and our eyes met and in that look that passed between us we both gave ourselves away; everything was said.

I was still in love with him and he was still in pain.

Leggy Blonde turned, too, but after a brief searchlight gaze, she turned her back on me. Richard didn't turn back, though, and I didn't look away until Faisel placed Jean in my arms.

I went back to the launch using the service stairs to give myself time to pull myself together. I wasn't thinking clearly. I hugged Jean to my beating heart. I needed to splash my face with water. I needed to call Elizabeth. I needed to take deep breaths.

I passed Charlie coming up the stairs.

"Good, I was looking for you."

"Well, you've discovered me."

"Listen, would you join me for a glass of cordial? The event seems to be going splendidly and I wanted to discuss a few things with you."

"Perfect," I replied as if I wasn't in the least bit conflicted or on the verge of an emotional breakdown.

Charlie pushed against a curve in the wall that magically opened onto the dimly lit secret staircase, which according to Michael, Lady Henrietta Posche had used to smuggle in her lover. Now painted a shade of Georgian orange, its wooden stairs were worn from the footfalls of centuries.

It was because of the secret passage that Charlie chose the onetime bedchamber of Lady Posche as his office. He said he loved the idea of all those illicit comings and goings, said it made going over the accounts seem more exotic.

"Michael gave me a copy of his book."

"You should read it," he told me.

"Of course I will."

"Some of the letters were found here in this room by the builders during the renovation."

"How amazing," I told him as I looked about, and tried to envisage the room as it was in the eighteenth century. Presently, it looked like a BBC period-drama set, book-lined, crystal-chandeliered... In fact, apart from the plasma screen over the fireplace tuned to Sky News Extra (for Jean), it was like walking into another time zone.

"You know, if these walls could talk we could sell tickets," he mused as he carefully eased the cork off a bottle of Dom. We both settled on the leather chesterfield with Jean between us.

"So you thumped the ex?"

"I did indeed."

"Hard?"

I took a sip of my champagne, smiling teasingly over my glass at Charlie. "I thought I'd broken my hand."

"Shocked, was he?"

"I didn't wait to find out." I smiled faux proudly.

Charlie raised one eyebrow. "So the candle of love has finally been snuffed?"

"The fire of passion utterly extinguished."

We both took a long sip of our cordial while taking an even longer look at one another. I was wondering if Charlie was about to give me a raise or a man-to-girl talk, so I preempted him by asking, "So is this one those talks where you give me a raise?" I was only half joking.

"I suppose it should be, shouldn't it?"

"Oh, absolutely."

"But no. I'm just wondering if you slapped Richard to mark the end of something or whether there's someone else?"

"I slapped him because he's an arse and I should have slapped him years ago."

"So, not because he's seeing someone else?"

I shook my head.

"Well, then. Hold your glass like a poem!"

"What?"

"It's the name of a book Lady Henrietta Posche wrote."

"Oh." I nodded absentmindedly. Charlie blushed, but that was probably because during our eye-to-eye contact, Jean Harlot, the little slapper, had clambered onto his lap and was snuffling his...well, let's just say her behavior was highly inappropriate.

"He's in the house tonight, you know," he remarked as I lifted my shameful pet off him and held her above my nose so that I could give her a jolly good ticking off. "Now,

madam, that is not the way a lady treats a man." I didn't want
to discuss Richard anymore.

"Oh, I don't know," laughed Charlie. "Depends on who
the lady is."

"Charlie," I scolded. "You're sounding quite pervy."

After that, we both seemed to relax and we talked generally, about the club and ideas he had for its expansion. He
was thinking of buying the house next door and knocking
through so we could have a pool. I suggested a few ways we
could launch the idea and raise more funds. Soon we were
toasting his dreams with our second glass of champagne and
giggling stupidly at the maddest things, which was very
naughty as I was still officially meant to be working.

"I'd better take Jean off for a last check of the launch," I
said as I stood to leave. "I'm meeting the girls at the Met.
Josie's bringing her husband. Actually, why don't you join
us," I invited. "Emmanuel's joining us, so we'll need someone to amuse him."

"Do you know, if that's a serious offer I just might. I feel
like I never get to escape this place sometimes."

"The girls would love it," I told him truthfully. "Maybe
you could pull Clemmie or Elizabeth?" I suggested. "They
both fancy you like mad." I know it was very unprofessional
of me suggesting that my boss shag my girlfriends, but we
both knew I was sort of joking.

"Best not to mix business with pleasure," he told me
sternly.

I giggled so hard I fell into him and it was definitely just
the "cordial" that had gone straight to my head, but I actually thought Charlie was about to kiss me and I was almost
ready to kiss him back. Poor Charlie, he must have been horrified, because he went bright red, and once we'd untangled
ourselves he started fussing with a cigar box.

"Erm, so I'll see you there," I told him, stroking Jean's ears, not wanting him to see me blushing.

"In about an hour, okay?"

"Right ho," I replied and scurried off.

Talk about embarrassing! I slipped through the secret panel and rushed down the stairs, and bam, slammed straight into Richard.

"Shit!" I exclaimed, because it's very humiliating to slam into a man you've just slapped across the face a mere few hours previous.

I muffled an apology, but Richard just looked at me in a forlorn sort of way and then said, "Lolly?"

The last time he'd said Lolly I'd slugged him, but now I wanted to fall into his embrace and rest my fuzzy muddled head on his shoulder. Not that I did, of course; apart from anything else, Jean was wriggling about in my arms.

"Hey, Jean Harlot, my baby!" With that, he took her in his arms and scratched her ears as if he did it every day. He had beautiful long tapered fingers and I was reminded of the marvelous things he'd done to my body with them only last Friday.

Without thinking, the words just came out of my mouth. "Make her go away!"

"Sorry? I was just giving her a stroke." He looked as if I'd just slapped him again.

"I'm not talking about Jean. Make *her* go away. Drop her off and come to mine."

"But I can't, she's moved in, Lola. I've asked her to marry me," he explained almost pleadingly. "Lolly, I'm sorry, but I do love you, I always will, but we can't…we can't go back."

Now it was me being slapped across the face. A slap of reality. Richard, for all his flaws and mistakes, was right. I took Jean from his arms. "Well, make sure you never meet up with me again," I told him, holding back a sob. "I mean it, Richard. I can't deal with this bumping into you all the time."

"Lolly, don't."

Tears began to fall down my cheeks. "I mean it, Richard," I repeated.

"Oh, Lolly," he sighed, pulling me into his chest and stroking my hair. "Please, Lolly, you know we can't go back to what we had, not really." He was right, we both had to turn around and walk away, go forward into the future and stop looking back, but I couldn't bear it. I couldn't bear the familiar comfort of having Richard's arms around me. I couldn't walk away when all I could think of lately was him and all the good times we'd had. The vows we'd made seemed as real and binding now as they did then. I wanted what we had back. I didn't want to know about Sally, I didn't want to know about sensible or about right and wrong. I wanted Sally to go away, to cease to exist so that I could have Richard back.

"Why can't we go back?" I asked, looking up at him.

"Oh, Lolly,"

"Why, Richard. I want you back. Make her go away."

ten

If your life is to be a poem of love, you must not disrupt the verse with doubt or vacillations.

Whether making love, riding in a carriage, instructing a servant, organizing a party, greeting a guest or discussing politics, every movement, every action, every word, should be in homage to that love.

I cannot but feel the touch of my lover's lips on each word that comes from my mouth, whether my conversation be with a parlor maid or my very own true love…

Extract from *Hold Your Glass Like a Poem*
by Lady Henrietta Posche

It was a bold gambit but I made a pact with my conscience. If Richard dumped Leggy Blonde and came to me, it meant we were meant to be together, like Anthony and Cleopatra, like Richard Burton and Elizabeth Taylor, like, well…like Kitty and Martin. If he didn't come then fine…all this madness of late could stop.

I knew, though, in the marrow of my bones, that he'd come.

I knew because underneath my mad obsession with Richard, I knew Richard…maybe even better than I knew myself. He would have to come, I'd thrown down a gauntlet and Richard had always been one to take on a challenge. I was so sure he'd come, I had even dressed Jean in her darling brown Hermés ribbon that really set off her eyes.

I slipped into my sexiest underwear, which was so cool the designer still didn't have a supplier. She was a member of Posh House and all her pieces were decorated with real gemstones, like garnets and rose quartz, which meant it was almost impossible to wash them but they looked divine. Mostly I had them hanging on my bedroom wall with pegs—like an art installation. But tonight I dusted them off—I was to be the work of art.

I took a bottle of Dom champagne out of my mini-fridge, which doubled as my cosmetics cabinet, full as it was of nail varnish and moisturizers. Apart from champagne, I didn't keep food or drink in my flat, there simply wasn't the space. I'd even converted my kitchen cupboard into book-shelves, and I placed Jean's copy of *Secret Passage to the Past* on it, because she wasn't a great fan of biography really. I placed the copy dedicated to me beside my bed, along with the opened bottle of Dom. Then I lit a tuberose candle and inserted the latest Dido CD into my laptop. I was always meaning to buy a stereo, but when you live a nocturnal life, you never seem to find the time to do that sort of shopping.

The buzzer went and I hastily made my bed as I heard the lift come up. Richard. He looked drained when I opened the door, but as I wrapped my arms around him and led him through to my bedroom, he returned my kisses with equal fervor.

And in those kisses I knew the truth: Leggy Blonde had lost and I had won. She might have the legs and looks of a model, but they were the looks and legs of a loser. He had chosen me, a girl of ordinary height, attractive enough though definitely no model—the outsider perhaps, but the winner. The only disappointment was that my prize was slightly damaged from the battle. After sex, Richard rolled off me and groaned. Not a groan of ecstasy but a groan of pain, of problems pushed aside now back and demanding to be dealt with.

I turned away and pulled the sheet around me. Not even

the sweet little scratching sounds of Jean hopping into the room could make reality any less miserable in that postcoital moment.

He said he couldn't stay the night.

I said he could.

He kissed me before falling back down against the pillows. Then my phone rang.

"Lola! What happened to you?" It was Elizabeth.

"Oh shit, I forgot, I was *soooo* knackered after work I just came home and fell asleep," I lied. "I'm sorry, I should have called." I yawned. "How's it going anyway, what's the DJ like?" I climbed out of bed and took the phone into the living room.

"The DJ's fine, but listen, Charlie's here, he seemed rattled that you didn't come. Slip on your heels and run down now."

"I don't know, Elizabeth, I don't really feel like going out, I think I need a night in."

She laughed. "That'll be the day. But not tonight. Come on, we have to celebrate your afternoon of violent assault. We've ordered champagne, everyone's here. Wait there, Clemmie wants a word."

"Lola, get down here now! Charlie's here."

"Well, I'm sure you and the girls can entertain him. The truth is," I lied, "I'm not sure I'm up for anything tonight, gem, I'm feeling a bit crap actually."

"He's here with some gorgeous blond creature, as it happens," she teased, whispering. "I always thought *you* should have a fling with Charlie."

"Nice!" I replied. "Especially as it sounds like he's with someone."

"You could make mincemeat of her, Lola, you know these thoroughbreds don't have the staying power. Besides, girl or no girl, he really wanted to see you tonight. Sashay on down, your glass awaits you, darling."

As I hung up the phone, Richard walked out in his trousers.

"You're not leaving?" I was aware of the slight whine in my voice.

"I can't do this, Lola," he stated simply, and I thought how he looked like a dog that's been beaten, not a man who had just been made love to. "We can't do this, Lola. You know that."

So I said goodbye, at a loss for anything else to say.

"I do love you," he told me as he was leaving. "I don't want to lose you in my life…I just can't…" His voice trailed off as I shut the door.

I didn't want to hear anything beyond the "I love you" part. The rest was just verbiage. So I ignored the doubts, the conflict, the nagging voices of doom in my head, the traces of a line of cocaine I later found left on the cistern of my loo, and clung to that. He loved me. I was like the proverbial child with her hands over her eyes, chanting, "If I can't see the monster, it's not there."

All that mattered was he loved me.

By the time I joined the others, Charlie and his gorgeous blonde had already left. I felt bad but I justified my behavior by telling myself that it had only been a suggestion that he join us at the Met, a suggestion made so that he could feel flattered and flirt with the girls. I mean, Charlie and I spent enough time together without socializing outside of work.

The girls saw it differently. "You invited him down, you should have been here."

There was no point hiding it, so I told them what had happened.

"You told him *what?*" Clemmie asked in disgust.

"To make her go away," I repeated as if it was the most marvelously daring thing to say in the world.

Even Emmanuel looked appalled.

"But the point is, don't you see, he did!" Why were they being so obtuse. Couldn't they grasp the point here: Richard had chosen me over her.

Elizabeth looked into my eyes. "The point is, Lola, he did a line, shagged you and probably did another line and left...back to shag her."

"Where he belongs," Josie added, pompously smug married that she is.

An image of Richard, my Richard, making love to Leggy Blonde took form in my mind then. I felt sick. Elizabeth shook her head. "I can't believe you. Worst of all I can't believe I'm starting to feel sorry for Richard."

"I feel sorry for his girlfriend," Clemmie muttered.

"She's not his girlfriend," I snapped, surprised by my own ferocity.

"Well, she lives with him now, doesn't she?" Clemmie pointed out.

I put my hands over my ears. "The point you're all missing is that he was *my* husband. We weren't just a fling, we didn't just date. He married *me*, we're still in love and she's just in the way."

"Can you hear yourself?" Elizabeth asked, removing my hands from my ears. "You can't keep going back. Richard's moved on, sure you can dial him up for sex the way I used to dial Mike, but that's not going to end in happily-ever-after the way you seem to think, Lola."

"That never stopped you dialing Mike," I reminded her nastily.

Elizabeth rolled her eyes in exasperation.

"Mike didn't have a live-in girlfriend," Josie pointed out.

"You're wrong. I know it sounds bad, and I do feel sorry for Sally—" I wasn't sure I did really "—but if Richard and I are meant to be together it's better for her in the long run, too."

"You're right, you're a veritable saint!" Elizabeth agreed sarcastically. "I only hope Sally appreciates your selflessness."

"Anyone want more drinks?" Emmanuel asked, obviously keen to remove himself from the booth.

"Look, darling," Elizabeth said, stroking my hair, "I know how easy and convenient sex with the ex can be, but that's all it is, convenient and easy. It's not love. Love is a celebration of all that's inconvenient and complicated."

I shook my head. Love my friends as I do, I knew they were wrong, so I declared the subject closed and we all had a dance and Clemmie pulled a cute Swedish boy with lovely thick sandy-blond hair.

By the time I arrived back home to feed Jean, though, I was agitated again. I wanted Richard back and I was sure I could get him back, too, if I played my cards right. So I called him at six in the morning.

He picked up after the first ring, "I was just thinking about you," he murmured sleepily. I wondered if she was asleep in the bed beside him, or perhaps pretending to be asleep, listening to him on the phone. I wondered if she was listening to his words and realizing that she wasn't as safe in his love as she imagined. "Sorry about last night, leaving like that. I was a prick," he said.

"I think we've said enough sorrys, don't you?" I told him.

"Maybe. So what's new?"

"Jean was wondering if you wanted to drop by on your way to work and put me to bed."

He laughed and told me to tell Jean he was on his way.

I answered the door naked, he picked me up and took me

to bed, made beautiful familiar love to me, and then kissed me all over and told me I was beautiful, and I knew that whatever else happened I would hold on to this moment forever. I was right. Richard and I were made for each other, but even in my rapture I took wicked pleasure in knowing he had chosen me over Sally, certain now that if it was what I wanted he always would. Our bodies were the perfect fit, we were meant to be together, there was an electricity with Richard that I'd never experienced with anyone else before. Even during all our time apart, Richard was always the man in all my sexual fantasies.

Before he left he made me a green tea with a cube of sugar, just how I like it. Then he kissed me tenderly. "I'm sorry I keep pushing you away, Lola," he whispered. "This will all work out, though, won't it?" he asked, as if needing reassurance.

"Of course it will work out. It has to," I replied simply.

"I love your nose," he told me, running a finger down my cheekbone.

I wrinkled my nose, embarrassed by the compliment.

He laughed. "I especially love the way I can make it wrinkle up by saying stuff like that."

As he stood in the doorway ready to leave he paused for a moment to tell me he loved me again. Then he left.

I hugged the pillow to my chest and muffled my squeal of triumph in case he heard me in the corridor. I'd won. I'd won! I'd won. Leggy Blonde had lost. Hoorah! Hoorah! Hoorah!

The phone rang just as I was drifting off into a deep sleep. It was Kitty.

"Aunt Camilla died in her sleep last night," she told me as I was still digging the earplugs out of my ears.

"Oh no! Oh no, poor Aunt Camilla."

"Yes, well, she was excessively elderly and she died peacefully."

The thought of Aunt Camilla doing anything that wasn't peaceful was impossible to conjure. Kitty started telling me about the funeral arrangements and how Aunt Camilla had left specific instructions that required cremation and her ashes being exploded in a large spray of fireworks over Surrey. "I can't even begin to imagine what the legalities of arranging a funeral such as this are going to be."

"Well, let me know if there's anything I can do to help."

"Joanna's going to be run off her feet with all the preparations," Kitty sighed, ignoring my offer. "Still, it might be quite fun. Do you know Aunt Camilla has arranged for a funfair to be set with rides, a marquee, Morris dancers and a band. And then at night there will be fire-eaters and magicians and everyone from her local village has been invited. Wasn't she the dark horse?"

"Not to me," I told my mother pointedly. As the sounds of central London going to work started up outside my window, I flicked through the book about Posche House, reading the letters of love Lady Posche had written to her lover, Edward.

eleven

Reading Henrietta's book, *Hold Your Glass Like a Poem,* one is often left feeling uneasy. For at no time does she hint at her adultery. In fact, she gives every impression that the great love and devotion she speaks of is for her own husband. There is no suggestion in her husband's private correspondence that he thought differently. Perhaps while resigned to his wife's adultery he held a vain belief that his beloved wife loved him as he loved her, or at least in her own way.

Certainly through her correspondence to her sister it might be gleaned that Edward's dissipation was felt more keenly by Hen as time wore on. Perhaps her feelings for her husband deepened through her awareness of his gentle steadfast patience.

Secret Passage to the Past:
A Biography of Lady Henrietta Posche
By Michael Carpendum

That afternoon Jean and I went down to stay with Kitty and Richard at Aunt Camilla's small cottage in Surrey. Although my aunt was a wealthy woman, she had always lived in a small but pretty wisteria-covered cottage in the village of Dumblesham. More recently, she had employed the services of a full-time nurse, a rather dreary middle-aged woman called Ms. Durram. Apart from Ms. Durram, though, my aunt had lived alone for most of her life, and perhaps because of this she had thrown herself enthusiastically into village life.

Driving into the picture-postcard community, I remembered coming to stay with my aunt just before I married Richard. She wasn't very well then, but as ever she insisted on looking after me as if I was still in short socks and pigtails.

She was actually my father's aunt, a very wealthy, very elegant old-fashioned woman in the best possible sense. Martin called her the last of the Grand Old Edwardians. I remember finding her formal-dining habits exotic, growing up as I had with parents who preferred dining out. When we did eat at home, it was always something from the delicatessen, like quails' eggs, carpaccio, fois gras, caviar or fresh oysters and lobster.

Aunt Camilla, on the other hand, always dined at table with napkins and three courses. The most extraordinary thing about her for me, though, was that while I'm sure she was quite fond of Kitty, she wasn't mesmerized by her the way everyone else was.

When my mother said her nutty things about spinsters and "the breathtaking tragedy of a life lived without passion," Aunt Camilla would either smile serenely, secretly wink at me or feign deafness. During divorces when we didn't "speak to that man's family," Aunt Camilla was always the exception. I think Kitty actually admired her ability to not enter the fray.

Kitty and Martin opened the door at the sound of my cab as if they'd been anxiously awaiting my arrival like parents in movies. I couldn't help thinking how sweet they looked standing on the doorstep. Kitty, tall and slender in her trademark mouse-pink chiffon and marabou: Martin, in his favorite tatty cardigan, which Kitty had knitted for him. Actually, Kitty had Joanna knit it, but it amounted to the same thing in Kitty's mind.

I'd always enjoyed the quiet sanctuary of my aunt's cottage, especially when my parents were going through some of their more traumatic stages of divorce or reconciliation. I don't know what was worse, the screaming (sorry, passionate) rows or the public displays of love that followed. During the divorces, I would inevitably be used as a weapon by Kitty to punish Martin, so it always came as a great relief when they'd pack me off to stay with Aunt Camilla. She never mentioned my parents' relationship and how it was affecting me, which was marvelous because back at home, Kitty and Martin spoke of little else—speaking about me as if I wasn't in the room.

I paid the cabdriver, and my parents wrapped me up in a group hug on the front porch. It felt rather odd but strangely nice. I imagined that any passerby might think we looked the picture of the average English family—with the exception of Jean, who had attached herself to Martin's trouser leg.

Once inside the cottage, all my childhood visits came to life in my mind, all the memories of memories; of baking sponge cakes and gingerbread men and eating them with glasses of homemade lemonade or freshly squeezed juice.

I had brought Richard here to visit Aunt Camilla after we married and he'd made a rude joke about the place smelling of camphor and digestive biscuits. Nor did he appreciate the way poor old Aunt Camilla kept referring to him as Oliver. The worst thing, though, was that Aunt Camilla didn't drink (I don't think she really approved of it) and so there was no alcohol in her house. Despite the fact we were only there for a Sunday lunch, Richard became quite animated about this lack of alcohol on the drive back.

"Who doesn't offer a guest a blasted drink?" he'd railed as we raced round the tight bends of the hedge-lined country lanes in our Ferrari. I was quite relieved by her alcohol-etiquette personally, as he was driving like a maniac anyway. I'd reminded him that she was quite elderly and a little bit potty, but he wasn't to be mollified.

"That's no excuse, bad manners are bad manners. Whoever heard of inviting people to Sunday lunch and not serving wine, let alone offering a restorative? For God's sake, we'd just driven all the bloody way from London. It's disgusting!"

It was the first time I'd ever seen my new husband so angry, and I really didn't want to fight, but she had offered us tea and homemade biscuits on our arrival, of which I gently reminded him. Hence, the "whole place smells of digestive biscuits" tirade.

"It smells just the same as it did when I was little," I told Kitty and Martin as I settled Jean down.

Kitty squeezed my hand. "I know, lavender water and old books," she sighed sadly. "We will miss her."

"Last of the Grand Old Edwardians," Martin declared.

"He's been saying that since we arrived," Kitty mocked with an eye roll, but she was smiling as she said it. "I think he's going through clock withdrawal."

We went into the kitchen where a deli feast was already laid out on a platter. Kitty bustled around with plates and napkins while Martin made tea. It seemed strange seeing them in this domestic environment, strange because they seemed so at home, so familiar with the rituals of tea making and food preparation.

"She never married," Martin remarked, lathering fois gras on his toast.

"Poor old Cam-Cam," Kitty added. "What an empty, soulless, pointless life."

"Well, she had her friends," I added, picking at my food. "She had Ms. What's-her-name the nurse."

"Ms. What's-her-name who packed up and left the moment she found poor Cam-Cam? Can you imagine the callousness of the woman? You simply can't get good help these days. The world is full of soulless people with no poetry in their hearts." Kitty shook her head and sipped her tea daintily. "It wears me out so."

★ ★ ★

After our supper, I washed up with Martin. My aunt didn't believe in modern contraptions like dishwashers. I washed, he dried, as if we'd done it together a thousand times before.

"She was very beautiful when she was younger," he began, placing a plate in the cupboard. "She was still a great beauty when I was a boy. I was quite enraptured by her."

I paused and looked at my father, shocked that he could ever have had eyes for anyone other than Kitty, but he was looking off into the middle distance, deep in his own thoughts.

"Apparently, when I was three I announced I was going to marry her."

"Oh bless."

He chuckled at the precociousness of his romantic notions as Kitty entered the room. It wasn't the first time I'd heard the story, but I laughed as I always did.

My father seemed to be in another place and time as he added, "And do you know, I stuck to my guns when they told me I couldn't marry my aunt. I told them, 'Well, if I can't marry her, I shall find someone just like Aunt Cam to marry!' And I did. Same long thin frame, hair like spun gold, just like a screen goddess," he continued. I wasn't sure if he was talking about Aunt Camilla or Kitty now.

Kitty ruffled his hair affectionately. "Oh, Martin, stop. You know it's a sign of impending madness when you repeat stories of your childhood over and over again."

"I expect it is," my father agreed, putting the last plate away. "I shall still miss the old thing, though."

"Last of the Grand Old Edwardians," Kitty teased, but she seemed pensive too. Later, as she curled up on the living-room sofa with some papers of Aunt Camilla's, I watched her and thought I'd never seen her so quietly still. Normally when Kitty did "still," it was in a languid, feline way—you could almost hear her purr. Now she was simply absorbed; her eyes veiled by her flamboyant reading glasses, poring over a file of papers.

Finally she looked up at me. "You know, her funeral arrangements are madly elaborate. Are you sure you didn't help arrange all this for her, Lola?" she asked. "It seems every last detail is taken care of, all the insurances, all the bookings. Absolutely fascinating. I'm really impressed."

I was stunned by the compliment. I was never really convinced that Kitty knew exactly what it was I did for a living, as she always seemed to go into one of her "despairs" whenever I spoke about my career.

"Here, take a look at these papers and see what you think, Lola. Even the guest list is drawn up as if for a celebration."

I read the hand-written pages with interest. Titled, *The Funeral Fete & Ball of Lady Camilla Dawne,* every detail was laid out, complete with contingency plans. The funeral itself was to take place on the Friday morning a week after her death, her cremation to take place the same day. The fete was to commence on the Saturday after her funeral, at 11:00 a.m. on the village green. She'd paid a premium so that her booking superseded any other bookings. She'd even set aside a further amount to reimburse any inconvenienced parties. She was such a loved member of the community that I couldn't imagine anyone minding in the least putting their occasion off.

Kitty was right, the proposed schedule was professional. I couldn't have done better myself. She'd covered everything with the attention to detail that I would have; there were plans in place so that anything that could go wrong would immediately be put to rights.

The fete was to last all day and included rides and festivities for children. In the evening there was to be a ball in a marquee. A deposit had already been placed with the caterers and the band. The guest list was vast and looked as if it had recently been updated. The finale was to be a fireworks display at midnight, with Aunt Camilla's ashes being fired off into the sky. Everything right down to the appropriate insurance had been accounted for.

"Talk about going out in a blaze of light," I remarked as I passed back the file.

"I'm just staggered at the vast organization involved with hosting an event like this," Kitty mused, putting on her glasses and looking through the documents again.

"Is it called 'hosting' when the host is dead?" Martin inquired.

Kitty ignored him as she looked up at me. "Is your job as complicated as this, Lola?"

"It depends. Yes, I suppose…"

"When you think about all the things that can go wrong." She shook her elegant head and looked at me carefully. "I simply had no idea how elaborate these sorts of events were to organize. You are a clever girl, aren't you, Lola?"

I blushed at the compliment, which was repeated about ten minutes later as the sun set over the village green opposite. I tried to imagine my aunt planning this celebration for her friends and family on evenings like this. I could see her now, sitting where Kitty was sitting, going over the details of the fete and the ball in her head, picturing how it would all look. I could imagine her, imagining her guests laughing and partying, while she burst into the sky in a flaming wheel of fireworks. I could imagine her getting quotes from caterers and auditioning bands and trying to imagine all the things that could go wrong and then making B plans to cover them.

"She was in love once, you know," Martin remarked, breaking our comfortable family silence.

Kitty took off her glasses and stared at him as if he was an interloper. "What's this? You never told me anything about her romantic soul."

"No?"

The mood of quiet contemplation was shattered. "No. Never." Kitty looked extremely pissed off.

"No. Well, I suppose I didn't. It was a bit of a sore point with the family."

"*We* are your family, Martin," she told him, her violet eyes flashing. "We three in this room." She looked to me for support as I prayed for the chintz sofa to swallow me up. "And as we knew nothing of this romance, how could it be a sore point with us?"

Poor Martin realized then what a tight corner he was in. Aunt Camilla's funeral file was set aside along with Kitty's glasses. He was holding a shovel and standing in a hole and he knew it. He had that look about him of a man who has suddenly realized he doesn't have the ability to climb out on his own. He looked at me to throw him a rope, but Kitty's accusatory gaze was tightly fixed. She was twitching now, like a tiger flexing its muscles before thrusting itself on its prey.

Martin coughed before beginning his explanation. "Quite. Well, there was talk of some fellow. Oliver, I think he was called. I don't think old Cam ever really recovered." He pressed his thumbs to the bridge of his nose as if he had a headache. "There was even talk of marriage, I believe, but no formal announcement was ever made. I was only a young lad, four or five, maybe even younger, when I first heard my father mention it. I might have got it wrong, I suppose," he suggested hopefully.

"And you never mentioned her broken nuptials to me, your own wife, because…?" I could tell by her controlled tone that Kitty was wildly annoyed. I thought of all the times she had bemoaned my aunt's spinster status, frequently comparing me to her, berating me in front of her, holding her up as an example of what happens to those that lead the unromantic life. I think Kitty was thinking the same thing. My mother can be insensitive but she doesn't set out to be. I am certain of that. Now she was feeling that she'd misjudged Camilla and she was blaming Martin.

My father blustered, "I don't know that I felt certain of my facts. As I said, I heard rumors, whispers in the nursery. It had all happened long before I was born, even. Once I saw a photograph when I was visiting her as a boy. It's not here now, I noticed that as soon as we arrived. It used to sit on her bedside. His name was Oliver, I only know that because it was written on the photograph. I remember reading it out loud. She became very cross. I asked my father about it but he wasn't disposed to discuss the issue. Bit of a dipso by all accounts. Couldn't say no to a drink. We might have a hunt round here for the photograph," he suggested, as if finding the snapshot of Oliver might mitigate his crime.

Kitty interrupted again but I wasn't paying attention. Besides, I knew all the signs…there was a row brewing and I was only in the way, so I let myself out, as I'd let myself out a thousand times as a child. They wouldn't even notice I was gone. I set off across the village green. There was a bandstand in the middle where I took a seat and wished I smoked. On the chair graffitied with declarations of teenage love, I looked up at the stars in the clear night sky, waiting peacefully for Camilla to join them.

Tyne O'Connell

She'd always called Richard Oliver, and because I don't smoke and because I was cold and feeling alone, I called his mobile.

He rejected me.

twelve

It was not uncommon for men and women of Henrietta's class to take lovers after marriage. Henrietta and her husband were unexceptional in this way; both had affairs, always conducted with the utmost discretion.

Henrietta's husband, Charles, had numerous lovers, though he always claimed he loved none as he loved his darling Hen. Apart from Edward, Henrietta had very few lovers, and one is left wondering whether she took them to bed for her own pleasure or for Edward's pain. Certainly the letters she wrote to her sister makes it apparent that while she was discreet about her affairs where her husband and the public were concerned, conversely she made certain she informed Edward of her every affair, sometimes in lurid detail.

Secret Passage to the Past:
A Biography of Lady Henrietta Posche
By Michael Carpendum

"I was with Sally when you called," Richard whispered when he called me back the next evening as I was traveling back to London.

"Is she with you now?" I asked, terrified he'd say yes but knowing he wouldn't, even if she were. I needed to talk about my aunt's death, and the person I needed to talk to was the man who had promised to love me through sickness and health, better and worse.

He sounded furtive as he replied. "No, I'm at a friend's dinner party. I can't talk now."

I didn't mention anything about the lack of voices in the background because he'd probably have an excuse for that, or worse, accuse me of prying, so instead I asked if I could drop in on him later.

"Not tonight, I've got a big day tomorrow," he explained.

I closed my eyes and rallied myself to save what little dignity I had and say, "Okay then, goodbye." I definitely wasn't going to plead. I never plead. "Only, I really need to see you," I pleaded (there was even a little whiney note on the end). "That is, it would be lovely to see you," I added brightly, in my best CCC style.

"Tell you what, I'll come to yours on the way home from work tomorrow, around six-thirty?" He made it sound as if he was doing me a huge favor. He didn't at all sound desperate to see me.

But I said yes anyway, even though an irritating voice in my head was yelling no. It was the irritating voice of Lola the professional, the voice of Lola, senior events manager, who had organized an event at the club that was due to kick off at six-thirty. It was one of my outside events—that is, outside my club duties—but the clients had paid to hold the party at Posh House. This meant I received a fee from the client and a small fee from Posh House.

It wasn't a particularly grand affair, but it was a prestigious client I wanted to impress. The Darague Chain, who owned some of the trendiest five-star resorts in the world, were launching a new one in Jamaica that they wanted their exclusive London client list to know about. Although it wasn't too large, I knew from experience that these sorts of events were particularly challenging as they mixed alcohol and canapés with speeches and dull presentations.

After a few glasses of wine and a half hour spent listening to boring speeches, the guests would inevitably peel off slowly, like a dwindling herd of buffalo, and it was my job to make sure they didn't stampede. I would normally arrive early at these sorts of events because nonmembers attending functions at the club had an unnerving knack for creating bad feeling amongst the members.

As it was one of my own events, I couldn't call in sick, so I hazarded (something I never do!) that as long as I asked one of the reception managers to keep an eye on things for the first hour, I'd be there by the second hour. The reliable Carl was duty manager that evening and Charlie wasn't due to drop in that night, so I should be safe. I spoke to Carl the next morning before going to sleep and he assured me it would all be fine. I told him I owed him one. Sorted.

Richard didn't arrive until seven-thirty. We had a long slow kiss at the door. Jean was watching the news. We were the perfect family. I told him about Aunt Camilla and he was really kind, sitting me on his lap and stroking my hair. Jean hippity-hopped over for a sniff and then hopped over to her little litter hutch. "Isn't she a good rabbit?" I remarked.

"Who?"

"Jean, our rabbit," I said, pointing to her in case he confused her with his other rabbits.

He scratched his head as he watched her bustling about the room. "Sorry, I keep forgetting."

"That's horrible," I scolded, giving him a playful smack. "Don't you remember you bought her for me on our first-month anniversary?"

"'Course I do, Lolls, I was just teasing. I said close your eyes, hold out your hands and say rabbit."

"She was so tiny then."

"They were good times," he agreed. "But…"

I didn't want to hear the word *but*. I wanted to put my hands over my ears and say, "La, la, la, I can't hear you."

"I told Sally about what happened…you know, with us the other night. Well, I had to, basically, as she caught us at it. And I feel terrible, Lola. The guilt, it's killing me. I'm sorry, I just can't do this."

I interrupted. "I should really be going to work," I told him in my husky sex-siren voice as I moved my mouth over his. He returned my kiss for a while but then he pushed me away. "I can't, Lolly. This is wrong."

"Fine," I said, climbing off his lap and gathering up my things. I was really late now. "I have to go now anyway, do you want to meet up later?"

He looked like a man in horrible pain. "Lolly, I'm sorry, I'm just confused. I don't want to hurt Sally. Fuck it, I don't want to hurt you, but well, we already know we didn't work out, and well…"

My phone rang. I pushed reject and slipped it in my bag. I was glad of the interruption. I didn't want to hear what he had to say. I wanted to stop him before he said something I'd regret.

"Lola?" he pleaded, standing up to grab me.

I threw his arm off my shoulder. "I have to go," I insisted as I went into the bathroom and brushed my hair. Richard was still in the living room, but the flat was so small I could hear his every move. I could almost hear his every breath.

"You can see my position," he continued. "Sally has just moved in. Before you rang me up that night, I was so certain she was the one, and then…" He put his head in his hands and groaned. His groaning thing was really beginning to get to me.

"As I remember, the night I rang, you were 'freaked' by her request to move in!" I reminded him.

"Oh, I don't know," he replied. "It's all fucked up. We can't go back. Can we?"

I closed my eyes and splashed my face with cold water. La, la, la, I can't hear you.

"Well, can we?" he asked.

I knew what he wanted me to say, he wanted me to agree that "No, we couldn't go back." He wanted me to be the one to set him free. He wanted me to take the blame and make him feel okay. There was nothing left to say apart from the obvious, so I applied my makeup as the phone started up again in my bag.

"Do you want me to get that?" he asked.

"Leave it," I told him. "It'll be work. I have to go."

He put Jean and me in a cab and waved us off as if we were his wife and child off for a big adventure. I checked my miss calls and saw I had four new messages. I was still listening to the panicked pleas of Carl—message three, when I arrived at the club.

"The police are in the back room interviewing Miss Hickory and the two staff who witnessed the assault," Carl explained as he escorted me through to the bar where the incident had taken place. "I don't think Miss Hickory wants to press charges, but the police may decide to anyway. She's very distressed. I had to call Charlie, Lola. Sorry."

"I know," I reassured him. "Look, this is totally my problem and I'm sorry to have put you through this."

Even from my vantage point at the bar doorway I could hear the patrons discussing the fracas. Torna Delz, a D-list celebrity, and her personal trainer had been invited by Darague to the event. Torna and her trainer were more famous for their bad drunken behavior and Torna's weight problem than anything they actually did. They had recently been the basis of several tabloid exposés.

Predictably, after having far too much to drink at the launch, they'd grown bored with the speeches and made their way into the members' bar. After a few more drinks, Torna, imagining her boyfriend, Keith, to be eyeing up one of the members—the glamorous author Tabitha Hickory— had thrown her drink over the author and flung a punch, which missed. In an attempt to restrain Torna, Keith accidentally hit poor Tabitha on the ear, knocking out her earring and bruising her lobe. It wasn't a serious injury but it was my fault.

Charlie tapped me on the shoulder. He was wearing a loose T-shirt and a pair of chinos, his hair was wet. He must have been at the gym. I was so used to seeing him in his owner-of-the-club uniform—i.e., long sleeves—that I was surprised by his tanned athletic upper arms.

"Upstairs," he ordered.

This was very bad and we both knew it. I knew it because it was my fault, there was no way around that, really, but then once we reached his office I threw my arms around him and cried, "I'm sorry, Charlie, but my aunt just died."

His body relaxed and his tone softened. "Oh, Lolly, I'm sorry."

"I'm so upset, I couldn't come in."

"Not to worry, my love, sit down and have a cordial."

Aunt Camilla's death might not have been the direct reason that I was late, but I found once I started talking to Charlie my misery was real. I poured out all my feelings, all the things I had wanted to tell Richard but hadn't had a chance to. I sobbed about the story of Aunt Camilla's death and how close I'd been to her and how she had never married because the man she loved, Oliver, was a dipsomaniac, and how she must have thought Richard was too because she called him Oliver and now she was going to be shot up into the sky in fireworks and she'd arranged the whole fete down to the last detail.

Charlie listened to the story, which came out of me in a torrent of half sentences and lengthy sidetracks. He stroked my back, comforted me and told me all was forgiven. If I was a cat I'd only have eight lives left.

Later, the police asked to speak to Charlie and I waited in his office and tried to compose myself while he went down. As it turned out, Miss Hickory wasn't going to press charges, her ear was slightly bruised; however, a report of the incident would be filed and no doubt something would appear in the papers. It wasn't what Charlie wanted for the club but he didn't say anything further to me about the matter.

After the situation had been dealt with, Charlie and I went down to have dinner in the restaurant. In the secret passage on the way down, I told him what had been going on with Richard and how I still thought I might be in love with him but that he had someone else. Charlie didn't say much, but in the silences I could hear some of the things I was saying echoing back at me, and I started to feel really stupid.

"Speaking of exes," Charlie added at one point. "Here come Hamish and Jeremy." Hamish waved and headed toward us. "I almost forgot to mention, Jeremy asked about you today. Seems he spotted you that night when we were playing secret agents behind the drinks station."

"Pull up a couple of chairs," Charlie insisted after the "hellos" and "God, I haven't seen you for ages" had been dispensed. I began to feel uncomfortable, sitting between my two exes, so I suggested we invite Elizabeth and Clemmie. I was worried that Charlie might mention something about Richard and I knew that Elizabeth would circumvent any attempt to revisit the Richard issue. Clemmie was already on a date, but Elizabeth said she'd see us in five. Then I had this horrible vision of Richard turning up—after all, Jeremy and Hamish were his mates. Oh, I just wanted to die.

Jeremy told me I looked gorgeous, which made me feel a bit better.

I laughed and Charlie told them that we'd had a bit of trouble at the club earlier in the evening, and that I was a bit upset about my aunt's death. Both Hamish and Jeremy were very sweet.

"Well, you look amazing," Jeremy insisted, and by the way he smiled at me, I suspected he was flirting. I often think that flirting is the ability to make someone feel as if they're the only person in the room, which was how Jeremy began to make me feel. That was why I fell for him in the first place. He had the same easy charm as Charlie, so that even the maddest silliest things made you feel that he really got you, the way no one else ever had.

Sadly, this didn't carry through to the bedroom; sex with Jeremy had always been less than earth-shattering. Hamish was talking to Charlie and as I leaned in to listen, I realized that Jeremy and I were still locked in one another's gaze. I blushed. I hadn't meant to stare, I was just in another world, but I knew that the look held significance for Jeremy.

"So how's the estate?" I asked Hamish, throwing the full force of my attention on him.

"Oh, didn't you hear, I'm selling up. Stony broke, don't you know. Not a penny to be made up there. Money just pours out of you like sweat. To tell you the truth, I'm bloody sick of the whole shooting match. If I see another sheep I'll go mad. No, I'm back in London now, trying to find something to do, living in my old flat on Ladbrook Square. You know it."

Oh, I knew it. I knew it intimately. Knew every corner. Back in college we'd come to London every chance we got and spent the entire weekend there, in bed.

As if reading my mind, Hamish added, "We used to shag like lunatics in those days. Don't know where we got the energy." He put out his cigarette and shook his head, as if remembering a particularly lively shag.

I was so relieved to see Elizabeth walk into the restaurant that I jumped up and waved at her dementedly. But if I thought that would dilute the atmosphere, I was wrong.

The first conversation Elizabeth initiated required Hamish telling his whole story again.

Elizabeth laughed as genuinely as she could—I guess to break the tension, which was so palpable it was like a sixth guest.

The whole evening was like that; every time I tried to steer the conversation onto something general, I ended up in a quagmire of memories. Charlie was looking at me significantly, but I had no idea what significance his looks were hoping to convey.

I kept mouthing the word *What?* but he'd just shake his head, nod at Hamish and Elizabeth and shoot me another unintelligible significant look. At one point I kicked him, but I missed and got Jeremy, who wrapped his leg around mine in a sexual way.

I suppose I'd asked for that.

Then Hamish asked Elizabeth if she'd like to go for a walk around the square with him and she agreed, giving me a look that I couldn't interpret, and suddenly Charlie's hints made sense.

"I've got to go check on Jean and do a bit of paperwork myself," Charlie added awkwardly as he fled the table, and suddenly Jeremy and I were left there alone, with the dessert plates being removed. I didn't know where to look, so I was immensely relieved when Charlie came back, until he said, "I'll look after Jean tonight if you two want to go off somewhere." Then Jeremy gave Charlie a wink, which I presumed was some sort of Masonic code the two of them had developed over their long years of friendship. Charlie didn't wink back, though he looked over at me and smiled a sort of sad smile. Maybe I was becoming an object of pity to him, and if that was the case, I only had myself to blame. I'd behaved ridiculously over Richard, and

Charlie knew it. But I was determined that all that was behind me now.

Jeremy suggested we go to Click, a private members' club at a hotel in Knightsbridge. I agreed, partly because I'd been meaning to go there since the launch and check out how it was going. The opening night had been fabulous and Elizabeth and I had danced till four in the morning.

As we were leaving, I saw Richard and Sally in the bar. Jeremy did, too, but he didn't say anything and nor did I, we just went outside and hailed a cab as if we hadn't.

I felt oddly excited on the journey there. I think I felt that by being with Jeremy I was cheating on Richard, and for some reason that made me feel more empowered. Jeremy told me again how gorgeous I was looking and held my eyes with his. When he took hold of my hand, his arm resting against my knee, I didn't push him away; in fact, when he squeezed my hand I squeezed his back.

The club was kicking and Jeremy made his way to the bar for drinks. I ordered a watermelon cosmopolitan. I wanted to get smashed. I wanted to stop my head buzzing. I wanted to stop the feelings I'd been feeling about Richard. Somehow, everything about my life seemed wrong, and being drunk seemed like a temporary, if dangerous, way out.

I didn't remember him being a good dancer when we were going out. Maybe he'd only acquired the skill after we'd split, I decided after my second drink. Who knows, maybe he'd acquired other skills, too. Either way, we danced the night away, and as we faded out of the club in the last moments of darkness, I was carrying my Gina heels. One cosmopolitan had led to two, which led to a third, and I wasn't surprised that we were kissing in the cab; I was just surprised

I was enjoying it. When Jeremy pulled away to ask the driver to skip my stop, I didn't argue. We kissed all the way home.

Unlike his dancing, though, the sex was just as I always remembered it: technically fine but deeply unsatisfying.

thirteen

"…'Tis a miracle to me that I can endure what is now over a week since Edward came hither. I go abroad in my thoughts by day and pace my bedchamber by night. I would not live another hour without his handsomeness were it not for my precious children. In sober earnest, my husband does spend his breath to very little purpose telling me that I am prejudicing my own health in this obsession, for he believes I have taken to settling my whole stock of happiness upon the affection of a drab cad of ruinous fortune.

To prove otherwise I have taken the Duke of Albany as my lover, although he is a cloth head and mean-spirited under the sheets. My dearest, 'tis only to you I say he is in every way odious to me, though all ladies seem to find him the pinnacle of wit. He is somewhat of a poet, nothing to touch Lord Byron, of course, but his verse is not altogether unhandsome. I have him recite poetry while he makes love to me, otherwise I should be unable to bear it."

Extract of a letter from Lady Henrietta Posche to her sister, Elizabeth

The first thing I wanted to do when I woke up—apart from empty my bladder and take intravenous painkillers for my throbbing head—was call Richard to tell him I'd slept with Jeremy.

I know, perverse, childish, perhaps even verging on the psychotic, but the desire was so overwhelming that I didn't question my motivations. This was my rationale: Richard was sleeping with Leggy Blonde—I wasn't so naive that I didn't know that. I was just managing to push the image from my mind and focus on other things. But I wanted to see if Richard could push *me* shagging *Jeremy* from his mind. I guess it was a sort of one-upmanship of emotional cruelty.

I didn't see anything troubling or dysfunctional about it. Then, why would I? I could sleep with other people if I wanted to…I knew that already, but here's the thing…Richard probably didn't! Men are like that, they never imagine the worst. They never go to bed at night with that racing analytical worst-case-scenario list of things that might go wrong. Me, I always imagined the worst.

I couldn't stop imagining him kissing Leggy Blonde.

I couldn't stop imagining him having sex with Leggy Blonde.

I couldn't stop imagining him telling Leggy Blonde that he loved her (not that he'd mean it, of course).

So now I couldn't wait for Richard to have those same tortured thoughts about me with Jeremy, his own mate. It wasn't just a desire to torture him, though. I wanted to see his reaction. I wanted him to show his hand, to realize fully what I already knew, that Richard and the Leggy Blonde were a flop, a nonstarter of a love story. Unlike the Richard and Lola Show, which was a smash-hit romantic comedy for our times...for all times. I was hoping that *this* (by *this*, I mean poor hapless, hopeful Jeremy) would give him the push to give Leggy Blonde the push. They don't call me the London genius of PR strategy for nothing!

Jeremy woke up soon after me and looked about as rotten as I felt.

"How much did we drink last night?" he asked, ruffling his hair as if trying to kick-start his brain.

"Enough to never want to look at a drink again?" I groaned. Talking made my brains rattle.

After slowly easing himself up and into a pair of jeans he went to the kitchen and brought us Virgin Marys and co-codamols, which we knocked back like vodka shots. "Greasy fry-up?" he suggested brightly as I fell back on the pillows.

"Definitely," I agreed, smiling weakly at him through the fog of my agony.

He was very sweet and even managed to dig up a spare toothbrush for me, and after a shower I felt almost well again, until he spoiled everything on the way out of his building by telling me how much he enjoyed being with me. When he entwined his hand in mine and kissed me on the cheek, I felt slightly ashamed.

I didn't want to be the one to rain on his parade though, so I prattled away semibrightly about how lovely last night had been, grateful I had a hangover to hide behind. We walked past white stucco terraced housing in the morning sunshine to a greasy spoon restaurant on Westbourne Grove for a proper fry-up. Jeremy bought us each some mindless tabloid reading material, which thankfully suspended the need for further conversation.

After breakfast, weariness began to engulf me, which gave me the perfect excuse to say goodbye. Jeremy stood by me while I waited for a cab, but my attempt at a friendly air kiss goodbye turned into an awkward tooth-smashing semi-snog, with me crossing my fingers behind my back while he scraped my disgusting morning-after tongue with his disgusting morning-after tongue. Any lasting hope that Jeremy might *not* have the wrong impression about what last night had meant to me were dashed when he said. "I'm glad we're back together."

Doesn't anyone know the rules anymore? What had happened to the sacred bastion of no-strings sex with the ex? I wondered. Did the booty call mean nothing to anyone? Society was clearly falling apart at the seams, I decided as I grunted a "see you later" and dived into the capacious carriage. I wasn't going to allow this little island of social etiquette to disappear into a sea of false sentiments.

Back at my flat I flopped onto my bed for a disco nap before work, because even though I'd had a good six hours' sleep at Jeremy's, drunk sleep never seems to count. I turned off my mobile, but just to be sure I set my alarm clock so I wouldn't be late for work.

★ ★ ★

I woke up in darkness, disorientated and fuzzy. After fumbling with my lamp switch and staring at my clock, it finally dawned on me that it couldn't really be four in the afternoon. Not when there were stars in the sky and it was May! The battery in my alarm clock must have died.

I turned on my phone and saw the time. Apart from missing drinks with the girls, I was already three hours late for work and still needed to shower and get ready—and my head was still throbbing.

I had eleven new messages. Three were from the girls asking where the fuck I was, four were from Charlie. I deleted all four without listening to any of them. The next message was from Kitty, asking me to call her back. The last one was from Richard. All he said was, "Richard here. Erm… groan…I'll try later, I guess."

It's incredible how much you can read into a message that essentially says absolutely nothing. For me, the message from Richard was as inscrutable as a horoscope.

So instead of diving under a shower.

Or calling my boss to plead for my job.

Or calling my friends to apologize for letting them down.

Or returning Kitty's call because, well, she never calls me.

I replayed the message; a dozen times or more. He'd said he'd try *later,* which meant…he was going to call *again!*

I arrived at the club in a fluster. I don't think Jonathan, who was on the door that evening, knew what hit him. I was too late to skulk off into my office and pretend I'd been there all the time, so I took the stairs Charlie style—three at a time—and pushed through to the secret passage and up into the sanctum sanctorum of his office.

He was at his desk. Jean was on his lap. Everything was

just as it should be, except for Charlie's face. Normally animated, he just stared at me with a studied, blank expression, as if deciding whether he could get away with sending me to the gallows. I swear, the way he was stroking Jean was pure pantomime bad guy.

I spoke first, in a stuttering high-pitched voice, my lack of composure bleeding guilt. "Sorry," I squeaked. "About the late thing. The batteries on my alarm died and I slept straight through." As soon as the words were out of my mouth, I realized how the-dog-ate-my-homeworkish they sounded.

Charlie didn't respond. He just kept stroking Jean, which began to annoy me. Notwithstanding my tardiness, I didn't like my rabbit being used as a makeshift sphinx cat. Why couldn't he just tick me off and be done with it?

Eventually I said as much. "Look, this is a bit ridiculous, Charlie, it's not as if I ran down my batteries intentionally, is it? It's not as if I've used the excuse before!" I started to gesture wildly, more certain of my position now. "After all, it's not as if I'm blaming the dog for eating my homework or something implausible like that, is it? Batteries run down, Charlie, that's the nature of the disposable world. That's why they're called disposable batteries, no doubt." I smiled, slightly relaxing now, quietly proud of how well I'd excused my lateness.

Charlie just kept on stroking Jean, though, as unimpressed as you like. I shrugged; the man was being totally unreasonable. "I am sorry," I lied, "but things go wrong, Charlie. Unforeseeable things happen to everyone! And if you don't mind, I would rather you didn't stroke my rabbit in that comedy-thriller-type fashion. You're being melodramatic. Everyone is late for work *occasionally*."

He picked Jean up out of his lap and placed her on his desk. "Except for you," he told me calmly.

The words hung there between us like a declaration of…I didn't know what. Vexation, I guess, although there was a threatening calmness to his tone. I suppose I hadn't ever been late before apart from the other day. I do take my job very seriously. I'm overly obsessive about it according to Kitty. Which, reasonably speaking, should mean he could cut me a bit of slack!

Jean hopped back into his lap and he gave her another stroke, totally disregarding my instructions that he cease to do so. "I'm not perfect." I shrugged, my indignation having successfully wrestled my guilt down again. I mean, I was only…okay, so I was four hours late, which was half of my shift, but still, how dare he stare at me pointedly while stroking *my* rabbit. He was going to have to pay me a lot more if he expected to get away with this sort of tyranny.

"So, if that's all, I'll go to work," I told him grandly.

"Presuming you still have a job?"

"Prrrwrrwhah!" I spluttered. "Are you firing me? And if so, will you kindly cease handling my rabbit!"

"No, Lola, I'm not firing you, but I will if you come in late again," he replied, placing Jean back on the desk once more.

"Fine. Well, as I said, if that's all, I'll get on with it."

Then he had the audacity to ask, "Aren't you going to ask about Jean?"

Talk about taking the biscuit. "Well, as she's sitting right in front of me and you're stoking her, there isn't much to say, is there?" I knew I sounded like a bitch, but all I wanted to do was get out of the room before Richard called, so I turned around and headed for the door again. "Do you want me to take her with me?" I asked as I put my hand on the door. I was quite hoping he wouldn't say yes because I was going to be running around sorting out anything that might have gone wrong during my shift.

"No, of course I'm happy to have her here," he snapped. "But, Lola, there is one more thing," he added. I turned around. "Your mother called."

My mother was not a big fan of making phone calls. I'd almost forgotten about Kitty's message to call her back. People called Kitty, Kitty didn't call people. In fact, I couldn't remember her ever having called me before. If she needed to summon me she always had Joanna or Martin do it. "Oh?" I turned back around to face him. He knew my mother's aversion to using telephonic systems to communicate as well as I did.

"Your aunt's funeral is on Saturday. She asked me to come. Apparently, my name was on your aunt's guest list. So if you like, I can give you a lift down."

"What if I'm late for work before then and you have to fire me? Won't that be a bit of an uncomfortable journey for us?" I asked.

He smiled. "Am I being an arse or are you being a bitch?"

And suddenly I felt the tension between us evaporate. "Both?" I replied, smiling back.

He held his hand up in a mock oath. "I promise not to fire you before your aunt's funeral."

"Yes, that would be very insensitive," I agreed, turning to open the door again.

"I almost forgot, Jeremy sent flowers, they're in reception. I gather there was a rapprochement between you two last night then?" he inquired cheekily.

I pushed on the door, trying to decide whether to reply or not. For goodness' sake, we'd split up an age ago and sex with the ex didn't count, everyone knew that. And as this thought sped through my mind, I froze because it suddenly occurred to me that Richard may see sex with me as sex with the ex. I was feeling very unnerved, and so I turned and said, "Would it be too hard for you to keep your nose out of my private affairs, Charlie?" Which even I couldn't believe I had just said.

He looked stung by my words…funnily enough. "Could you not even pretend to respect me, Lola?" he asked.

It was the maddest question I'd ever heard, and apart from anything else, I had passed the point of being able to think rationally a long time ago. I was too upset by my random thought about Jeremy to think about how I treated Charlie. I mean, of course I respected him. I adored him. It was just that I was distracted. Everything seemed to be getting in the way of Richard, from Leggy Blonde to my job, and now I had a potential Jeremy fiasco on my hands. I didn't have time to confab with Charlie all night, so naturally I gave him a pretty irritated reply. "Where did that come from, Charlie? Look, you've just ticked me off for being late for work, completely ignoring my, up to now, blemish-free record. All I'm doing, or rather *trying* to do, is leave this room and do my job. Call me mad, but I thought that you as my boss would consider that the highest respect I could give you as an employee."

Charlie looked at me and smiled a sad sort of smile. "I don't want you to respect me as your boss, Lola. I mean as a friend? Couldn't you even pretend to *like* me?"

Men! Arrgghh! They are sooooo needy! Show them you love them and they run for miles, treat them carelessly and they bleat like lambs. I shook my head as if he was a lost cause I could no longer waste my valuable time trying to rescue. He wanted something from me but I didn't know what, and I didn't have time to find out. More than ever, I wanted to be out of his room for Richard's call and I didn't know what to say to sort things out fast enough, so I just pushed open the door and left.

He only had himself to blame.

There were two events at the club that night, neither of them was particularly large and a quick check with security and the front desk reassured me that chaos so far had been kept at bay by a mixture of luck and good staffing. After checking the incident reports, I focused on some networking that I needed to do at one of the events I'd organized for an Italian clothing designer. Or rather I tried to focus. Charlie's chat had unnerved me, only I wasn't sure why. Our whole talk had made me feel jumbled up inside. I mean, of course I respected him as a friend. Obviously I had done something though to put his nose out of joint. Was he annoyed about me sleeping with Jeremy perhaps? Or leaving him to look after Jean? Did he think I took him for granted…did I take him for granted? All these questions would have to be dealt with later, I decided, spotting Joel, the record executive I wanted to talk to, at the other end of the room.

Then my phone rang.

"Lola, it's Richard, I called earlier."

My heart was beating with what he was about to say, but then he went on to say he didn't know what to say but that he needed to see me. The phrase "needed to see me" seemed to echo on forever. I was meant to be meeting the girls after work, but I agreed to meet him at my flat first. I decided I finally knew what Kitty and Martin meant about passion. What I felt for Richard was so absorbing, so overwhelming, I didn't have room in my life for work or friends right now. My real focus had to be Richard.

"It's fucked up," Elizabeth told me when I called to say I might be late because Richard was dropping by.

"Excuse me?"

"This sudden obsession with Richard, it's madness. You're letting your friends down and your job suffer."

"Look, I was late once!" It was actually twice, but I hadn't told her about the alarm thing because that was just an accident that could have happened to anyone. It wasn't like I'd been deliberately late.

"Twice. Charlie called me earlier. He told me you went off with Jeremy last night."

I was angry about everyone talking about me behind my back. "Well, if you know about Jeremy why are you accusing me of being obsessed with Richard?"

"Because it's fucked up, and I'm really worried about you. We're all really worried about you."

I was worried about me, too, but I didn't share it with Elizabeth because I had a plan, and as long as you have a plan everything will work out fine; that's my life motto.

After I got off the phone from her, Jeremy rang. I rejected him but took Kitty's call a second later.

"We've found a copy of Camilla's will," she explained. "The original is with her solicitor. Darling, you know she was quite well off."

"Yes," I replied, more interested in the group of record executives confabbing in the corner. I still hadn't got a chance to speak to Joel, so I made my way toward him now.

"I suppose you were her favorite, I always thought it was the spinster connection."

I accepted a mineral water from the tray, my hangover was starting to kick in again and I needed to hydrate. "Thank you, Kitty."

"Maybe it was because of the Oliver chap, perhaps there was more to it. Anyway, that's not the point. She's left quite a bit of money to you."

I waved at Joel and made a sign to show I wanted a word.

"Can we discuss this later, Kitty? It's just that I'm at work and can't really talk now."

Joel gave me a kiss on the cheek. I gave him a signal to show him I was getting rid of someone on the other end of the phone and he laughed.

"It's over seven hundred thousand pounds actually, and then there is her cottage, which she owned outright. Now, of course, there will be an enormous amount of death duty to pay, but still it will make for a very nice little nest egg."

fourteen

Henrietta's love for Edward does not appear to have affected her wifely duties. She fell pregnant within the first year of her marriage, and by all accounts enjoyed motherhood immensely. She wrote to her sister, Elizabeth, extolling the virtues of children. In all, she had three children, each of them, as far as she was concerned, were sired by her husband; a son, Frederick, and two daughters, Elizabeth and Katherine.

When she was seven, her youngest daughter, Katherine, became perilously ill with scarlet fever, and Henrietta ignored the doctor's advice and tended to the child herself. Edward, who had again forsworn gambling and was once again a frequent guest at society parties, was extremely put out by her motherly duties and soon sought solace in the arms of her closest friend, Matilda, the Duchess of

Carlone. Although it seems implausible that Matilda could have known of her friend's devotion to Edward, Henrietta never forgave her and she was never invited to Posche House again.

Secret Passage to the Past:
A Biography of Lady Henrietta Posche
By Michael Carpendum

I arrived home at eleven to find Richard waiting for me outside my flat door. Not my building, my actual flat. He didn't have a key to the building, so someone must have buzzed him in. Typical of Richard to be able to charm my fellow residents to ignore the police sticker inside the lift warning that allowing strangers into the building was an open invitation to thieves, muggers, murderers and rapists.

Richard looked more like a dog that had been beaten than a criminal, though, and I immediately regretted sleeping with Jeremy as I juggled the flowers he'd sent me to open the door. The flowers had been accompanied by a card declaring "Glad you are back in my life." I felt guilty as I'd folded the card in half and slipped it in a bin.

I wrapped Richard up in a cuddle and he nuzzled my neck and I realized I wanted to make him feel better not worse. Actually, I wanted to make *us* feel better. I wanted to heal the scars, tend to the wounds and make us whole again, and no amount of conflict or warning signs seemed to be capable of making that feeling go away.

Once inside, Jean demanded I put the news on for her while Richard went to the loo without so much as a word. I figured he was taking cocaine—well, the flat was so microscopic I could hear him snorting the stuff. I listened to the sounds of ritual cocaine use, the tap running while he snorted his line off the cistern, then a flush of the toilet as if he'd actually been emptying his bladder. But I justified his cocaine usage. He was going through a rough time, so I was prepared to forgive him. I mean, lots of people take cocaine, especially successful people like Richard, I reminded myself. Apparently, tests had shown that there wasn't a five-pound note in circulation that hadn't been touched by nose candy. We were probably all inhaling the stuff by proxy, I told myself. I hardly knew anyone who didn't do a line *occasionally.* "I shouldn't be so judgmental, should I, Jean?" I asked my rabbit, who studiously ignored me as the headline music started up.

When Richard reappeared, he was eager to chat, eager to laugh. The Richard of old, the Richard I had fallen in love with. The Richard who never tired of conversation, never took anything seriously, the Richard who could always make me laugh. Of course, I wondered whether the cocaine was the conduit to the personality I loved so much. But I wasn't troubled enough to find out the answer. I had other things to worry about. Like my own guilty conscience about Jeremy.

Besides, I was glad Richard was happier. I watched him as he stood over Jean's litter tray and scratched his head. He was always so fastidious about her tray when we lived together. "I forgot how much work she is," he remarked, smiling at me. "Shall I change this?"

I laughed. "It's fine, I'll do it later," I promised, but he set to work anyway. Seeing him carrying out such a mundane domestic task pulled on my heart more than any amount of flowers or words. He'd always been wonderful at things like that when we were together, and it truly felt like coming home.

After he bleached his hands clean, he sat me on his lap and I told him about my inheritance, and to be fair to him, he cast off his own problems and gave me one of his boa constrictor hugs. As I gasped for air he spun me round, just the way he used to when he came home from work—he used to say he couldn't believe how lucky he was to have a wife like me. This was the man I loved, the man with boundless enthusiasm and endless capacity for fun. Jean looked up from her news broadcast and scowled. She hates being interrupted when the headlines are on.

With all the excitement I utterly forgot about Jeremy and my nasty torturing-Richard plot. I suddenly saw what an awful person I'd been; Richard knew how he felt about me, he was just struggling with the problem of sorting his life out and didn't need the specter of Jeremy to make him realize how much he loved me. I felt horribly ashamed of my cheap ruse to make him jealous. But I was putting all my awfulness behind me now. My unexpected windfall was just the incentive I needed to be compassionate and understanding about Richard's problems. I even felt more compassionate toward Leggy Blonde, especially now I was certain she was going to be cut out of the picture.

"We should have champagne to celebrate!" he insisted, and even though normally I would agree, I really couldn't face alcohol so soon after my horrendous excesses with Jeremy.

"I've got a bottle in the fridge, but I got totally trollied last night, so you'll have to toast me alone," I explained, doing my hangover face, which is a mixture of pathetic self-pity and remorse. It always used to make Richard laugh and propel him into a mad nurturing frenzy.

"Rubbish," he cajoled. "You can't win all that money and not drink champagne." He lifted me off the ground in another hug.

"I haven't *won* it," I pointed out. "Poor Aunt Camilla died." I thought of her broken engagement with the man called Oliver who drank too much, and felt strangely irritated by Richard's enthusiasm as a wave of loss engulfed me. But then he broke open the champagne, poured two glasses and I dutifully drank one. He didn't seem to care whether I drank or not after that, happily polishing off the bottle himself in short time, although to be fair he did make me a pot of green tea.

"I love that you drink green tea," he said as he watched me sipping my brew. I fluttered my lashes coquettishly, smitten that a man could love me for something as simple as drinking tea. "It's so comforting."

I didn't reply that I loved that he snorted cocaine, but there was no escaping it now. He didn't even slope off to the loo to conceal it anymore; instead, he began racking the lines up on Jean's vanity mirror.

"You're riding the dusty wagon pretty hard at the moment," I remarked when he asked to borrow Jean's mirror.

He looked up from his task with a grin on his face, joking, "I have to if I'm going to spend any time with you, madam." At least I hoped it was a joke. He wasn't actually asking me to accept responsibility for his drug taking…was he? "You keep very antisocial hours. I'd be falling asleep by now, and then what sort of company would I be?"

Before I could answer, he added, "I can't believe Jean has

her own mirror," cleverly segueing the conversation off his cocaine and onto my favorite subject, Jean.

"Well, she has to look her best. She doesn't want to be laughed at by the other rabbits!" I told him casually as he chopped up his lines.

"Sure you don't want one?" he asked.

"No, I'm happy with my tea," I replied with exaggerated primness.

But here's the thing…for once I wasn't putting my hands over my eyes and pretending it wasn't happening, and that had to be progress. I decided that once we were back to-gether we could deal with his drug problem; besides, once things were settled he'd probably want to take less himself. He'd definitely cut back when we were together…until his business went bad.

Besides, Leggy Blonde was still the main specter that had to be dealt with finally, so later when I heard him on the phone in the loo, I panicked that he might be talking to her. When he came out, and said he'd had a call from Marcus, a guy from work, I was immeasurably relieved.

"He has to drop something off to me. Would you mind if he dropped it here? I hate to ask, only I don't feel like going back to mine…not now?" His face was so adorable I would have said yes to a troop of circus tumblers dropping round to my flat.

"Oh God, no, definitely have him drop it off here," I gushed with relief, not even caring what it was this Marcus fellow was dropping. He could move his offices in for the night, because all I cared about was that he'd asked to stay the night, which meant Leggy Blonde was going to be spending the night alone.

Marcus turned up an hour later, and Richard went down-stairs to collect his "papers." When he came back he kissed me passionately and then tried to cuddle Jean, who bit him nastily on the hand.

"Jean," I scolded. "Don't be such a bitch or I'll take you to the vet and have your teeth filed!"

She ignored my empty threat and hopped back over to watch an advertisement for a charity that rescued sad and abused pets. I've been threatening her with teeth filing, and neutering, forever, and I think she'd worked out that I was all talk.

"Right, shall we have another pot of green tea?" Richard asked. "I think it's high time I got to grips with the attraction of this brew, don't you?"

We were a freeze-frame of married coupledom, snuggled up on opposite ends of the sofa, our legs entwined, sipping green tea, watching the news with our rabbit. Just like any normal married couple.

I wasn't really interested, but he spent an hour explaining how he was taking over a smaller software company. It sounded madly boring, but he seemed so excited I didn't want him to stop. I loved the way a gorgeous man like Richard could get so excited about the maddest, most insignificant things.

When the light began to creep through the blinds, I suggested we go down to Berkeley Square for Jean's bunny run. Finally, I felt I was winning the battle; Richard and I were like the married couple we always should have been, watching our Jean as she hopped her way about the square.

"She might be a he," Richard suggested as he nuzzled my ear.

"What do you mean, she might be a he? Her name's Jean," I reminded him.

He coughed nervously. "I didn't really ask about her sex, I just bought her from a kid on the tube." He grinned his naughty-schoolboy grin, the one I had always found so adorable.

Until now! "What do you mean you bought her from a kid on the tube?" I demanded. I didn't like the idea of my Jean being procured randomly on the public transport system. In my imagination he had planned the surprise of giving me Jean. In my imagination he had driven long and far into the countryside to find a bunny-breeding field and looked at hundreds, if not thousands, of rabbits before choosing just the right one for us. In my imagination many a rabbit had been rejected before our Jean was chosen.

"Just one of those beggars that go down the aisles hustling for change. I was alone in the carriage with him and he was irritating the shit out of me. You know how they hassle you and hassle you until you pay up. In the end I said I'd give him five quid for the rabbit if he left me alone. I didn't think he'd actually give it to me. These bloody beggars, they have no sense of sentimentality!" He shook his head at the outrage of it all.

I swallowed back my immediate reaction before replying carefully, "So, actually, you didn't even mean to buy me Jean."

"What's that supposed to mean? You love her, don't you? Does it really matter where she came from?"

"Of course I love her. She's ours. I thought she was a carefully planned first-month anniversary present," I told him, trying to hide the hurt in my voice.

He shrugged then shook his head as he wrapped me in a cuddle. "She was. That is, I *was* planning on buying you a rabbit or at least something nonallergic, and then I ended up with her." He kissed me on the nose. "It was fate, in a sense."

"Hardly much planning if you only bought her as a means of being left alone by the boy hassling you on the tube," I pointed out crossly.

He pulled away as if he was pissed off. "Lolly, don't get weird on me. It's five o'clock in the bloody morning. Some of us have to be at work in a few hours. I'm not in the mood for one of your sulks."

I heard the warning voice of Elizabeth in my head, "When a guy says 'Don't get weird on me' he means don't expect anything from me, because I'm only in this thing for low-maintenance, low-input sex and casual affection."

I picked Jean up and kissed her tiny nose, listening to my own voice, which reasonably pointed out that Richard was right. It was five o'clock (if not later) in the morning, and did it really matter where Jean came from?

Richard put his arm around Jean and I on the walk back to the flat and I nestled my head on his shoulder. He kissed me at the door and asked if he could see me tonight.

I nodded, still conflicted about what he'd said about buying Jean from a refugee, but I pushed all that from my mind. I was used to staying up all night in my job, but Richard wasn't.

I had a good day's sleep and made sure I was at work on time, and when Charlie invited me in for a cordial at the end of the night everything seemed to be back to normal. In fact, when I told him about my inheritance he joked that I should invest some of it in shares of the club. Jean and Cinders watched the news as he proffered the bottle of Veuve.

The memory of my drunken night with Jeremy had started to fade and it was a nice feeling having things back on track with Charlie, so I agreed. We toasted my aunt and settled into comfortable conversation while Cinders licked Jean maternally. I decided to share Richard's theory about Jean being a boy, which in effect meant I told Charlie the whole sordid story of how Richard had come to purchase her.

He was silent for a while, staring into the bubbles of his glass before remarking, "Did you tell him about your inheritance?"

"What's that got to do with Jean's gender?" I asked hotly.

"Nothing, just a thought." He continued to stare into his champagne as if he might divine something from the upward flow of tiny bubbles.

"Well, of course I told him, why wouldn't I? It's hardly a national secret."

Charlie shrugged. His long legs were resting on the desk, he looked the very image of the relaxed gentleman as he took a small sip of his cordial. But I didn't like the tension that was crackling in the room, the tension of unasked questions and unspoken opinions, so I asked straight out, "Do you have a problem with Richard or something?"

He looked me straight in the eye as he replied, "Or something."

"Don't be cryptic, Charlie, just say what's on your mind."

He swung his legs off the desk and replied, "Okay, quite frankly, I think Richard's a cokehead."

I laughed—one of those hollow laughs. "That's preposterous."

He raised one eyebrow at me questioningly.

I shrugged my shoulders at the absurdity. "God, everyone takes the occasional recreational line in our world."

Again he gave me the raised eyebrow. "I'd hardly call his use occasional or recreational…in any world. He's flashy, Lola, and fake, he's everything that's loathsome about the new rich."

I was floored by the venom in Charlie's words. "You're such a snob, Charlie!" I told him contemptuously. "How dare you sneer at Richard? At least he got where he is today by hard work. Not everyone can inherit it," I reminded him pointedly, although I'd just come into a windfall by way of inheritance myself (though nothing on the scale of Charlie's family money).

"Oh, has he? Well, in that case, can you tell me, Lola, where you suppose he is today?"

"And what's that supposed to mean?"

"Nothing," he replied mildly, looking out the window as if done with our conversation. "It was an idle question."

"Well, it didn't sound very idle to me, it sounded energetically pointed. Richard works really hard and doesn't deserve to have snide comments made about him."

He spoke more gently. "Look, Lola, just think about it, he hasn't paid his membership for over two years and his bar bill is astronomical. Were he anyone else, I would have canceled his membership."

"Well, don't give him special treatment on my account," I told him as I gathered Jean up into my arms. "Look, I'll see you tomorrow. I'm meeting Richard."

"Ask him how Marcus is for me, will you?" he called out to me as I was about to push on the door.

"Excuse me, you mean the guy he works with?"

Charlie shook his head. "Forget I said anything. It's been a long day. Your mother asked me to your aunt's funeral tomorrow, I'm driving Elizabeth down, you sure you wouldn't like a lift?"

"No, thank you," I informed him grandly. "I'd prefer to go with Richard." And with that, I flounced theatrically out of Posh House and took a cab home.

fifteen

"…I begin to wonder if even you, my darling Eliza-beth, can countenance this latest allowance I have made for Edward. While I was nursing my daughter he made love to my closest friend, Matilda, even going so far as to write her a sonnet, which, in her ignorance, she showed to me.

I have adored her since first coming to London, and her many kindnesses to me have meant much to me over the years. Yet so sickened am I by the thought of her lying in Edward's arms, I cannot bear to look upon her and have refused her each time she has paid a visit. She, of course, has no idea why I am punishing her in this way, but if I relent and see her, I should betray myself. What else must be sacrificed on the altar of my love, dearest Elizabeth? Please try and come down to London. I still cannot leave as Katherine is so weak…"

Extract of a letter from Lady Henrietta
Posche to her sister, Elizabeth

Richard turned up at my flat on the day of Aunt Camilla's funeral in a Mercedes convertible he'd hired specially. I know he was only trying to be sweet, but I told him I'd have preferred to have arrived at the crematorium in a more somber vehicle.

"Like a hearse, you mean?" he asked, giving me a kiss on the nose.

"No, not a hearse, it's just that this roof-down, wind-in-our-hair thing…it doesn't seem quite funereal."

He put his hand on my knee. "Look, we haven't been out of London together for years and I just wanted to make the most of it. Besides, your aunt wasn't the somber type, and from what you told me about her heavily scripted funeral fete, I think she would have approved. This car struck me as the perfect car for a village fete."

I gave his hand a squeeze, settled into the expensive comfort of the tan leather seat and turned on the CD player. He was right, and I loved the way he was using words like *we* and *together* in the same sentence. It was a glorious late-spring day and I was probably still vexed by Charlie and his insinuations about Richard. Also, Jeremy had left several messages on my phone. Seriously, having a love life can be very demanding and stressful.

Richard drove with his foot down the whole way, so that we arrived outside ten minutes early. I felt a horrible shiver go through me as we climbed out of the car and looked toward the ominous faux-Tudor crematorium. Richard looked at me and made a face. "Bit ghastly, isn't it?" he remarked.

Clemmie and Josie weren't able to make the funeral due to work commitments. Clemmie was looking after Jean for me and they were joining us at the fete tomorrow. But Elizabeth had insisted on coming, as had Charlie, and I was relieved when their car pulled up alongside ours, because Richard and I were just sitting there in strained silence. "These places give me the creeps," Richard said when I would have much rather he put his arm around me.

Charlie ran chivalrously round to open the door for Elizabeth, who climbed out of his old Aston Martin looking slightly flushed. Her long dark hair was tied up in an elegant chignon, and in her A-line black dress and chocolate-brown shawl, she looked very Audrey Hepburn. I was wearing a horrible black pantsuit I'd bought specially, as the only dark-colored item of clothing I owned was my black-sequined cleavage-bearing top. I'd tied my hair back in a tight bun. I looked like the funeral director.

"Hello, Richard," Elizabeth said in as cursory a way as she could without being outright rude. She'd always been immune to his charm and always made sure he knew it. Then she turned away from him and spoke to me as if he didn't exist. "Darling, we were trying to catch up with you the whole way! God, you were flying around those hairpin bends like a Formula One car!"

"Yes, well, it seems a shame not to open up the throttle on the old girl when you get out of London," Richard explained as if the car were his own. I felt both embarrassed by his stupid remark and guilty for feeling embarrassed. Poor Richard, I knew how being around my friends always made him feel uncomfortable. No matter what he said or did, they'd never really *got* him.

Charlie smiled at me and put his hand on my shoulder. "Okay, old girl?"

"Fine," I told him. He hadn't even made eye contact with Richard, so I wasn't going to reward his bad manners with civility even if he was trying to be kind. Instead, I put my arm protectively around Richard and suggested we all go in.

All four of us looked at the daunting building.

"I guess we have to go in at some point," Richard agreed.

Charlie was dressed in plain dark Armani linen suit. And as he took Elizabeth's arm to help her totter across the uneven bitumen in her heels, I thought they looked like the perfect couple, and even though the two of them had every right to be the perfect couple, should they choose, like everything else that day the idea seemed upsetting. I suppose funerals are like that.

Kitty and Martin were in the entrance vestibule of the crematorium, greeting people as they were going in. Richard and I both lingered behind for a bit while they spoke to Elizabeth and Charles. The whole setup was weirdly office-like in that there was already another group of mourners coming out, dabbing away tears and supporting one another in their grief. Kitty was in black, wearing a big black hat and swathed in her trademark chiffon. She told us that the ceremony was to start in three minutes, sharp.

Martin shook his head. "Horrible business this." I wasn't sure if he meant the burning-of-the-body business, the tight schedule or the whole death issue. He looked very handsome, though, beside Kitty, attired in uncharacteristic formality, a white carnation in his lapel.

Richard leaned in to kiss Kitty on the cheek and Martin gave me one of his big bear hugs.

"We'll miss the old girl," he said.

Kitty and Richard agreed, with Richard adding, "Yes, on the few occasions I met her she made an enormous impact." I know Kitty and Martin didn't know about Richard's true feelings toward Camilla, but his falseness made me cringe, so I took his hand and led him into the crematorium.

There was a malingering misery inside, partly due to the horrible green swirly carpet that was several decades past its due-by date, and the nasty deep red-flocked wallpaper. Worst of all, there were still a few stragglers from the last funeral sitting on the nasty dark green plastic folding chairs sobbing quietly into handkerchiefs. I didn't know whether to comfort them or hurry them along. Elizabeth looked at me and made a face. I knew what she meant. The whole effect was like a cross between a London registry office and a nasty B and B. A clearinghouse for dead people, and our slot was next.

By the time Kitty and Martin joined us in the grandly named "mourning parlor," we had a party of about forty people, all uncomfortably looking about in bewilderment at the surroundings. Eventually we were ushered into the funeral room by a small man in a dark suit heavily sprinkled with dandruff.

Camilla's coffin stood on a silk-swathed podium in the center. It was covered in white lilies and wreaths and on top was a large silver-framed photograph of Camilla as a young woman. She was laughing, her eyes looking into the eyes of a handsome man with a pencil-thin mustache. Scrawled across the photograph in a dark pen were the words,

Forever yours, Oliver, x

I wondered about Oliver. About where he was, alive or dead, and whether the two had ever had contact after their initial break. The ceremony was sad in a civil-ceremony sort of way, but most of all it was very weird. Apart from my parents, Richard, Charlie and Elizabeth, none of us knew one another. A man in a suit said a few words about Camilla that could have applied to any elderly woman and then a woman turned on a cheap CD player and we all sang along as best we could to "The Way You Look Tonight."

Notwithstanding the horrendous cheap grimness of everything, all of us were crying. The words "darling, never, never change," seemed to drag sobs out of everyone, and Richard reached out and took my hand as the curtain crept slowly and eerily around the coffin and the last of the Grand Old Edwardians was taken from us on a conveyer belt.

"They burn them in the night," Richard explained unnecessarily as we left the building, passing through another funeral party waiting their turn. "The body screams, you see."

I looked at him, chilled with the shock of what he'd just told me.

"The lungs still have air in them and they make a screaming sound as they burn them. I'd never invest in property near a place like this." He shuddered. "Worse than an abattoir."

I was rescued from commenting on his macabre facts by my father, who put his arm around me. "It's a sad old business," he sighed. After that, we all stood there for a bit in the car park, the men holding their keys, the girls holding their hats, all of us lost for words.

Eventually Elizabeth wrapped me in a hug and told me how much she loved me and then Charles hugged me, and for some reason I didn't want to let go. His reassuring strength and the comforting smell of lime that hung about him made me feel safe.

"I know she was old but I am going to miss her," I told them. The thought of her being burned chilled me and I must have kept on holding on to him as I thought about my aunt, because in the end Richard pulled me away and said, "Come on, Lola. We'll see you all tomorrow at the fete, then."

I felt numb as I allowed myself to be prized from Charlie and led away.

"We're staying at the Old Castle Bed & Breakfast if you want to drop in this evening for a drink and a chat," Elizabeth called out kindly, but Richard didn't turn back.

We drove back to my parents' in silence, Richard's hand resting on my knee, and I recalled going to Kitty's mother's funeral as a teenager; a traditional funeral where the coffin was lowered into the ground and we were able to say a proper goodbye. Afterward, Kitty, Martin and I and a few other close relatives had greeted people at the reception. It was held at my grandmother's house, which was later sold. As the guests came through the door, they all offered some form of condolence, mostly the "I'm sorry for your loss. Let me know if there is anything I can do" sort of thing. One woman, though, had the temerity to take Kitty's hand and say, "I don't really know what to say."

Kitty's reaction had had a profound effect on me at the time. She had pulled herself from her grief and looked the woman straight in the eye and said, "Well, why don't you go off and give it some thought, you gauche creature!" The woman looked shocked and muttered something about it being a figure of speech. So Kitty pointed her crime out more neatly. "I'm dealing with the loss of my mother and yet you arrive here to ask me for *my* help in scripting words of sympathy? Next time try something sympathetic like, I'm sorry for your loss! Most people seem to be able to manage that much at the very least."

The woman, of course, scuttled off shamed while the other guests mentally applauded. The reason I was remembering that day was that I was worried Richard would say something gauche. Not because he was gauche, but because being around my family and friends seemed to bring out the worst in him. Surely he would behave, I tried to reassure myself. Surely he wouldn't…

"I don't know what to say," he told Kitty as she answered the door. She had clearly been crying and I simply wrapped her in my arms instinctively, although a part of me froze waiting for the derision to be heaped on Richard.

Instead, she held me while Martin came to the door and shook Richard's hand. Richard asked where he should put our bags and went off, utterly insensitive to his own insensitivity.

Kitty seemed uncharacteristically rattled. "I suppose I should have invited Charlie and Elizabeth to stay with us, there's plenty of room, I can't have been thinking clearly," she remarked. I assured her it was fine, and added that they might feel more comfortable in a B and B, given the circumstances.

"Now, come on, girls," Martin cut in. "Let's stop all this doom and gloom now. We've said our goodbyes and Cam-Cam wouldn't have wanted long faces. In fact, she's left us with the strictest instructions not to cast a shadow over her passing. She's going to be shot off into the stars tomorrow night and we should all pay our respects by enjoying ourselves."

Despite my father's heartiness it was not the most comfortable evening. Martin and Kitty were both subdued, but that wasn't the worst of it. Richard kept attempting conversation, seemingly mindless to the mood of the rest of us. He was like a playful red setter at…well…at a funeral. I know he was only trying to cheer us all up, but despite Martin's reminder that Camilla wouldn't have wanted us to be glum, we all felt emotionally subdued.

During our supper of oysters and champagne, or as Kitty referred to it, "a no-nonsense snack," Richard inquired about Oliver. "I always thought of her as an old spinster," he added.

Kitty froze but said nothing.

I waded in to save him. "Well, they had some sort of romance when she was younger."

"So is the guy still alive?"

Martin shook his head. "I very much doubt it," he said, and then left the table for more bread. Nothing more was said, and out of fear of further strain I suggested that Richard and I might go to visit Charlie and Elizabeth at their B and B and Kitty leaped on the idea with enthusiasm.

"What a lovely idea."

"But if you'd rather we stayed," I prevaricated.

"No, no, no, you must join your friends. I feel dreadful that I didn't invite them."

"Yes, you young ones go off. I'll call you a cab, shall I?" Martin added.

Things at the Old Castle were no better, though. Charlie and Elizabeth were curled up on a sofa, a backgammon board between them, laughing and chattering companionably when we arrived. It might have been my imagination, but they didn't look thrilled to see us.

"Oh, we didn't think you'd come," Elizabeth sighed. But it seemed to me that what she wanted to say was, "We didn't *want* you to come."

"No? Well, we did, here we are, but if you'd rather…" My sentence trailed off as I took in the look of barely concealed hatred on Charlie's face as he stared at Richard. Thank goodness Richard was blissfully unaware of the subtext as he was looking around the room.

"Which way are the toilets?" he asked.

I confronted Charlie about the way he was looking at Richard while he was out of the room. He claimed not to know what I was talking about and offered me a drink.

We stayed for a couple of games of backgammon, but talk was strained mostly due to Charlie's demeanor. He barely said a word and hardly looked up from the backgammon board—whether he was playing or not. After a few attempts at polite conversation, Richard fell into silence, too, quietly reading the *Times* while I played backgammon with Elizabeth and Charlie watched on.

I had a sense of Charlie's eyes on me the entire evening, and at one point I even met his stare, but he didn't turn away. He just looked unflinchingly (judgmentally, I suppose) into my eyes. Elizabeth caught his look but I don't think Richard noticed. Elizabeth spent the rest of the game glancing from Charlie to me and giving me significant looks that I didn't understand and didn't have the emotional energy to interpret.

When Richard suggested we call a cab at eleven-thirty, I dived on the idea with relish. We held hands in the back of the car but neither of us spoke. By silent agreement we went straight to bed. I remembered the last time we had stayed in this bed together. We'd been married a few months and we had both decided it would be too weird making love in my parents' house.

Richard claimed, "It's only fun making love in your parents' house when you're not supposed to."

I agreed even at the time although my reason had been I wasn't in the mood, but when he added that "Sanctioned sex is a bit of a turnoff, don't you think?" I'd been shocked.

Looking back on that conversation I still felt uneasy. Because after all, that's what marriage was…sanctioned sex. We did spoon now, though, which was nice, and as I was falling asleep, Richard asked me if I'd like to marry him again. Just like that. "Let's get married."

I waited in case he was going to say something else, but he didn't, so I said, "Are you sure that's what you really want?"

"I was never sure about getting divorced, Lolly, you know that."

I snuggled in to him. "Me neither," I agreed, and that seemed to settle it. "You've still got your ring, haven't you?" he asked.

I breathed the words *of course* into his ear.

"Me, too," he added, interlocking his hand in mine.

It wasn't exactly a passionate declaration of love or the most romantic of proposals but it felt timely, and it felt right. It really did feel right. It felt like the past years apart from Richard had been swept away, as if nothing but our being together mattered at all. There was a continuous thread running through our relationship and that was what I was clinging to.

"I do love you, Lolly," he whispered, his breath hot in my ear.

"I love you, too," I told him as our breathing slowed.

I thought about Leggy Blonde and wondered how things

had finally ended between them, whether she had walked out or whether he had told her it wasn't going to work. I was desperately curious, actually, and longed to ask what had happened to Sally, but I didn't. I had obviously been right all along about Richard's feelings toward her. She hadn't really mattered to him after all.

The heavens opened and for the rest of the night a thunderstorm raged. The rain slicing diagonally down, belted against the window, muffling Richard's slight snore.

sixteen

After the death of his father, Edward came into a small inheritance. Though by no means enough to make him a rich man, it seems for a period at least this money enabled him to pay off his debts and he was once more welcomed back into polite society. Unbeknownst to Henrietta, though, during this time he not only continued his gambling but became addicted to opium. Henrietta either chose to ignore his addiction or bore it as she had his gambling. However, in many ways, it was the beginning of the end, as his debts soon once more went unhonored.

Secret Passage to the Past:
A Biography of Lady Henrietta Posche
by Michael Carpendum

Despite our concerns following the heavy late-night rains, the sun was as bright and strong as if it were August. Richard and Martin had set off early to assist with setting up the fete. By ten-thirty, when Kitty and I arrived, the green was buzzing with local villagers and Aunt Camilla's friends and family. There were children's rides, face painting, Morris dancers and stores offering food such as fairy floss, hot dogs, toffee apples and soft drinks, all for free.

Being in my aunt's village, I was reminded of all the times I'd walked across this green with her, chatting about life and fashion and men. Richard had been helping to set up the fete since first light with Martin, while Kitty and I had come along later. Walking through the crowd to search for him, I couldn't help imagining that I'd caught a glimpse of my Camilla in the crowd.

I saw Richard by the bungee-jumping ride and watched as he helped the smaller children into the rubber bungee seat.

He was wearing a pair of threadbare blue jeans I'd once bought him and his green Converse All-Stars. My heart melted.

"Bunjee jump, miss?" he inquired in an East End accent as I slipped my arms around him and kissed his neck. Next minute he was strapping me into the seat and bouncing me up on the cushions. I felt as if I was flying as my body bounced twenty feet into the air. I somersaulted on my second bounce and Richard whistled through his teeth and clapped.

When he finally grabbed me, I ran my fingers through his hair and mucked it up, and even though his eyes were hidden behind his Ray•Bans I knew they were smiling at me. Afterward, he brought me a toffee apple, which we licked together, our tongues occasionally touching in a tantalizing tease, until he eventually kissed me full on the mouth.

"I'd better get back to work," he said, breaking the kiss. I watched his tall, lean frame as he headed back to the stand. I felt connected to him in the way I'd wanted to feel connected to him since I first saw him that night with Leggy Blonde at Posh House. Martin joined him, and the two of them helped an older lady into the bunjee seat. They looked so sweet together, just like a father and son-in-law.

Even though Aunt Camilla had always carefully avoided the subject of Richard after our divorce, I felt certain she would have supported my decision to remarry him now if she were here. On the subject of remarriage, I hadn't had a chance to tell Kitty and Martin about Richard's proposal, as we'd had such an early start, but I knew they'd be delighted. They were the king and queen of romance, the poster children for remarriage, after all!

Elizabeth, Josie and Clemmie, well, that was another matter. As for Charlie, given his behavior recently, I really didn't care what he thought. In fact, I'd more or less decided to tender my resignation, partly because of his feelings toward Richard but mostly I'd decided it was time for me to take the plunge in terms of setting up the PR company I'd always dreamed of owning.

With my inheritance I could finally make my dream a reality. Once the tax man had taken his chunk, I'd still have enough to pay off my mortgage, have a bit of a blowout on Bond Street and enough left over to set up Lola PR.

"Darling, there you are, I've been looking all over for you," Jeremy panted. I cringed as I checked out the white bony legs that appeared from his shorts. They were the most horridly lurid checked shorts, the sort a golfing surfer might wear. Had I actually had sex with those legs? Sometimes I really do despair of myself, but more to the point, what on earth was Jeremy doing here? My aunt had a lot to answer for.

"Oh, Jeremy, darling, how lovely to see you." I kissed his cheeks, my stomach knotted with fear that Richard would now discover I'd recently shagged him. Oh no, everything was going to go wrong now. I had an awful queasy feeling, which I was pretty sure was a premonition of impending disaster.

"Yes, what an extraordinary thing," he exclaimed, looking around the noise and carnival atmosphere of the fete. "I received this invitation in the post, I didn't really know what to make of it," he explained, brandishing his invitation. "I left you several messages but I guess you've had a lot on." He snaked his arm around my waist just as I noticed Richard coming toward us.

Ever the quick thinker, I took swift action and threw myself into a small puddle. I hadn't actually meant to land in the actual puddle, of course, merely to fall lightly near it so that Richard wouldn't catch Jeremy with his arm around me. But Jeremy wasn't prepared to let me fall, and as I struggled to disengage from his arm around my waist, he tried to grab me back. I pushed him away and lost my footing, which landed me slap bang in the middle of the puddle, covered in mud. Jeremy looked befuddled as he helped me up. "I tried to catch you, Lola, but you threw me off."

"Lolly!" Richard called out, racing over. He'd taken his glasses off and looked madly concerned.

"Don't know what happened there," said Jeremy, dabbing at my face with a handkerchief. So typical of him to carry a fresh white handkerchief, I thought irritably. "One minute she was as upright as you like, and the next…splat!"

"What the hell do you think you were doing, man? I saw you with my own eyes, she tried to fight you off."

"What?"

"You pushed her straight into that puddle!"

Jeremy looked horrified. "I was just trying to help. I was putting my arm around her, just being affectionate, and then—"

"Bloody funny way of showing affection, pushing a girl into a pond like that. What the hell is wrong with you?" Richard demanded, looking as if he was about to hit poor Jeremy.

"What would I push her into a bloody pond for, Richard?" Jeremy reasoned, clearly beginning to get a bit hot under the collar as well. "Besides, it was a puddle not a pond."

"She looks like a drowned rat, you idiot!"

Thank God, Kitty arrived on the scene in her chiffon-flowing glory. "Lola, what on earth is going on?" she asked, brandishing a giant swirl of pink fairy floss—as a fashion accessory, I suspected. "Why on earth did you jump into that puddle? You silly, silly girl."

"I didn't jump," I remonstrated as Kitty shook her head and tutted and brandished her fairy floss.

Richard, the darling that he is, stood up to Kitty for me. "She was bloody well pushed by Jeremy here. I saw it with my own eyes."

"I was trying to catch her, only she fought me off," remonstrated Jeremy.

Kitty shook her head. "Stop all this showing off, now, Lola, and come and help with the rides. Charlie's running the coconut shy single-handedly." She gave Richard an accusatory look as if to say "and you?"

Jeremy slipped his hand in my right hand and Richard slipped his hand in my left. This was becoming farcical, only not in a funny way.

Josie approached me next; she had Jean on her little diamante leash, and owing to the damp ground, the rabbit's fur was all muddied. "Couldn't you have held her?" I scolded.

"I tried to, Lola, but she keeps humping me. In fact, I'm sure she's a he, not a she at all. I mean, it's not normal for a girl to hump everything like that."

I pulled my hands away from Richard and Jeremy, picked up my muddy rabbit and clasped her to my chest while Jeremy and Richard slipped their arms back around my waist.

Richard asked Jeremy what he was up to. Jeremy put the same question to Richard and immediately they were head-to-head, virtually circling each other like gladiators.

Josie looked at me, mystified. "What an earth is going on?"

Kitty suddenly reappeared, grabbed my arm and dragged me off, leaving Richard and Jeremy unsupervised. "Will you stop behaving like a lost infant and give Charlie a hand, Lola!" she ordered, propelling me forward toward the Ferris wheel. "He seems to be the only one with any sense of community spirit here today!"

"But, Kitty, you don't understand, Richard's been here since dawn setting up, and doing the bunjee jumps…"

She totally ignored me, pushing me toward Charlie as village children ran past clutching their fairy floss and toffee apples, squealing with delight. I felt like a small child myself. "He's asked me to marry him," I blurted, deciding this was an emergency and I should play my trump card.

But Kitty didn't seem in the least bit fazed. She continued to push me toward the coconut shy, where I could see Charlie lifting a small girl up so that she could have a reasonable shot. "And I really need to go back to him, because I slept with Jeremy to make him jealous, only Jeremy doesn't know that's why I slept with him and I never got round to telling Richard and now he's asked me to marry him and if he finds out about Jeremy *now,* he'll think I'm a total slut and won't want to marry me and…" My voice trailed off because we'd arrived at the coconut shy and Charlie was facing me and had clearly heard the last bit of my rant.

"You're marrying him, then?" Charlie asked. He was holding the hand of the most adorable little girl with beautiful doe-brown eyes and a head of chaotic black curls. Kitty crouched in a pool of chiffon and chatted to the little girl as if she wasn't eavesdropping on our conversation.

I held Jean to my chest more tightly as if facing up to the Big Bad Wolf. "Yes, are you surprised?" I huffed.

"Yes, as it happens…although *horrified* might be a better word."

Talk about the arrogance of the man. "Actually, *congratulations* is more traditional," I pointed out.

"What about his girlfriend?"

"Commiserations?" I suggested brightly. I wasn't going to have him rain on my parade.

"Admirable sense of sisterhood, Lola," he chastised.

The little girl looked at me and pointed at me. "Sister!" she repeated happily.

"She's not my sister and I don't know what your problem is," I pointed out. "What's Leggy Blonde got to do with me?" I shrugged, like a philosophical Frenchman. "Richard and she had a fling before we hooked up again. I'm not responsible for every girl in the world!"

"Who is this Leggy Blonde?" Kitty asked, standing up to rejoin the conversation.

"Leggy Blonde," the little girl repeated, pointing her finger right at me.

"Forget about Leggy Blonde," I snapped a little harshly. "She's not the issue."

The little girl looked hurt and I felt ashamed as Charlie picked her up.

Kitty gave me a wide-eyed look of incomprehension, patting a sweep of blond hair from her face.

"Leggy Blonde," the little girl in Charlie's arms repeated, but Charlie ignored her, adding, "Well, what about Jeremy, then? What's he going to think when he finds out you only slept with him to make Richard jealous?"

"I didn't tell Richard," I replied, blushing at being called on my shameful attempt at making Richard jealous. I couldn't bear that Charlie had guessed what I'd been up to. My duplicity seemed so much worse when I imagined it through someone else's eyes. I looked searchingly through the crowd for Richard and Jeremy but saw only a sea of villagers. Jean was wriggling, so I placed her back on the ground.

"Lola!" Kitty scolded. "You're sounding like a total slut, darling!"

"What's a slut?" the little girl inquired, bending her head down in order to look up earnestly into Charlie's eyes.

Kitty took her from Charlie and placed her on the ground, crouching and looking into her wide dark eyes. "A slut is a girl of very loose morals," she explained earnestly.

The little girl turned to me and pointed. "You're a slut," she announced loudly enough for everyone in a thousand-mile radius to hear.

"Can I have a go on the slut?" asked a small boy of about four years of age whose mother looked at me as if I was a witch that needed burning. She picked her boy up and carried him off while I stood there clutching my muddy rabbit in my muddy clothes. Charlie looked at me as if he didn't know me, while the little boy's voice echoed in the distance—"I want a go on the slut. I want a go on the slut!"

"Right, then, who wants to win a prize on the coconut shy?" called Charlie, and all the children around forgot about the slut and started jumping all over him with cries of "Me! Me! Me!"

Kitty put her arm around my waist and led me away. "So he proposed again, did he?"

"Last night."

"And how do you feel about it, *really* feel about it, Lola?" She stopped and looked deeply into my eyes the way only Kitty can (basically because on anyone else it would seem melodramatic!).

But I ignored her piercing gaze—well, actually, I diverted her gaze by looking soulfully into Jean's eyes and making mad little clucking sounds at her. "What do you mean, how do I feel about it? I thought you'd be pleased."

"My pleasure in your proposal should be immaterial. I asked how *you* felt. Do you really think he is your passion, darling, that's the point."

"What do you mean is he my *passion?* What sort of thing

is that to ask?" It was exactly the sort of thing Kitty would ask, but I was annoyed with her asking anyway.

"Do you *ache* when you can't be with him?"

I flashed back to the aching I did after I saw him with Leggy Blonde, although deep down it had been niggling at me recently that prior to seeing him with Leggy Blonde there hadn't been a whole lot of aching really. Actually…I'd been quite happy with my life; happy with my job, happy with my friends, happy with my flat, happy with my occasional flings, happy with my rabbit. When I thought about it, I'd been quite the quirky single girl. Independent and happy with it! "Of course I ache when I'm not with him," I said, though.

"Well, then, that's all that matters," she said and walked on as if the matter was settled.

I scuttled after her. Jean's little ears went back with irritation (she hates it when I scuttle), but I couldn't help feeling a bit miffed. "You might say congratulations. After all, you're always going on at me about the tragedy of my life and how I have no passion. You're the one who's always despaired of me, saying I 'wear you out so' with my lack of passion."

Kitty stopped and turned. "Yes, I have felt at times that your life was empty, I did worry that you lacked passion or purpose. But then, I used to think Aunt Camilla's life was empty, too. Maybe I was wrong about both of you." She smiled at me and put a hand out to stroke Jean's ears. "One thing I do know is that passion isn't something you need congratulations for. It's a painful disorder, an uncontrollable emotion, a purpose, a raison d'être without which I can't live. If you have the soul of a poet, as I do, you can't live without the suffering that passion brings."

"You make it sound like a disease," I said as Jean subtly rubbed her back end on my arm.

Kitty pulled her hand away and looked soulfully into the middle distance as only a woman who has played Juliet a thousand times can. I wouldn't be able to look into the middle distance soulfully if my life depended on it. Actually, even thinking about it made me have to think of something sad to stop myself falling apart at the seams giggling. "It is a disease, I suppose," Kitty sighed. "A disease of the soul. And like an addict I can't live without it."

"Oh," I replied, almost bursting with laughter as Kitty put a hand out wistfully. "I don't know anymore if it's for everyone, though," she conceded.

Even though it was Kitty, I was stunned by her speech nonetheless. She'd clearly been madly affected by my aunt's death, and specifically about the discovery of Aunt Camilla's secret love, but I hadn't expected her to question passion. I hadn't anticipated that she wouldn't dance with pleasure at the news that Richard and I were to be remarried.

I didn't have a chance to dwell, though, because a small boy charged into me, sending poor horny little Jean flying. Kitty and I ran to her aid, but she must have been okay because she started hopping away swiftly through the crowds. We gave chase, and when finally I gathered her into my arms, I became aware of a fracas going on at the edge of the green.

Richard and Charlie were yelling at one another.

"Isn't that Richard?" Kitty asked, pointing to a corner of the green.

I watched with horror as Richard pushed Charlie, then I saw Charlie storm off.

Kitty and I both raced over with Jean. "What's going on?" I asked Richard when we finally reached him.

"Oh, the guy's a prick, don't worry about him," he replied, seemingly quite casual.

"What were you arguing about?"

"He was at me for the pissy membership subscription. I told him I'd give him a check. I mean, for Christ's sake, it's hardly on the top of my agenda today." Then he put his arm around me. "I'm about to marry the girl of my dreams, that's all I care about."

As I nuzzled into my fiancé's arm, I remembered then that Charlie had mentioned something about Richard's membership subscription being overdue, but normally the membership secretary would have contacted him. It wasn't something I'd expect Charlie to involve himself in, no matter how annoyed he was. "Seems odd that he would bring it up here," I remarked.

"The guy is odd," he replied before giving me a kiss on the head.

"Well, let's not worry about it now," I reassured him. "Come back and enjoy the fete."

"Yes," agreed Kitty. "I will take Jean for a walk."

When she had gone, Richard took me in his arms and kissed me long and slow on the mouth.

"Let's go and have a go on a ride," I suggested.

He kissed me again. "In a moment, I'm just waiting here for Marcus."

"Marcus?"

"Ah, some rubbish with work, don't worry about it."

I wandered disconsolately after Kitty, but I *did* worry about it. I worried about it a lot. It was something Charlie had said to me about Marcus, but I couldn't remember what.

seventeen

"Since the death of his father, Edward has been as he was when I first met him. I wish you could see him, Elizabeth dearest, he is lighter of spirit, as if a dark cloud has been lifted. He has even forsworn gambling. My heart could burst with the joy I feel at having my darling Edward returned to me.

There is only Edward, no one else. I am walking as if in an opium-induced trance. No one else seems to exist for me. Tomorrow he is taking me to the studio of an artist. He is certain he can convince me to have my portrait painted. I do wish you could come down to London to see him as he is now. I promise you, he is as he ever was…"

Extract from a letter from Lady Henrietta Posche to her sister, Elizabeth

Elizabeth came running up to me later and said Charlie was going to go back to London, to which I'd said good riddance, although I didn't really mean it, and Elizabeth pretty much accused me of as much.

"Of course I mean it!" I insisted. As if I was the sort of horrible person who could easily dismiss someone who'd gone to the trouble of coming all this way down from London for my aunt's funeral!

She rolled her eyes as though I was deranged. "Anyway, not to worry, I've persuaded him to stay for the ball, but he's decided to go back to the hotel. What was Richard's problem anyway?" she asked. "I heard they had an argument."

"Richard's problem? It was Charlie who started it. He was hassling him about his stupid membership subscription, can you believe it?"

"No," she replied simply, and there the matter was left.

Richard joined us at the Ferris wheel about an hour later,

and as I watched him lope over in the faded blue jeans I'd given him, I toyed with the idea of asking about Marcus. After air kissing Elizabeth and placing a soft wet kiss on my mouth, he rolled his sleeves up and asked Martin what he could do.

Even Elizabeth said she was impressed at the way he threw himself into the activities. It was fantastic, notwithstanding the village teenagers who must have heard of the incident earlier and kept asking how much it cost for a ride on the slut.

At around two-thirty, Martin gave a speech, a eulogy of sorts, only without the sadness. Kitty stood by his side, adding screen-goddess glamour to the fete while Martin told the story of how he had thought Camilla the most elegant woman when he was a boy and how everyone that came in contact with her had been touched by her charm. The speech was lighthearted and short, which was perfect, because by that stage I think everyone was fairly tired and ready to head home. A light drizzle had begun to fall, and as Richard took my hand and kissed it, everyone started clapping—at first I thought they were applauding Richard and me, but of course the applause was in honor of Aunt Camilla. Still, it was terribly romantic.

I spotted Jeremy as we were leaving, but I pretended I didn't and went off with the girls in another direction. Richard kindly offered to help Martin supervise the packing up of the fete so that the marquee could be erected for the ball that evening. Kitty went back home, as she needed a rest. I went back to the hotel with the girls, completely forgetting that Charlie would be there.

His lanky frame was stretched out on one of the sofas in the sitting room. He was reading the *Times* but put it aside as we entered, and asked us how the fete had gone. He was all smiles, which made it impossible to be cross with him.

"Ah, my sirens return," he declared as Josie, Elizabeth and Clemmie jumped on him like puppies and he wrestled with them like a big brother.

I sat demurely on the sofa opposite and stroked Jean.

Once he'd calmed the girls down, he asked Jean how she'd enjoyed the festivities and I answered for her because she was busy nibbling a piece of carrot I was feeding her.

I stayed for a cup of tea and then went home. There had been no mention of his argument with Richard and I hoped that the matter could be dropped, although I did toy with mentioning the membership issue just so that I could explain that if money was an issue I could easily pay Richard's subscription. I really didn't want any bad feeling between my friends and Richard now that we were to be married. I wanted them to be pleased for me and rally around the way friends were meant to rally round when you found the man of your dreams—or in my case refound him. The main thing was, we were always meant to be together and we'd simply had a bad patch. After all, Kitty and Martin had had four bad patches in all and yet no one could possibly imagine they weren't right for one another.

In the end, though, I decided that Aunt Camilla's funeral was not the time to speak of engagements. This was her day and I wasn't going to be the one to steal her limelight.

Back home Kitty and Martin were in bed—at five in the evening! I suppose it was lovely that they were still so sexually attracted to one another after all these years, but I rolled my eyes at Jean and she gave me a look as if to say, "I know, isn't parental sex disgusting!" I cleaned her up in the laundry sink and dried her off with a blow-dryer, then settled her in the kitchen with some rabbit food and went off to have a shower.

Richard arrived back as I was getting out. I rubbed my naked body up against him but he pushed me away. He was in a bad mood. He said he'd lost the papers that Marcus had brought and was going to have to have them brought again.

"Can't you leave it until tomorrow? I mean, what use can the papers be to you tonight when we're going to be at the ball?"

"You don't seem to understand, Lola. Not everyone has a pile of money to fall back on. Everything I have is riding on this deal."

I smarted at the reference to my inheritance. "No, Richard, I *can* understand they're important, but couldn't we deal with it tomorrow? It seems a waste to have Marcus travel all the way down here again."

"I've got to sign them, Lola."

"Oh. So why didn't you just sign them when he came earlier then?"

"Look, this really isn't your concern," he snapped.

"Fine," I agreed and went off to get dressed. He apologized later and of course I forgave him—I mean, he must have been exhausted after all the work he'd put in at the fete, but I couldn't help clinging to my hurt. Mainly because I was thinking about the significant emphasis Charlie had put on the name Marcus the other day while we'd been having a cordial in his office. I determined to tackle him about it at the ball and sort the matter out once and for all.

Camilla had decreed that everyone must wear white to the ball and had specified my outfit, an old white deco wedding gown, cut on the bias with a long train.

"She'd planned to wear it when she married Oliver," Kitty explained.

Martin added, "No one ever knew they had planned to elope, but for some reason they never did."

"Do you really think he died?" I asked, wondering if perhaps he was still sadly holding a candle to Camilla all these years.

"Almost certainly," Martin replied. "Although that's beside the point. She was the one who pulled away, and while I've no doubt she continued to love him, there was nothing to suggest she ever regretted that decision. She was an eminently sensible woman old Cam-Cam."

I couldn't help feeling a certain regret on her behalf, though, as I admired myself in the mirror of my bedroom. The tiara that went with the outfit was a family heirloom and I felt like a fairy queen. Jean had given me her highest accolade by humping my leg, which was more than I got from Richard.

He'd been pacing the floor for half an hour, and when I came out, all he'd said was, "At last. Can we go now, then?"

Martin and Kitty ignored his remark and told me I looked stunning.

We had a driver take us to the ball in Martin's Bentley. Kitty announced our engagement on the way. Martin congratulated us but it sounded hollow. In fact, it reminded me of when I told them I'd got a first at Bristol.

Two fire-eaters flanked the outside of the marquee. We walked down a silk-draped tunnel a bit like a bridal bower. Inside, the silver-framed photograph of Camilla and Oliver met us, standing in a wreath of white lilies on a white silk-covered table by the seating board. Inside, the marquee was beautiful; tea lights flickered on every table set with white linen, white crockery and crystal glasses. The effect was stunning and romantic.

I was horrified, though, when I scrutinized the seating

plan. I was to be seated at a table with Charlie on one side of me and Jeremy on the other. The seating arrangements were all Aunt Camilla's, so I could hardly ask to change. Elizabeth was on the other side of Charlie, and Hamish was on the other side of her, followed by Clemmie, who was next to Richard, and Josie, who was next to Jeremy. What on earth was Aunt Camilla thinking when she'd organized these placements? I wondered.

A jazz band was setting up in the corner and waiters were strolling through the gathering crowd holding trays laden with glasses of champagne. Clemmie grabbed two and passed one to me. I turned to Elizabeth as she was grabbing two and whispered, "I can't sit beside Jeremy and Charlie," but of course she had no idea what I meant. She passed the other glass to Josie.

"You look stunning," Charlie told me as he pulled out my chair.

"Like a fairy princess," Jeremy extolled.

"Or a bride," Hamish added cheekily.

Richard was looking fidgety. He plonked himself down without pulling either Josie's or Clemmie's seat out. I noticed Hamish was ogling Elizabeth, who looked edible in a Versace white satin dress without a back. He told her he'd never seen anyone make a backless dress look so good. I consoled myself that at least that was one ex I didn't have to worry about.

Unfortunately, the same couldn't be said of Jeremy, who tried to put his hand on top of mine. It was time to speak frankly, although Richard had already left the table and gone outside.

"Jeremy, you know how fond I am of you, but I don't want—"

"She's marrying Richard again," Charlie interjected.

"What?" the entire table gasped.

"Yes, it'll be just like old times," Charlie toasted, without the doubts that were only too clear in the way he looked at me. "To the happy couple."

Jeremy looked at me as if I'd slapped him.

"Thanks," I said to Charlie, giving him my most ferocious look.

Hamish asked, "Speaking of the happy couple, where's Richard? Not off to see Marcus again, is he?"

"Do you know Marcus?" I asked, beginning to burn with curiosity about this poor fellow making all these trips out of London on the weekend.

He smirked. "I've met him once or twice."

Jeremy winked and tapped the side of his nose.

"It's his dealer's name, obviously!" Elizabeth told me irritably, as if I was the only one in the world who didn't know.

"So Richard's still on the old Colombian marching powder, is he?"

"He never came off it," Elizabeth replied, staring at me, daring me to contradict her.

A nasty silence hung over the table and I think Elizabeth realized she was responsible. "Remember Clive?" she asked, smiling wickedly.

The name drew a complete blank.

"We shared a house with him at college?"

I nodded, even though I'd never really got to know him that well as I was too busy dating Hamish at the time.

"I remember him," Hamish agreed. "Red-haired guy, totally wired all the time."

"Oh, I remember now, the long-haired heavy metalist?"

"The ligger," she added.

"He was the most pretentious twat that ever played air guitar," I explained to the others.

"Most of all he never paid for a thing. He was always nicking everyone else's food without putting anything in, taking money from everyone's room and 'borrowing' clothes without asking."

Clemmie went, "Oh God, we had a girl like that in college, she changed her name to Mizzie or something stupid like that. She thought it sounded more glamorous."

"Well, there was nothing glamorous about Clive," Elizabeth assured us. "He even used to nick all our socks! Imagine, socks!"

"Not just Damien's—the other guy we shared with—but our socks. Girls' socks," I added. "But he still thought he was the king of cool. Although, actually, come to think of it, he *borrowed* ten quid from my room at the end of our *house* share then bizarrely enough, he paid it back."

"Hence my story," she replied. "I bumped into Damien recently, and he told me how he got his own back on Clive, see."

We all leaned in so we could hear Elizabeth's story above the music. "Apparently, Damien was telling me that he got so sick of Clive nicking stuff and never pitching in for food, that he played this joke on him. You know how he was always drug mad but never bought any himself?"

"Oh I remember well," I agreed, taking another sip of my cosmo—it was nice pretending I was back in a pre-Richard world.

"Well, one afternoon when Clive was due back, Damien laid out a few lines of sherbet on a mirror."

"Sherbet?" Josie asked, looking confused.

"Yeah, you know sherbet dip? The sweet fizzy powder you licked off a licorice stick?" Elizabeth explained.

"Oh my God, I loved sherbet dip," Josie enthused.

"Not up your nose you wouldn't," Clemmie told her.

"Anyway, so listen. Damien chopped up the lines on the

mirror then he just left it in the living room with this big note saying, 'Warning! Do Not Touch. Back in a minute! D.' Then he went into his room and waited for Clive to come home."

"Oh my God," Clemmie laughed. "I can imagine what happened."

"Yep, Clive snorted the lot, and his nose totally exploded with fizz."

And for some reason, imagining the long-haired, heavy-metalist Clive snorting a line of fizzy sherbet made me laugh harder and longer than I'd laughed for ages.

The drinks waitress came and refilled our glasses.

"Hang on, though, why didn't Damien tell us?" I asked as we composed ourselves.

"He promised to lock it in the vault after Clive begged him and promised to change his ligging ways," she explained.

"Ah, for the problems of college," Josie sighed wistfully. "Things were sorted out so easily then." A sentiment which was toasted by all.

Later, Hamish asked about Richard and how we got back together.

"Yes, tell us how this love of ages was rekindled," Charlie probed, already sounding slightly drunk.

I twirled my glass nervously. "Well, I don't know that it ever really stopped, actually, the feelings we had for one another, I mean. I think we threw in the towel after all the troubles Richard had with his business." I looked Jeremy in the eye as I added, "I'm really sorry, Jeremy, I didn't mean to give you the wrong idea."

He looked quite white but smiled stoically. "Well, to the happy couple, I guess," he declared then drank his glass of champagne down in one.

This was going to be the most horrible funeral ball ever.

Richard came back and sat down.

"How's Marcus?" Charlie inquired lightly.

"He's not here yet."

"I haven't seen Marcus in ages," Hamish said, leaning back to give Richard a wink. "Let me know when he gets here, I wouldn't mind a line frankly."

Richard looked at me nervously, realizing that I'd rumbled his lie. The band started up with the Noel Coward number "World Weary" and he asked me if I wanted to dance.

"We haven't even eaten," I told him, unable to meet his eyes.

"Congratulations on your engagement," Jeremy said bitterly.

"What engagement?" Richard asked suspiciously.

Charlie raised his glass, "To Richard and Lola!" He was looking at me as he toasted—I couldn't read his expression, but there seemed an enormous gulf between us now that I desperately wanted to bridge. Of course, Charlie had behaved badly, but he had always been my rock, my best male friend, and the thought that my remarriage to Richard could cost me the security of that friendship saddened me.

"Long may their marriage last!" Hamish added. "Well, longer than last time."

Josie giggled, which Hamish found hilarious. Elizabeth and the others clinked glasses and smiled at me.

Richard looked slightly irritated as he ran his finger between his collar and neck. "Right, if you don't feel like dancing I'm going to go and check on Marcus again."

"I've got some cash if you need it," Hamish told him, following him out.

Kitty arrived and leaned between Charlie and me. "You're all here then, I see! Haven't seen you since Lola's wedding," she told Jeremy.

"Her *last* wedding, you mean."

Kitty smiled enigmatically around the table then wafted off in a cloud of Chanel No. 5 and a wisp of chiffon that left little to the imagination.

Richard and Hamish returned as the entrée plates were being removed. They were both very involved in some convoluted story about property prices in London.

"So Marcus got here okay, then?" Charlie inquired coolly.

Richard sneered. "Oh, shut up, will you, Charlie."

Everyone was laughing about something else, ignoring the tension between Richard and Charlie, but I didn't find any of it in the least bit funny. I looked about the table at all my friends in their white finery. Everyone seemed to be happy apart from Richard and me. I looked at him now as he necked his champagne. I always knew Richard took cocaine, lots of people in the media world took a line here and there, but I was angry that Richard would summon his dealer to my aunt's funeral and that he couldn't go without it for one lousy weekend.

"Just off to the toilet," Richard declared as the last drop of champagne was lost down his throat. He seemed completely oblivious to what I was feeling.

"I'll join you," said Charlie.

"Yeah, I wouldn't mind a line myself," said Hamish, but Charlie put his hand on his shoulder and pointed out that they couldn't both go.

"Fair enough," agreed Hamish, and I noticed Elizabeth gave him one of her lovely flirty smiles.

So here I was with my three girlfriends and my two ex-boyfriends while my future husband was riding the dusty wagon with my boss.

"We're an odd little group, aren't we?" Hamish said a short time later.

Jeremy agreed, but in such a way as to make it clear he didn't think we were odd in a good way.

The plates were cleared away and still Charlie and Richard hadn't returned.

Hamish was starting to fidget. "They're taking a while, aren't they?"

I stood up and said I'd go and check on them.

"I'll come, too," insisted Hamish.

The four Portaloos were outside on the edge of the green, with a small queue beginning to form outside each one. I joined one queue and Hamish joined the one beside me. "You don't suppose they're doing the lot, do you?" I ignored him, keeping my eye on the Portaloos to see who was coming out. After someone had come out of each of the loos, Hamish and I decided to go and look for them. We didn't have to look far. Richard was lying in a fetal position on the grass behind the loos, moaning.

I crouched and saw his nose was bleeding.

"Oh my God, who did this?" I asked, cradling him in my arms. Hamish went back to the loos to wet his handkerchief so that we could clean Richard's face up.

"That fucking boss of yours, who do you think?" he told me angrily.

"What? Richard, what is going on, really?" I asked, stroking his hair. "This isn't about a bloody membership subscription."

Half an hour later, I was sitting in a taxi with Hamish and Richard, taking Richard back to my parents' place, when Aunt Camilla was shot off into the stars. I pressed my face against the taxi's window and watched silently as she filled the sky and as the last spray of diamante frosting melted into the night.

"There goes one of the greats," the driver said more to himself than anyone else, and I began to cry, for her and Oliver, and for me and Richard.

eighteen

"I must resign myself at last to Edward's addiction. He has lately been so drugged that his skin has developed a yellow pallor. Sometimes I find myself counting his breaths while he sleeps, afraid that he will stop. He weighs so little now, that I can quite easily carry him into bed. He is like a child and an old man in one body. He has the most frightful dreams and sometimes when he stares at me after waking from one he has no recollection of who I am. Indeed, I have to struggle to remember that beside me is the man I have loved since childhood."

Extract of a letter from Lady Henrietta
Posche to her sister, Elizabeth

When I woke up the next morning Richard was already up preparing breakfast. His face didn't look too bad; in fact, the only evidence that he'd been in a fight was a slight redness around his nose, as if he had a cold. Kitty and Martin wandered into the dining room holding hands.

"Your face doesn't look as if it will even bruise," Kitty assured Richard as he poured her tea. He looked slightly annoyed rather than relieved by her observation, so I waded in to his defense.

"It was still horrendous of Charlie, though!" I pointed out loyally as I sipped my tea. Truthfully, I was still vexed that Richard hadn't as yet offered a reasonable explanation as to why Charlie would want to hit him.

"Never had Charlie down as a pugilist," Martin mused, as if he kept a logbook of pugilists in his study.

Richard went, "I suspect he's losing it slightly."

"He seemed very much in charge of it when I spoke to him," Kitty argued.

Richard sat down and added calmly, "I've heard the club's in trouble."

"That's ridiculous!" I said, reddening at the attack on me, because that's what it amounted to. I was, after all, the person in charge of promoting the club and ensuring its success.

Richard took my hand in his. "I'm not suggesting it's because of you, Lolls, he's just not that good at the financial side. And if you ask me, he's jealous."

Kitty snorted, "Jealous of what?" It was a bit rude, but she had a sort of point. I mean, Richard wasn't someone that aroused jealousy from someone like Charlie, who was just as good-looking, richer and madly popular. She patted her platinum hair then admired her exquisitely manicured nails. "Perhaps I shall have Elsa in to do my nails today."

But Martin seemed to realize what Richard was really saying. "Are you suggesting that Charlie's jealous of you and Lola, Richard?"

Richard replied, "He's more or less said as much. I mean, it's obvious the way his eyes follow her around."

I balked at the sheer madness of the idea. "That's ridiculous, I've known Charlie for years, we're just good friends. There has never been the slightest hint that he feels anything other than professional respect for me," I told them indignantly. "Besides which, I'm not his type." I was about to say his type was leggy blondes but stopped myself in the nick of time.

"Is he *your* type, though?" Kitty inquired vaguely.

I looked at Richard for help but he was studiously reading the paper. I suspected it could be written in Chinese for all the information he was taking in, because it was obvious he was listening intently to the conversation.

I pretended to ignore Kitty's question, but Kitty wasn't letting me off that easily. Her eyes were still fixed on me and try as I might to look away, I knew she wasn't going to let her question go unanswered.

Eventually I rolled my eyes and groaned. "Don't be idiotic, Kitty. The point is, I don't see how I can continue working with him after this episode."

Kitty laughed. "An episode makes it sound like an ongoing soap opera, darling."

"Well, it's not," I told her firmly. "Now, can we drop this discussion about Charlie, it can hardly be making Richard feel very comfortable."

Richard looked up from his paper. "You won't need to work at all now, not with your inheritance."

Kitty and Martin looked at one another significantly.

"I like working," I argued. "I was thinking of starting up my own PR company. Lola PR. I have enough contacts and—"

"Lola adores her job," Kitty waded in, for once not pronouncing the word *job* as if it was something distastefully shady.

"You could always come into business with me," Richard offered. "I need a good PR."

I blushed as another look passed between Kitty and Martin.

"I don't do IT PR, though."

"Sounds like a nasty disease," Kitty said as another significant look passed between her and Martin.

"Maybe we should be heading off," I suggested, not wanting to go where Kitty and Martin's look was heading.

"Yes, we want to miss the traffic," Richard agreed.

As we gathered at the front door for our goodbyes—apart from Richard, who was outside putting the bags in the boot—Kitty took my hand. "Have a talk with Charlie about

all this before you do anything rash. There's usually two sides
to every story, darling."

"Well, whatever his 'story' is, I can hardly work for him
when he feels this level of violent animosity toward my husband, can I?"

"He's not your husband yet," Martin reminded me.

Kitty kissed me. "Be true to your heart, darling, let your
heart guide you, not your head."

I finally began to relax on the drive back. Richard was
very good at taking my mind off my worries. He began by
doing impressions of the different drivers we passed, and
soon my mind was off the issue of Charlie and back on
how much I loved Richard. We were much better together
when we were on our own, I decided. As we drove into
London, he suggested we go back to his place instead of
mine. I agreed immediately. We swung round to mine first,
though, and picked up Jean's little house and a change of
clothes for me and arrived in Shepherds Bush around four
o'clock.

"Excuse me, Jean, would you mind waiting in the car for
a moment?" Richard asked politely.

Jean gave him one of her huffy looks, which he took as
a yes. Then he picked me up out of my seat and carried me
inside, all the way up the narrow steps, where he opened the
door and walked with me in his arms over the threshold.

He kissed me long and tenderly on the lips and I felt so
light I didn't even notice when he put me down on the floor.
Delight turned to shock, though, as I looked around my new
surroundings. The house was virtually devoid of furniture;
it was as if Richard had moved out.

"You've been robbed!" I gasped.

He laughed nervously as he took my chin in his hand and

raised my face to his. He kissed me on the mouth. "Not quite robbed," he said, looking at the floor like a child about to be chastised. He didn't seem as surprised as I was.

"What do you mean, not quite? Where's all your stuff?"

"Sally must have already been around."

"What do mean. Are you saying she stole it?"

"Not stole it. Not quite."

"But if she took it, that's theft. You should call the police," I insisted.

"Calm down, Lolly. Look, most of it was hers anyway. I didn't think she'd pick it up this quickly, that's all," he said, running his hands through his hair anxiously as he surveyed the room. All that remained was the large ghastly lurid abstract painting that was still on the wall, an old standard lamp I recognized as the one he'd owned when I met him and a few boxes.

I sat down on the floor and tried to absorb what he was telling me. "But you only *just* asked her to move in. What happened to what was already here before?" I questioned.

"Ah well, I wasn't quite honest about that, see, Lolly." He sat down on the floor beside me and took my hands. "Actually, the thing is, it was me who asked to move in with her. I had a bit of a problem with the business recently. The truth is, I virtually lost my shirt in a software venture, so I asked if I could move in with her."

"No." I shook my head. "I remember the morning I rang you up you told me the two of you had had a row because she'd asked to move in with you!"

"Mmm. I did say that, didn't I?" He looked ashamed.

"But it wasn't true, though?"

"We had had a fight, that was true, but it was over me moving out not her moving in."

"So why did you lie to me?"

He ran both his hands through his hair. "She had a problem with my cocaine. I didn't want to go into it all. Look, can't we go on from now, from this moment?"

I wanted to say that it was him with the cocaine problem, but there were other more pressing issues to clear up. "I'm not understanding this at all, Richard. I need more."

He nodded as if accepting this point.

"Whose place is this now?"

He put his head in his hands. "Okay, truth? You want the truth?"

I wasn't sure I did but I nodded anyway.

"She owns the house. That is, she did own it, she's since put it on the market. The buyers have already exchanged, but she's told me I can stay on until just before completion to sort of watch the place."

I wasn't liking this. Where once there had been questions without answers, now every question seemed rhetorical. "So you lied to me from the very beginning, basically."

He was still running his fingers through his hair. "Look, Lolly, you called me out of the blue. I wasn't planning any of this. You caught me by surprise. Obviously I didn't want to go into the whole complicated business of what was happening between Sally and me with my ex-wife. Be fair, at that point I didn't think we'd be ending up like this, did I? I just wanted to get you off the phone that morning!"

I felt sick. "I've got to get out of here." I stood up to leave.

He grabbed my hand. "Lolly, please don't go." I looked down on him, stretched out pathetically in this empty room. He looked as if he was about to cry. "Please, Lolly, I need you."

"Richard, I can't deal with this. I can't—"

He grabbed my hand. "Lolly, please. I know I'm fucked up. Do you think I don't know what a mess I'm in, with my business, with you, with the drugs? I don't know what to do about anything anymore…apart from you. When you came back into my life, I finally saw what it was I really wanted. You're the only thing in my whole fucked-up existence that makes sense to me. I love you, Lola, that's the only thing I'm sure of anymore." Then he began to cry. "I'll get help. If you stay with me, I'll get off the coke, I promise," he pleaded.

So I stayed. Apart from anything else, going would have meant a scene, and I was too tired and too shocked to deal with a scene, so I went outside and retrieved Jean from the car, snuggling my face in her soft fur. She looked at me with her worried little face and I didn't have the heart to tell her that we'd be spending the night in a house without Sky News. Maybe that was how Richard had lied to me, I tried to tell myself, not because he was a duplicitous arsehole like it seemed, but because he didn't have the heart.

I spent the night in the empty house that belonged to Leggy Blonde. While Richard spoke of his despair and made promises about solutions, I cried and nodded, and despite my fears, I chose to believe him.

Lying in bed that night—in the bed Sally had been kind enough to leave—I began to think of her not as Leggy Blonde but as a girl who'd loved a man who, let's face it, was a lying cokehead. A lying cokehead I loved. Because I did love him. It was as complicated and as simple as that.

Neither Jean nor I could sleep. She was hippity-hopping around the room, frustrated by the lack of news headlines, and I was lying awake wondering what I was doing and what I was going to do. Richard, on the other hand, snored obliviously in the deep sleep of the innocent.

I stroked a lock of hair from his eyes and kissed his forehead. He looked so vulnerable when he slept that I was duped into believing he was the man I knew he could be, rather than the man he really was. Perhaps I'd always been duped where Richard was concerned, but I was in too deep not to make myself believe that whatever problems we had we could solve together. That's what marriage was all about, after all.

So I pushed aside any second thoughts I might be having and convinced myself that as long as we loved each other everything would work out, because I would make sure it did.

nineteen

Despite the decline in Edward's health, evidence shows that Posche House parties continued to define fashionable London. If anything, the parties became more outlandish; fancy-dress parties were frequent and the guest list was a who's who of London life. Lady Posche was considered unusual in her class in that she rarely left London, although her husband, Charles, was a keen lover of country pursuits and spent a good deal of time at his rambling estate in Norfolk. Yet the two never broke their habit of writing to one another daily, and their letters are full of declarations of love. Perhaps the true reason Henrietta couldn't leave London was that she could not bear to be away from her lover, Edward.

Secret Passage to the Past:
A Biography of Lady Henrietta Posche
by Michael Carpendum

I awoke around midday. The revelations of the day before drained into my consciousness like swamp water. I had gone out with a determined plan to win my ex-husband back. I had delved into the past and got far more than I bargained for. Now I knew how Alice in Wonderland felt as she fell down the rabbit hole.

I think the word is *fucked*.

Richard had already left for work. There was a note on the pillow where he'd slept, a Post-it that read, Sorry, R x.

Downstairs in the empty kitchen there was an Alessi kettle on the marble work top but no food for Jean and no tea or coffee for me. I had thought of this house as Richard's own when I first came here, but now as I looked at it, stripped of all the decorative efforts of a woman I'd dislodged from her own home, I felt deeply depressed and a little bit afraid. I envisaged her arriving unexpectedly, the way axe murderers do in movies.

I didn't delay another moment, gathering Jean and all our things together for a hasty exit. Laden with all our belongings, I struggled out, slamming the door on the empty house, and set forth into the street in search of a cab. It took forever to find one, and when I did, the driver forcibly embroiled me into a diatribe against London traffic, his wife, and how they both wanted to move to Spain but he hated the dogs and cats that were everywhere. I've never even been to Spain and I don't know what their views on rabbits are but I felt it was best to go along with whatever he said. Jean was unnerved, though, I could tell.

My mobile battery had run down over the weekend, so when I arrived back at my flat, I plugged it in to recharge and climbed into the shower. While I was toweling myself down, I checked through the messages, and as I was listening to one from Clemmie, the doorbell rang.

"Hi, it's us!" my three friends shouted into the speaker.

"We come bearing gifts!" they laughed as they burst into the tiny cupboard that was my flat, dressed in tea dresses and cheap diamante tiaras. Each of them was holding an enormous bunch of flowers. Elizabeth came in last, struggling as she was under the weight of a jeroboam of champagne. She kicked the door closed with the heel of her Choo's.

"Darling, congratulations, we feel terrible about being so horrible about Richard these past weeks, so we're going to make it up to you," she announced.

"Exactly," agreed Josie. "In fact, Emmanuel told me I'd been beastly toward you and that I was to invite you and Richard to ours for dinner. So there."

"We're to come, as well," Clemmie added, settling the flowers in my kitchen sink.

"Everyone who matters is to come," Elizabeth declared expansively. "I'm bringing Hamish."

They wrapped me in a group hug and I desperately wanted to embrace them back with the same enthusiasm. I did! I wanted to embrace their good wishes. I wanted to believe what they believed, that everything between Richard and me was fairy-tale-perfect and that they were the only problem in an otherwise perfect union. But actually, it wasn't perfect. I now had the man I wanted on a plate, prostate at my feet, vulnerable, suppliant and...

"Thank you," I heard myself saying. "It means so much to me that you're pleased for me...for us."

"Of course we're pleased for you. If Richard is what you want, darling, Richard is what you must have," Elizabeth stated.

"Exactly!" agreed Clemmie. "Now, when's the big event and can we be your bridesmaids with lovely sexy dresses?"

"Jean's already signed up for the post of chief bridesmaid," I told them.

"Oh, Jean Harlot, always the bridesmaid never the bride!" Elizabeth picked up Jean for a cuddle. Jean, who'd been quite happy watching the headlines, squirmed with irritation.

"So, breakfast at Claridges," they chorused.

An hour later, I was frocked up in a little floral tea dress, with strappy Manolo sandals and Aunt Camilla's diamond tiara, and we set across the road to Claridges. Jean was wriggling in her bag while we tucked into afternoon tea, because of course they stop serving breakfast at Claridges at some ungodly hour of the morning. If I were a councilor, I would campaign for breakfast to be available at any time of the day or night. Scones and cream are nice in their way, but when you want a kipper, you want a kipper and that's all there is to it.

As the harpist strummed her harp, we tucked into scones and cream and with well-practiced sleight of hand I was able to slip all the garnishes from the finger sandwiches into my bag for Jean. I was starting to believe that things with Richard and I were perfect in every way until Elizabeth burst my little pre-bride bubble of girlie fun when she asked through a mouthful of cress sandwich, "So, what are you going to do about Charlie?"

I took a sip of tea while I strengthened my resolve. "I'm going to resign."

"Just like that?"

Clemmie put her cup down noisily on the saucer at the shock of it all. "After all you've been through together?"

"Yes, how many years is it? Five?" added Josie.

"Don't you think he deserves a chance to tell his side?"

Elizabeth put her hand over mine. "Yes, he's always been there for you, Lola. Are you sure you're not acting on re-flex?"

Clemmie waded in. "He was there when Richard dumped all over you the first time." Elizabeth and Josie looked at her censoriously.

I put my hands over my ears. "Richard did not dump all over me!"

Clemmie was unbowed. "No? He made you give up work to study interior design and then went bust and you were left without a job. Did it never occur to you that Charlie might have employed someone else in that time? Did you ever—"

Josie put her hand over her mouth with the shock of it all. "Oh God, wouldn't it be awful to think that someone got fired so you could have your old job back?" she ex-claimed.

"Well, it was only his sister, actually," I interjected.

Elizabeth shook her head. "So? He still replaced her with you."

I suppose that was true. Charlie had mentioned something about how bringing me back on board "had slightly vexed his sister," but then as I thought about it, Charlie always understated things, especially unpleasant things. Besides, I told myself, there were plenty of other openings at Posh House. She didn't have to leave entirely. We could have worked together.

"Look, can we stop talking about bloody Charlie," I snapped. When you're confused or in a corner or in the wrong, it's remarkable how easily righteous indignation comes. I see it all the time with bolshie guests. I've heard the implausible, the impossible and the illogical used to justify misdemeanors from theft to violence. Sometimes listening to the sheer madness of the justifications holds me spellbound.

I think there should be an award for most imaginative excuse. There could even be categories like at the Oscars. If so, I would have won it for my speech about how Charlie's attack was inexcusable on any level and, regardless of how kind and lovely he may have been to me in the past, knowing how he felt about Richard, the man I was going to marry, I couldn't countenance working for him a moment longer. I didn't mention that Richard, the man I was going to marry, was a homeless coke addict who had lied to me repeatedly since the day I met him.

If I imagined that the girls were going to put up more of a fight in Charlie's defense, I was mistaken. "Well, I'm sure you'll do what's best," Elizabeth agreed, calling for the bill.

"Fair enough," agreed Josie. "Sorry if we, erm…hassled you."

Clemmie shrugged. "Yes, the point is, we're behind you.

We all felt guilty about our reaction to you getting back with Richard and just wanted you to know that we want you to be happy, to know that you have…"

"Our blessing," added Elizabeth, putting one hand on my head and making the sign of the cross with the other, "to marry Richard."

So there it was; as far as they were concerned, I finally had overcome the last obstacle that stood in the way of remarrying Richard. I finally had the support that I'd been begging them to give me since I first saw him that night with Leggy Blonde. How were they to know that their longed-for approbation came at the very same time as my doubts? How could I discuss those doubts now? Now that they were finally telling me I was right to have none?

I had longed for their approval, dreamed of them congratulating me on getting back together with Richard, done everything in my power to convince them that he really was the right man for me. And now that they were saying and feeling all I had wanted them to say and feel, how could I admit to having the doubts they'd urged me to have? I had set a train of events in motion that evening, and now as the train was derailing, I had no one to turn to for help. The train was out of control and I was on it careering toward something terrifying. There was only one person left in the anti-Richard campaign, and that was Charlie. Which meant there was only one thing to do.

Outside Claridges I climbed into a cab as the girls waved me off.

"Posh House," I told the driver, and then I settled back into the seat and gathered my thoughts for what I was about to do.

twenty

Charles returned to Posche House to support his wife following a letter in which she expressed her concern over the health of Edward. However, by the time his carriage arrived, Edward had already left the house. His health was by all accounts extremely bad. By this stage he was suffering hallucinations and breathing difficulties, but such was his addiction to opium he managed to drag himself back to one of London's many opium dens.

Henrietta was devastated and turned to Charles for support. Charles stood by her and offered what comfort he could, but unbeknown to her he was considering having Edward horsewhipped for his treatment of his wife, should he dare to show his face in Posche House again, a threat that he openly expressed to her sister, Elizabeth, in a letter.

Secret Passage to the Past:
A Biography of Lady Henrietta Posche
by Michael Carpendum

In a fantasy mental slide show, this is how my resignation would have looked.

I would jump out of the taxi to pay. The driver would remark—in reference to my lovely Dolce & Gabbana tea dress—"special occasion, love?" I'd laugh insouciantly; a girl of confidence and fortune. I would overtip, the driver would say—"Thank you, love, have a good one"—and I would stride confidently through reception.

Carl or Beth, or whoever was on, would shower me with still more compliments about my dress. I'd be charming, of course, distributing air kisses all round. I'd tell them how lovely they all looked—if it was Carl, I'd flirt slightly; gay men love to practice their flirting skills. I'd release Jean from the confines of her bag and ask them to look after her (so she wouldn't put me off my carefully planned speech). I would then skip up the stairs and through the secret door and up the tenebrous passage to Charlie's office. He'd be there, as ever, his long legs resting on his desk, his arms folded behind his head, a wistful look on his face. He'd say, "Ah, Lola, how lovely to see you." To which I'd reply, "Well, you might feel differently after you hear what I have to say, Charles."

Then I'd explain that following his violent assault on my fiancé I was tendering my resignation.

He'd probably weep.

Not that I'd ever seen Charlie weep, but in my fantasy he'd at the very least be holding back a tear. Sniffling, wiping his eyes, that sort of thing. He'd apologize profusely. Admit how horrendous and shamefully sickening his behavior toward Richard had been and beg me to forgive him, offering to apologize to Richard and give me a raise. Then we'd have a cuddle and I'd tell Charlie about Richard's coke habit and how he was broke and homeless and he'd sit me down and tell me everything would be all right.

This is how my resignation actually went…

I tripped as I fell out of the cab and scraped my knee. My tiara fell to the ground. Then as I scrambled in the gutter to retrieve it, a creep going past made a pervy comment. Sticking the tiara back on my head, I asked the driver what the fare was. He told me it was three pounds twenty and I handed him a fifty, telling him to make it five. He said he didn't have any change and so I ran into reception to get a smaller note.

Instead of one of the regular staff, there was someone new and ultraofficious on reception, Madame Too Big for Her Boots. As I had no swipe card and she didn't know who I was, she refused to assist me in finding change, telling me that the club didn't keep money on the premises, which was rubbish. It took me forever to explain who I was. In the end, the horrible girl rang Charlie to see what she should "do about me." Charlie must have told her to hand over the change, but when I eventually got back to the cab, where the meter was still on, to find I now owed nine pounds sixty, so I just gave him a tenner and he groaned about the heat.

Back in reception, Madame Too Big for Her Boots informed me that Charlie was in a meeting, wasn't to be disturbed, and I was to wait. By this time I had taken Jean out of her bag and was stroking her ears, so I suggested I'd wait in the courtyard, to which she almost had a fit. She told me it might be better if I sat on the hard wooden pew in reception and asked me to keep Jean in my bag. After an hour I was cheered by a text message from Richard saying "R luvs L." Eventually, Charlie called down and Madame Too Big for Her Bloody Boots had one of the security staff lead me to his office via the main stairs—as if I was planning on stealing something.

He knocked on Charlie's door and asked if it was okay to let me in! Then when he got the okay, he asked me to hand over my "animal." The whole affair was going from bad to worse, but I gave Jean to the security guy and asked him to take care of her. To be fair, he did give her a little stroke and even laughed when she began to hump his arm.

"Lola, I'm surprised to see you," Charlie said once I was standing before him. He was standing up, the light from the window illuminating his athletic body from behind. He was wearing an old T-shirt emblazoned with The Cure on the front. It had a hole in it on the shoulder and I could see the brown skin of his broad shoulder underneath.

"Well, erm…that is…I am…"

"Let me guess, you're resigning?"

"Well, I was, erm, that is…"

"No hard feelings, I hope?" He smiled and extended his hand for me to shake. I'm pretty sure we had never shaken hands before, but I shook it like a Japanese businessman and smiled back at him.

"I anticipated you wouldn't feel comfortable working for me anymore after the weekend's events. Slightly surprised, actually, that you felt the need to tell me to my face." He passed me an envelope and smiled one of his lovely easy smiles. "Here, I thought you might appreciate this." My eyes traveled down his long lean arm holding out the envelope. His skin was always such a lovely tawny color.

All this formality was beginning to distress me. I didn't open the envelope, but I presumed it was some sort of final payment, so I shoved it in my bag. "Yes…well, thank you. That is, I think this is better, don't you?" I tried to match his easy smile, but my eyes were about to brim with tears, so I bit my lip.

He looked like he wanted to hold me, and I felt like I wanted to be held, but both of us remained rooted to the spot like actors staying on their chalk marks on a film set.

Eventually he turned away and looked out over the courtyard, leaving me with the back of his neck to study as I pulled myself together. I heard Cinders panting. She was standing at my feet looking up at me, probably wondering where Jean was. I gave her a pat and she licked my hand.

"Well, bye then," I said to Charlie's back as my eyes teared up again.

"Yes, goodbye, Lola," he replied without turning around.

So there it was, a chapter of my life was closing. I turned away as well then, and walked toward the door. Cinders followed me, only to be called back by Charlie. "One last thing though, Lola."

"Yes?" I asked, turning around hopefully. Hoping for something I couldn't define, an escape perhaps from the train of events I had set in motion. Suddenly I wasn't so sure about setting up my own company. Nor was I sure I could bear to lose Charlie in my life, and it was only really now that I saw my resignation for what it truly was. The end of an era; the end of a friendship that had sustained me through the past five years. I wanted to turn back the clock and change my mind, but my hopes were dashed when Charlie said, "You'll appreciate that I've had to cancel Richard's membership. I've written to inform him, but I just thought I should mention it to you."

I didn't know what to say, so I pushed open the door to the secret passage and rushed down the dimly lit wooden stairs, collected Jean from the security guy who was playing with her in reception while Madame Too Big for Her Boots looked on in disapproval. I thanked the guy, put Jean in the bag Charlie had once given me for her and ran out onto the street.

I hailed a cab and cried the whole way home.

Inside my flat I switched on the news for Jean and threw myself on my bed and cried my eyes out. When Kitty called, I wailed, "How could he have let me go so easily?"

"Did you ask him why he hit Richard?"

"No, he didn't give me a chance. It was awful. Kitty, it was as if he couldn't face me, couldn't wait to be rid of me," I sobbed.

"I guess it's what you wanted," she reminded me.

My friends were no less surprised. Although Elizabeth and Clemmie were horrified to discover (as was I) that I hadn't discussed terms with Charlie. As PR for Posh House, I had signed an exclusivity agreement which meant I wasn't allowed to contact any of my clients or contacts that I'd met during my time at Posh House—in short, I wasn't allowed to contact London's A-list.

"I can't believe you resigned without preliminary discussions, Lola," Elizabeth told me. "I don't see how you plan to start your own PR company when you can't contact any of your Posh House list."

That was when my first doubts began to creep in. Doubts that only became more incessant when Richard came over after work. He gave me a cuddle and reassured me it was all for the best, but then he said, "Besides, the man's insane. I don't want a wife of mine working for a violent-tempered bastard like that."

I had this urge to scream, "No! Stop! I want to get off!" As much as I loved Richard, I loved Charlie, too (only in a different sort of way, obviously). I couldn't have him spoken about as a violent-tempered bastard when I knew he wasn't. But then, I couldn't say that to Richard because I knew it would hurt his pride. Just the same, doubts began to work away about what I was sacrificing in order to have Richard back, which was just crazy because deep down I knew Richard and I were right.

I told myself it was sheer perversity and anyway I was in too deep. I had effectively wrestled Richard from Leggy Blonde and now that he was broke and in need, I didn't really see how I could explain that a part of me wasn't ready to marry him again, especially when he was struggling with his addiction. I had plotted and planned every detail of getting back together with Richard and yet in my master plan I hadn't built in a contingency back-out strategy, so I said nothing and hoped the doubts would go away.

Richard stroked my hair and said, "Besides, we should be celebrating. I'm taking you out to dinner. I have a surprise for you that I think you'll like."

I didn't really feel it would be appropriate to remind him that he was for all intents and purposes broke and homeless and in no position to take me out to dinner much less buy me surprises. But I walked with him down to Scotts, a seafood restaurant on Mount Street, where we ordered two dozen Irish rock oysters, a lobster and a bottle of Dom, my favorite champagne. I laughed at his jokes and tried to follow the conversation, but the truth was, all I could think about was Charlie and how much I already missed him.

We were finishing off the lobster when he said, "I have an announcement, Lola."

I sat up straight. He had on his most serious face. Maybe he was going to tell me that he'd been thinking things over and decided that he wasn't in a position to marry me now that he was broke.

"I've made a decision."

I nodded, prepared and partially relieved that he was having second thoughts about marrying me again. He was going to tell me that he wanted to take things slowly, not rush into anything. I put on my most open I-can-take-it face.

Instead, he said, "I've booked myself into the Priory."

I stared across the table blinking. The Priory was a luxurious country hotel for alcoholics and addicts to detox and get twelve-step help for their problem. The fact that it cost an astronomical sum of money did occur to me, but because I was so proud and relieved that he was finally being honest with me and admitting he had a problem, I grabbed the hand he reached out to me and kissed it.

"Getting you back has made me want to be a better person, Lola. I feel like I've got a new lease on life and I don't want to do anything to blow that."

I smiled and nodded while he motioned for the waiter and ordered another bottle.

I was thinking to myself—another bottle?—when you're

about to check in to the Priory? Is that wise? But of course I didn't say anything because, after all, maybe it was normal to splurge the night before you detoxed. At least he wasn't in a lather waiting for Marcus, I reminded myself. He hadn't gone to the loo once since he'd arrived. In fact, as far as I was concerned, he could drink all the Dom he wanted.

"So when do you go in?" I asked him as the waiter poured the champagne into his glass.

"Tonight," he said. "No point hanging about, is there? I would have gone today but I wanted to talk it over with you first." He gave my hand a squeeze. "I do have a tiny favor to ask of you."

"Anything," I said confidently.

"Would you mind not trying to contact me there? Only they recommend that you cut yourself off entirely from absolutely everyone."

"Sure, whatever is best for you, darling, I am just so proud of you."

"Also, if you could keep it to yourself. I don't really want anyone else to know. I've told my partner at work and he's going to drive me up later this evening, but other than that I don't want anyone to know."

After I'd picked up the bill, Richard asked me if I'd mind if he went straight back to his place to pack a few things for the Priory, so I hailed him a cab and we said our goodbyes on the pavement. He kissed me tenderly on the lips and told me once again that he was doing this for me and then he climbed into the cab and disappeared into the night.

I rang Elizabeth and asked if we could meet up. "Clemmie and I are already at the Met, walk down now."

When I arrived, Elizabeth was dancing with Hamish. I knew it was stupid, but I felt a tiny bit weird. I mean, not jealous weird; it was just odd seeing my ex in my world, because this was my world and I'd never seen Hamish at the Met Bar, which meant Elizabeth must have invited him. Then Elizabeth put her arms around his neck and he put his around her waist and they kissed.

My girlfriend was pulling my ex!

When they came and sat down, they were holding hands. Hamish kissed me lightly on the cheek and asked me if I wanted a drink. I asked for a green tea and waited for him to go before I spoke to Elizabeth.

"You two look pretty cozy," I said, giving her a playful nudge. "I didn't know you had a thing for Hamish."

"Do you mind?"

"No," I told her, and as I said the word I knew it was true. "No, not a bit," I added. "He's a really great guy."

"So you're sure you're fine?"

"Better than fine. Richard has checked himself in to the Priory." I knew he'd told me not to tell anyone but I was bursting and besides, what kind of best friend would I be if I didn't tell my best friend absolutely everything.

"Oh, darling, that's the best news."

"It is, isn't it? Only promise not to tell anyone. I shouldn't have really told you even, but I was bursting."

"How are you feeling about your resignation now?" she asked, changing the subject as Hamish came back with drinks.

"Okay," I lied. "Sort of sad in a way, though. I kind of thought Charlie would try and talk me out of it."

"Did you want him to?"

"I didn't realize I wanted him to at the time but when he didn't, I felt awful, like everything we had together and all the stuff we'd been through meant nothing to him."

Hamish laughed, and both Elizabeth and I gave him a censorious look. "Sorry, but you make it sound like you broke up with a boyfriend rather than your boss."

"They were really close," Elizabeth explained.

"I thought of him as one of my best friends," I added.

"Best friends don't pay you money," Hamish pointed out.

"Yes, but we all loved Charlie, didn't we, Lolly?" Elizabeth said. "I suppose this means we won't see him anymore. Maybe after things calm down you can go back."

"He's got someone else, in fact," Hamish said, taking a sip of his beer.

At first I thought he meant another girlfriend, and for some reason I was relieved when I realized he meant someone to replace me as PR.

Elizabeth looked as shocked as me as she said, "God, that was quick. Lolly's not even cleaned out her office, let alone discussed terms. As I said, what are you going to do regarding your clients, and your contract prohibiting you from contacting anyone you know through Posh House?"

"Which, at a rough estimate, is everyone you know," Hamish added unnecessarily. "In fact, you shouldn't even be speaking to me," he joked.

I was too overwhelmed by events to think about the practical side of it yet. Now that the full enormity of what I'd done was sinking in, I realized I was going to have to go back to Charlie and hope he'd be prepared to negotiate a settlement enabling me to contact at least some of my Posh House crew. Otherwise, it was going to be a case of you'll-never-work-in-this-town-again.

"Wait a minute," I said. "If he's already employed someone before I even properly resigned, it's as though he knew I'd resign. Or worse, he was planning on firing me."

Hamish took a sip of his beer. "Tall blonde, apparently. I haven't seen her myself but I heard rumors at the club."

twenty-one

"My darling Hen, to marry for love were no re-proachful thing if we did not see that ten thousand couples that do it and yet hardly one can be held an example that it may be done and not repented afterward.

Yet, my dearest one, my only Henrietta, the love I feel for you hardly happens once in two ages. We are not to expect the world should discern we were not like the rest. I shall tell you stories of the agonies I have felt each time you have taken him to your bed another time, in a time where you and I can sit alone without the world, when the last embers of the party have expired and there is just you and I, Charles and Henrietta, man and wife.

My dearest darling passion.

Forever seems too short a time to share with you."

Extract of a letter from Lord
Charles Posche to his wife, Henrietta

I left Hamish and Elizabeth to their evening and went home early. The flat felt empty and smaller than ever. The very familiarity of the tiny space, Jean's wall-mounted plasma screen, her rabbit chalet, her little water dispenser, began to close in on me the moment I walked in. I sat down on the white leather sofa in the white boxlike space and tried to take an interest in world events with Jean, but it was useless—after catching the headlines, I realized I didn't know where the remote was or whether I even owned one. Jean was the only one who watched television; in fact, looking about the place, I decided it was more Jean's flat than mine.

Since my split with Richard two years ago, my life had revolved around Posh House. My life was all there and suddenly it seemed that everything reminded me that I wasn't going to ever be part of my own life again.

This flat had merely been a place to change my clothes and crash out before going to Posh House: a pit stop. As a home, though, it was woefully small and inadequate. I already missed Charlie, and the thought that I'd no longer have access to his languorous charm, his easy wit and toff drawl, plunged me further into misery.

For Richard's sake I had done the right thing in resigning, although it was a bit rich the way Charlie had been so casually accepting of it all. I mean, he could have put up some sort of fight. He hadn't even told me he was going to miss me. He hadn't even mentioned Jean, all he'd done was hand me my severance and hurried me out.

I took the envelope he'd handed me from my bag and opened it. Let's just see how much I was worth to him. Only it wasn't a check at all, it was a letter, a very old letter, written in ink on paper that had worn to a tissuelike fragility over age. The spiderlike writing poured from a hand drenched with love for a woman. I read each sentence over and over, trying to gain some meaning, some sense of why Charlie had gifted it to me, or if he had even meant to. It was signed Your Loving Husband, Charles, and after my heart missed a beat, I realized that it had the Posche seal on it. It must have been one of the letters discovered in the wall of the secret passage when they renovated the building.

I dug up my copy of the book *Secret Passage to the Past* and flipped through it. It was peppered with letters, but I was too impatient to search for this particular one. I reread the letter. There was one paragraph in particular that spoke to me.

I shall tell you of the agonies I have felt each time you have taken him to your bed another time. Perhaps in a time where you and I can sit alone without the world, when the last embers of the party have expired and there is just you and I, Charles and Henrietta, man

and wife, you will finally know the regard with which
I hold you.
My dearest darling passion. Forever seems too short a
time to share with you.

The letter fell from my hand. Was he suggesting, through
this letter, that he had actual romantic feelings toward me?
I couldn't deal with the answer, so I decided Charles was
merely jealous. Perhaps he was taking the piss, reproaching
me for finding love and leaving him in the lurch. I decided
that I was giving the letter too much credence because I was
lonely. I needed to speak to Richard. I wanted so badly to
tell him how proud I was of him for seeking treatment. I
wanted to tell him I missed him. I wanted him to reassure
me that we were doing the right thing.

As a substitute for the contact he'd begged me not to make
with him, I logged on to the Priory Hospital website. I knew
the hospital quite well as it was near my parents' home; a
beautiful white gothic colonial-looking building with rambling green grounds and comfortable hospital accommoda-
tion. It was famous for the celebrities that went there to deal
with drug, alcohol and eating disorders, although I had no
idea of the treatment involved.

I searched the site to find out how drug dependency was
treated. It was all fairly straightforward, discussing the strate-
gies used to help the individual cope without drugs. The
paragraph that struck me most, however, was where it explained the methods used to help the individual (the word
addict barely appeared) recognize the problem that led them
to become drug dependent and to overcome these problems
by developing self-esteem and positive attitudes.

I couldn't remember a time when Richard hadn't used cocaine, but then when I first met him, London was snowing

with the stuff and so commonplace it wasn't so much a drug as proof of success. I read down the page about the importance of receiving support and understanding from friends and family. That was me, I was about to be his wife, which made me both friend and family.

Jean was watching a news item about the improved security measures being introduced at airports. I had to wonder how much support she'd be prepared to offer to Richard and decided that the bulk of the burden was probably going to be all up to me.

His parents hadn't even bothered to come to our wedding and their contact with their son was sporadic at best. I had only ever met them once and found them cold, odd people. They had taken us to dinner at the Basil Hotel where they were staying. Conversation, such as it was, had centered on politics and how England was falling to pieces. His mother had asked with pointed disinterest about my job and I had briefly described it while Richard and his father discussed property prices. I was relieved when dinner was over, as it was the most uncomfortable meal I had ever sat through.

Richard never really spoke of his parents and it was always left to me to hassle him to write or call. At the time, I had told myself that my parents were odd as well, but they were always there for me. It was clear from reading the website that families were encouraged to become involved in the treatment process, yet Richard had specifically told me he wasn't allowed to contact me. He'd told me he didn't want Hamish or Jeremy or anyone else to even know he was there, yet the website extolled the educational sessions that ran parallel to the patient's treatment.

So why had he asked me to stay away to give him time? Why hadn't he asked me to go to these education sessions, especially after he knew I'd thrown in my job and had plenty of time. I was about to take those "better or worse" vows again. My place was in those sessions and I couldn't help feeling cut out.

Frustrated with the way I was feeling, I took Jean down to Berkeley Square so she could have a run and I could clear my head. It was still dark but the square was illuminated by the moon. I heard the security guys outside Annabel's laugh as Jean, in a fit of heated excitement, almost sent me flying as I scaled the fence. I waved goodnaturedly and they waved back, as if my world was still turning on its axis and everything was totally as it should be.

Sitting on my usual bench, I tried to unravel why I was so riddled with doubts. I was pleased Richard was getting the treatment he needed, but at the same time I felt as if he was cutting me out, and if I was going to be his wife, I needed to be part of his recovery.

And then there was the issue of who was paying for the treatment. Naturally I was happy to pay, but he hadn't asked me to and yet I was fairly certain he didn't have private medical insurance. Jean sniffed and humped her way around the trees in the square, and as the sun came up I decided I had to talk to him. Maybe he was trying to protect me, maybe he didn't understand that I wanted to support him, and if that was the case, I needed to clear up the misunderstanding. As night gave way to dawn, I gathered Jean up, popped her in her bag, climbed over the railings and went back to my flat to call the Priory.

I spelled his name for the third time. Again the helpful woman at reception told me there was no record of a patient by the name of Richard Arbiter Bisque. I decided it was probably an anonymity thing, places like the Priory are bound to be madly discreet about their "guests," so I rang his mobile next. He picked up but he was clearly annoyed.

"Look, I can't talk now," he whispered. "I can't believe you've called me when I told you not to."

"I just wanted to make sure they were treating you well," I lied.

"Well, they are, but I can't talk now," he snapped.

"When will I be able to visit you at the Priory?" I asked. "If you want me to go to any of the sessions with you—"

He cut me off midway through my Florence Nightingale moment. "I don't know. Don't call me again, though. I have to go." He hung up.

I couldn't stay in the flat. I was shaking. He was lying to me. He wasn't at the Priory, so where was he? I began to fear the worst, and out of a mixture of despair and hope I called Kitty for reassurance.

I knew it was a mistake as soon as I heard my rambling monologue trail off and the heavy sigh on the other end of the line. "Darling, I have the manicurist with me now, I can't focus. If Richard's gone to ground, you're going to have to wait for him to reappear. That's what addicts do, I hear."

"He's not an addict, Kitty!"

"Well, if he's decided he's addicted to drugs and is taking treatment for his addiction, what else is he?"

I tried to appeal to her sense of grandeur. "Yes, but we're talking about cocaine here, Kitty."

"Yes, there is a small comfort that he's taking a class-A drug, but nonetheless I fear the worst, Lola."

"That's not what I mean. Look, it's not as if he's using heroin. It's not as if he's a junkie."

"Oh, I wouldn't know the difference," she sighed. "I find all this narcotics business terribly sordid, don't you know."

"But I'm going to marry him, Kitty. We're in love!"

"Oh, Lola, are you? Are you really? I didn't want to throw cold water over this affair during Camilla's funeral fete, but watching you with him, I didn't feel like I was observing a grand passion. I saw no sparks and now you're telling me yourself that Richard is addicted to drugs, which means you are not his obsession, they are."

I hung up the phone and wrapped my arms around myself, chilled by Kitty's neat summing-up of my relationship with Richard. She was wrong, she had to be wrong, because my obsession these past weeks was to win him back, and now instead of a sense of achievement all I felt was the helplessness of a scenario that was driving me crazy. I lay in bed and thought about Richard and me. We were meant to be together, I couldn't stop believing that. My whole strategy had been based on that one immutable fact.

If he wasn't the one, I'd made a huge mistake and dismantled my life for nothing. He had to be the one…wherever he was. Although, if he wasn't at the Priory, where was he? I eventually fell asleep fully clothed and only woke when I heard my phone ringing in the afternoon.

"Lola? It's Charlie."

I propped myself up on my elbow and gathered my thoughts. "Charlie." Repeating his name staved off conversation long enough for me to wake up.

"Yes, from Posh House? You used to work for me."

"I know who you are," I replied overly crisply as I remembered the letter of Lady Posche he had given me. "What do you want, though?"

"You."

My heart began to pound. "Me?" I asked, just to check I'd heard correctly. And then I remembered the letter. The letter now safely placed back in the book. Charlie wanted me! Of course he did. All those years together, I'd been blind to how he'd felt.

"Why?" I asked.

"You haven't cleared your office out. Also, there are probably a few things we need to go over. I was wondering if you could find the time to drop in later this afternoon or early evening?"

I felt my heart stop with the embarrassment of what I'd been about to imagine as I gathered myself together and told him I'd see him at six.

twenty-two

"...I am afraid of alarming you, but things with Edward deteriorate with each passing day. He is fearfully ill and I am once more pretending the illness is mine. I don't want to disturb your shooting, but perhaps you could advise me on what I should do about his condition.

I am dissembled. Concealing him is become increasingly difficult, he is now too weak to move. His breathing is labored. I fear arousing the suspicion of a doctor, so I call no one. I love and respect you too much to bring scandal upon your good name. I shall await your council, anxiously, your loving wife, Hen."

An extract of a letter from Lady Henrietta Posche to her husband, Charles

"How random is that!" I complained to Elizabeth as I explained Charlie's phone call.

"I don't know why you're in such a lather, to be honest. The two of you have a lot of sorting out to do, especially if you plan to set up your own PR company, but even if you intend to work for someone else, you have to establish what access to clients your contract with Charlie stipulates."

"I suppose that's true but, Elizabeth, there was something else, remember I told you that he had the check all ready for me when I went in to resign?" Elizabeth nodded. "Well, I opened the envelope and it wasn't a check at all but an old letter from the archives of Lady Posche."

"Really! Shit, that must be worth something."

"I guess, but it's weird as well because it was sort of like a love letter."

"A what letter?"

"I've probably got this all wrong, but it was a letter from

Lord Charles Posche to his wife, only it was a letter of long-ing, as if he wanted her to know how much he loved her. Oh, I don't know, do you think—"

"Charles is in love with you?"

"No. But it was a bit cryptic."

"Cryptic for in love, you mean."

"Do you think that's possible?"

Elizabeth turned away and bit one of her nails. "He said something to me. I promised I wouldn't tell you."

"That's not fair."

"It's not about this. At least, not directly, anyway. I mean, I don't know, he's never said a word to me about his feelings for you, I swear, although I've seen the way he looks at you sometimes. We all have."

"What did he say?"

"I can't, Lola."

"What did he say?" I insisted.

She shook her head. "Why don't you ask him yourself about his feelings for you? After all, you've resigned, so you have nothing to lose, right? Besides, it's a very personal gift, so give him something in return and at least end things nicely."

"What did he tell you?"

"It's better you ask him yourself, Lola."

"That's not very loyal."

"That's not fair and you know it. It's better you hear it from him, for your sake." I pried a bit more but gave up. Elizabeth can be very stubborn like that. I knew I wouldn't get any more out of her.

"I need something personal for a man," I told the girl at Prada half an hour later.

"How about a wallet?" she offered.

The guy at Gucci was no more imaginative, so I ended

up on Mount Street at William & Son where they had the most beautiful leather goods, backgammon boards, chess boards, soft calf boxes crafted in a wide array of colors. I found myself fingering a deep orange leather envelope with a small heart etched onto it in silver. It seemed the perfect envelope for the letter to Lady Posche.

"Can I help you?" inquired a kindly-looking older gentleman who was holding a black Labrador just like Cinders, who was straining on a leash to jump on me.

"She's a puppy," he explained. "You'll have to forgive her, she's still very enthusiastic about people."

"She can probably smell my rabbit," I told him, patting my bag. "Jean loves dogs."

He laughed and so I explained about the gift from my boss and the sort of gift I wanted to reciprocate his kindness with and he agreed that the envelope I was holding would be the perfect gift.

So, armed with my beautifully wrapped gift, I took a cab, still unable to get the letter out of my head. I wondered if I'd have the courage to bring the letter up. I wondered if he'd have the balls to tell me what it all meant.

This time Carl was on reception and suggested I go straight up, as Charlie was on his own.

I took the secret staircase the same deep orange as the envelope. I couldn't help imagining Lord Charles Posche and how he must have felt about Lady Posche smuggling her lover up these stairs, or if he even knew, and I wondered about my future, about Richard's secrets and our future together.

A future in which I would never take this staircase again.

I tapped on the door and heard Charlie call out, "Come."

I used to find it funny when he said that. Elizabeth had once remarked it would make her orgasm to hear Charlie call that word out to her. I entered to find him standing by the window, looking speculatively out over the courtyard. I was used to seeing him in this pose, but in the few days away from him, I had forgotten how much presence he had. He exuded solidity, as if he'd been internally constructed by master craftsmen rather than assembling himself amateurishly like the rest of us.

I let Jean out of the bag and she hopped straight over to Cinders, who gave her a friendly lick. I had calculated that we would spend this meeting in negotiations, but now all I felt was heaviness, sadness for the distance that Richard had put between Charlie and me.

Before that night when I'd spotted Richard laughing easily with Jeremy and Hamish, and then later when I'd spied him arguing with Leggy Blonde, Charlie and I had been so close. I remembered that night so vividly now, the way he'd crouched behind the drinks station with me, and later how he'd sensed my agony at seeing Richard with another girl and called me a car. He had been a good friend as well as a brilliant boss. He'd been there for me whenever I needed him and now I was walking away from all that.

"So, Lola, how are you bearing up?"

What did he mean by "bearing up"? I could only presume he was speaking of my aunt's death. "Fine. She was very old."

"Yes, she was. But actually, I was speaking of the Richard thing, how are you managing there?"

"The Richard thing?" My love life had officially become a thing.

I sat down, confused now. It sounded as if Charlie knew about Richard seeking help for his cocaine addiction.

"I thought you might need an extra friend," he explained.

"Yes, he's well," I said, determined to be a paragon of discretion after my phone call with Richard this morning.

Wherever he was, I had to trust he was fighting for his sobriety.

Charlie interrupted my thoughts. "It's a rum business for everyone."

"What do you mean, a rum business?" I asked, pronouncing "rum business" in an exaggeratedly toff way.

"Well, him going back to Sally after proposing to you!"

"Back to Sally?" I repeated.

He repeated the sentence. "Back to Sally."

I looked up into his clear blue eyes but I wasn't absorbing his meaning at all, so I asked again, "Back to *Sally?*"

He looked as confused as I was. "Yes, he's gone back to Sally, didn't he tell you?"

I watched Jean sniffling about with Cinders. I looked out over the courtyard buzzing with the hum of members' conversations. My hands were wrapped around the gift I'd brought for him.

"Lola, are you okay, I presumed you of all people would have known?"

"Richard's in the Priory," I told him, even though I knew at that moment that he wasn't.

"The Priory?" he repeated, as if I'd said the fifth dimension.

"I think it's very admirable," I told him sanctimoniously.

"Lola, he's convinced Sally to take him back. God knows why. I suspect he's got nowhere else to go, but I promise you, I wouldn't lie to you about something like that." He came over to me, crouching at my feet. I stared at my hands, turning the gift over and over. He put his hand over my hands to still them. "Lola?"

I turned to face him. "And how would you know where Richard is? I doubt he'd confide in you after you hit him on Saturday. You're the last person he'd discuss his private affairs with. Or is this your secret confidence with Elizabeth?"

"My what?"

"Elizabeth told me you told her something that she wasn't to tell me."

Charlie reached out and stroked my hair. "Sally's my sister, Lola. I, well, that is to say, I wasn't sure if you knew or not. I presumed Richard would have told you and, well, I suppose when I doubted that he had, I didn't want to be the one…"

It's difficult to describe the emotions involved when struck with a revelation like that. All I can say is they were so powerful that I couldn't register them. Instead, I shoved the gift into Charlie's hands. "This is for you," I announced. He looked embarrassed as he took it, which was perfectly understandable as that was when the Leggy Blonde walked in and I turned to walk out.

I looked at her as I passed her, looked her up and down and up again. Although she was leaner and blonder than Charlie, she had the same easy smile, which she rested on me now. And then she blushed as she took in my shock. So here she was, flesh and blood. The Leggy Blonde. A slide show of all the times I'd seen her, having an argument with Richard that first night I saw her, walking in on our lovemaking, and here in Posh House snuggled up intimately with Richard on the sofa, stroking Jean.

I looked over at Charlie. The whole thing felt like a setup, like a joke had been played on me. Why had he never told me about his sister and Richard? Why had he let me go on believing? Why had he let her go on believing—or had he not, had she been privy to things he should have shared with me?

Like Charlie, she looked and sounded as if she'd been bred

rather than brought up; like fine bloodstock, there were no rough edges, no evidence of flaws. "You must be Lola, I've heard so much about you," she said, extending a hand. How typical of her to be so civilized; how typical of her to be the one to extend the hand of friendship to the other woman—because when it came down to it, that's what I was to Sally. The competition.

And I couldn't bear her civilities, they only highlighted my incivilities. I wanted to slap her, but then again maybe underneath her good breeding she wanted to slap me. So I took her hand and shook it politely as I said, "And you must be the woman doing my job...*and* my fiancé." I couldn't help myself, the words just came out of their own accord—delivered coldly, with perfect CCC control.

I looked her in the eye, daring her to blush, but instead I was blushing myself.

"I didn't know until a couple of weeks ago and then I left him," she explained, beginning to lose her composure. "It's him. I can't seem to help it. I love him and, well, he..." I heard pain in her voice, the pain I'd experienced so much with Richard. The pain of disappointment and resignation and inevitability.

So I left because I knew I couldn't keep up the CCC thing. Only, halfway down the secret passage as the tears began to flow, I remembered Jean and had to go back in and fetch her, which was very embarrassing.

Charlie and Sally tried to stop me. Charlie even grabbed my arm. "Wait, Lola, don't go like this."

"Please, Lola, don't go," agreed Sally. "I know how you feel. I feel the same way."

I looked at her with hatred then. "No, I don't think you do," I told her, even though I suspect she did. "He was my husband," I added, as if this gave me some special status.

"I've told him I can't do it anymore, Lola. I just wanted to talk to you, to explain, to—"

"Please, Lola, stay, listen," Charlie entreated. But I left, knowing I would never go back, never stand in this room again, because now it had finally dawned on me that going back was what had landed me in this mess in the first place.

twenty-three

"…I doubt much that what I shall reveal to you can make much sense; I find my head so heavy that I cannot feel my heart. All I know is it continues to beat, though it would be better for all were it to stop. If I did say once that my love for Edward should have nothing to do with my marriage to Charles, 'twas when his carriage toward me gave me such an occasion as could justify these words.

It was my intention to charter a course of domestic felicity, for I considered my love for Charles worthy of a wife. In this I did Charles a grave injustice, for I must conclude I have no value to Edward now, at times I wonder if he knows who I am, for his hallu-

cinations are such as to render him unaware of anyone or anything."

Extract of a letter from Lady Henrietta
Posche to her sister, Elizabeth

The journey home was dominated by complicated feelings that jumbled together like a mass of slithering eels. Richard rang me soon after I'd got back into the flat.

"How's it going?" I asked brightly, giving nothing away.

"Great, but it's you I'm interested in, how are things?"

I told him I'd just got back from sorting out some final business with Charlie. It seemed slightly unreal to me that I was able to lie to him so easily, but then years of staying CCC under pressure had clearly paid off. Also, I wanted to hear what he had to say because I was absolutely certain that Sally would have called him after our meeting.

But he didn't betray himself in the slightest. He told me that he was already beginning to feel better and the Priory doctors expected him to be able to leave Friday.

"Sorry I was so short with you this morning," he explained. "But they are pretty strict about outside contact. You could be my dealer for all they know," he joked.

"Marcus?"

"What?"

Can't you even follow your own lies? I was thinking. "Nothing," I replied, feeling a surge of anger and embarrassment for the way I'd been so blind. "So you are feeling better, things going well at the Priory? Met any nice addicts?" I was speaking in a faux-jolly, nasty sort of way. I sounded like a pin being dragged down a blackboard.

But Richard appeared not to notice. "I'm missing you," he whispered sexily. "I really miss you, Lola. I'm doing this for you, for us, you know that." The saddest thing was that I truly believe if you had put Richard on a lie detector monitor at that moment it would show he was telling the truth. Because I truly believe that Richard believed all his lies— which is ironic, because despite all the evidence, I had believed all Richard's lies, as well.

I know it sounds mad knowing what I now knew. It *was* mad…but I wanted to believe him too, more than I have ever wanted to believe anything in my life. I wanted to believe him the way I had always believed him, ignoring the nagging voices of my own judgment telling me he was lying.

I watched Jean as she hopped toward her water bowl. Richard was saying something to me but it didn't seem to matter what. He was so wrong in every way and my pulse raced to tell him what I really thought of him. But instead, all I said was, "Well, you'd better get off the phone or they'll catch you. You wouldn't want to create suspicion."

"No, you're right," he agreed solemnly. "I'll call you tomorrow if I get a chance, otherwise I'll see you Friday, babe."

I pressed end. "Babe? Can you believe I loved a man who can call me babe?" I asked Jean, who was looking up at me. Her eyes seemed to brim with understanding as she hopped over and gently began humping my foot. I picked her up and held her above my head. "Oh, Jean, what have I done?" I asked her, but she wriggled around, eager to be put down again. Rabbits do their best but they are not a girl's best friend.

So I called my best friends.

Elizabeth and Clemmie met me at the Met Bar at eleven. I arrived first, unable to spend a minute longer alone in my flat. Swiping my card outside, I began to relax as I entered the familiar buzz of the deep red bar. I saw another friend, Niki, sitting with a couple of actors I had organized various parties for at Posh House, so I just said a quick hi and slipped into the booth closest to the DJ's station, and when the drinks waiter came, I ordered a Bellini. I couldn't quite define what I felt but I did feel something, a mixture of things, really: a soup of shame, shock and despair. Mostly despair.

I looked around the tables of wealthy men and women chatting. There were a few people getting down to the music and a couple kissing at one of the tables in the middle of the bar. I watched them as I sipped my Bellini and wondered how they'd met, how long they'd been together and whether they thought they'd last forever and whether they would.

There was no escaping the reality that Richard had never loved me. Worse than the reality that Richard had never loved me, though, was this: I was beginning to think that maybe, just maybe, I had never loved him. Sure, I'd been in love with the idea of love, with the idea of happily-ever-afters. I'd been in love with the idea that I could have what Kitty and Martin had; an unquestionable passion for another human being that carried on despite interruptions, a love that withstood everything—even divorce.

The girls slipped into the booth with me and ordered cosmopolitans, after which I think they were stuck for words. They'd probably already said all the things they wanted to say now. How Richard was a cokehead, a liar, a prick. There wasn't any ground we hadn't covered in the anti-Richard field and yet here they were, desperate to pick up the pieces of their girlfriend's heart—the girlfriend they'd warned was going to have her heart broken if she persisted with her obsession with Richard. But they didn't say, "We told you so."

Actually, they didn't talk about Richard or Sally or Charlie or me. Instead, we talked about old times, safe times, before all this had happened. Elizabeth started the ball rolling with how she had bumped into Clive that day.

"Clive the sherbet head?" I asked, remembering the story she had told at Aunt Camilla's funeral ball—about the one bright moment of the evening.

She nodded. "Fizz Nose himself," she joked.

Andy the barman approached our table then and handed out taster cocktails. "Something I'm working on," he explained. "See what you think," he told us as we dutifully knocked them back.

And promptly spat them out again. All of us giving Andy the barman the thumbs-down. "Not too good?"

"Andy, what is in that, it's disgusting!" I told him, taking a sip of cosmopolitan to take the taste out of my mouth.

"Yes, what's in it?" Josie asked, sniffing her glass suspiciously.

"Absinthe, vermouth, gin. I was reviving the Piccadilly cocktail, from the Savoy cocktail book."

"Well, don't," I told him firmly, "it died for a reason."

"A very good reason," Elizabeth added.

twenty-four

"Good God, what an unhappy person I am, what in-judicious dreams and fancies led me to believe that I could treat a man such as Charles in such a disoblig-ing manner. For now I can see my love for Edward for what it truly is; the reckless and selfish fantasy of a child that has prevented me from loving my hus-band as he deserved.

I have begged Charles to dispose of me as he should, please, such is my shame, yet each day he writes to me of his undying love. My darling sister, I have made the most dreadful mistake..."

Letter from Lady Henrietta Posche to her sister, Elizabeth

Over the next couple of days I gave a lot of thought to Richard and why I had believed so resolutely that I was still in love with him. Because that's the thing about the past and going back; that's the thing about memory. We remember what we choose to remember. We remember memories of memories.

I had remembered how things could have been rather than remembering how they were. Richard's cocaine usage and his lying had run like a bright acrylic thread through our time together, but I had convinced myself that if I tugged hard enough I could pull that thread out. Well, I had tugged, but all I'd succeeding in doing was pulling the fabric apart.

In the beginning he had swept me off my feet. He had loved me as no one ever had before and I was dissembled by the idea that someone could *get* me the way Richard made me feel he got me. But had I really loved him or was I just in love with the idea of his love for me, which as it turned out seemed to be fueled by cocaine and convenience more than any real affection. Maybe I did love the man I knew he could be. But he wasn't that man anymore, and the more he aged the less likely he was ever to become that man.

These were my sane thoughts.

The insane thoughts ran along the lines of: the cheating, lying, arsehole bastard, I'm going to kill him. I'm not going to sit back and allow him to overturn my life. How dare he make me vulnerable, ruin my career and destroy my friendship with Charlie.

By the time he arrived at my flat on the Friday, though, I was quite composed in a cold, murderous, vengeful, deranged sort of way.

He shouldn't be able to get away with messing up my life, I'd decided.

He should be made to pay.

By the time he rang my buzzer, everything was prepared. Jean was wearing her best Hermés ribbon, the brown nicely offsetting her eyes. I was wearing my new dress from Miss Sixty and there was a bottle of Dom on ice in the living room. On my bedside table there were several lines of the finest-quality A-grade sherbet chopped up and spread out like long lines of cocaine, on a mirror. I had placed a razor blade and straw beside them for added effect.

"Welcome back," I cheered as he walked in the door and swung me around. I noticed the bags he had with him, but didn't comment.

"Oh, Lolly, I've missed you!" he said, placing me down on his knee.

"So how was it, did you have to scrub the toilet with a toothbrush and march in line with all the other coke-heads," I asked, trying to keep an expression of fixed concern on my face, though secretly I felt that boot-camp tortures and scrubbing toilets with his toothbrush didn't come close to the punishment he deserved. I kissed him again on the nose, just narrowly suppressing an urge to bite it off.

He laughed insouciantly, no idea at all of the dangers that lay ahead. "No, it wasn't so bad actually, it was quite nice to have a break and just chill out. You know how it is."

"So it was *just* a break?" I inquired lightly. "Not perpetual abstinence then?"

"I'm not saying I'm going to hammer it like I was, but well, you know what they say…"

I raised my eyebrows suggestively. "Never say never?"

He kissed me passionately. "I was hoping you'd say that. See, you get me, Lola, that's what I love about you."

I wondered at his capacity for keeping up this playacting. Then again I wondered about my own. I was matching him step for step, lie for lie, complicit in his game. He was like a reckless poker player, so certain he held the winning hand. "In fact, as you've been such a good boy," I told him, ruffling his hair, "I've prepared a surprise for us for later. A well-done-Richard prize." I kissed him on the cheek.

"Really?" He seemed genuinely surprised. "I thought you were really against it. In fact, you were the reason I went to the Priory." It was the first time that evening that he'd looked surprised.

I opened the champagne and poured us both a glass. It was really quite remarkable the way we were both sticking to our lines in our charade, Richard pretending he was just back from a week at the Priory, me pretending I wasn't planning on murdering him. In a hideous sort of way, we were fantastically well suited. "I did think it was a bit much the way you were so coked out of your head at Aunt Camilla's funeral fete, but I don't want you going all twelve step on me either," I told him, passing him his champagne. "I presume you can still drink champagne?"

"Are you kidding?" he asked, grabbing the glass. I could almost hear the saliva rushing to his mouth. "Shall we have a toast then?"

"To Richard," I said, raising my glass. "For all your hard work getting straight."

"To Lola, for making me want to," he toasted, snaking a hand around my waist and sitting me on his knee.

I kissed him lightly then wriggled off. "Actually, Richard, I've just got to go off to the shop to get something, but I'll be back in a second."

"I'll come with you," he offered.

"No, you stay here. It's only across the road. Why don't you unpack your things," I suggested, pointing toward his luggage. Then I dashed off before he could question me further.

Once I was out of the building, I wandered down to the local shop and bought a bottle of Evian, which I took across the road to Berkeley Square and drank, watching the workers crisscrossing their way across the pathways toward their tube stations. Eventually I decided that Richard would have found my trap, and set off back to the flat.

I could hear the cries of pain from the moment I stepped out of the lift. What I found inside was not the scene Elizabeth had described when she spoke of the trick Clive had played on Damien, though.

Blood not sherbet was foaming out of Richard's nose, quite a lot of it. He was clearly in desperate pain and suddenly I was jolted out of my desire for revenge and in a state of high panic. I truly didn't know what to do. I hadn't calculated a plan B for this sort of eventuality. First I tried Elizabeth on her mobile but she didn't pick up.

Richard was still howling with pain, so I held his head under the kitchen sink and ran cold water over his nose and face to try and wash out the sherbet. The sink quickly filled with his blood, though, and I really began to despair. What if he died, what if he bled to death in my flat? What if in my effort for adolescent revenge I ended up killing him?

His eyes were bloodshot and he'd stopped crying, but I didn't take that as a good sign as he'd also gone a bit bluish. I envisaged calling an ambulance and describing what I'd done. I thought of calling the Priory but remembered that was never real, just part of the elaborate parlor game of head-fuck we'd been playing with one another.

So I called Charlie, easygoing, capable, good-in-a-crisis Charlie, and told him what I'd done. Richard was lying on the floor in a pool of blood, moaning, and Jean was hopping around him looking very worried. What if he choked on his own blood?

I was still gabbling away when he told me he'd be with me "in a jiff."

Only Charlie would respond to a cry for help with a phrase like that, but he was true to his word and minutes later he arrived. He buzzed the door and asked me if I could get Richard down in the lift on my own. I sobbed that I couldn't and that in fact I was pretty sure Richard was dying, so he came into the building and moments later he was crouched beside Richard, who was now in a substantial pool of blood.

He dialed 999. "Ahm, hello, look, we've got a bit of situation, chap in his thirties, seems to have snorted a few lines of sherbet. Lot of blood, bit of a mess, actually."

Jean hopped over to me and I picked her up. She had a little bit of blood on her paws from where she'd gone over to see how Richard was.

I nuzzled my face in her fur while Charlie replied to further questions. "Yes, that's right, sherbet, you know, the white sweet powder stuff you lick off a licorice straw…yes, I know it's a sweet…well, the chap's lost consciousness and there's a fair amount of blood… No, obviously you're not meant to sniff it."

Minutes later we'd managed to get Richard into Charlie's Aston Martin and were tearing through the streets on our way to Chelsea & Westminster Hospital.

twenty-five

Your life is your poem. Each action, each decision, becomes an immortal word or phrase within the verse of one's life. It is essential therefore to decide at the earliest age the style of poem your life will depict: a poem of love, a poem of loss, a poem of tragedy, a poem extolling virtue perhaps.

From the moment you make the decision on your poem's theme, no movement, no word can be too inconsequential to ignore. The way you catch a pretty gentleman's eye in the reflection of a looking glass, the way you tilt your head when you are in conversation, the way you laugh, the way you hold your glass, the way you love, the way you bear your sorrows, your losses, all these things form the phrases and verses in the poem of your life.

Extract from *Hold Your Glass Like a Poem*
by Lady Henrietta Posche

The hospital staff saw Richard the moment we brought him in. Charlie and I struggled to complete the official forms, and after a long wait a young female doctor came out and spoke to us as if we were his parents. She explained that the blood loss had looked worse than it was and that Richard's cocaine habit had been the reason he'd had such a marked reaction to the sherbet, and that casualty staff were rinsing his sinuses out, but that we could see him soon.

Charlie sat with me under the cold lights on the hard hospital chairs. We didn't really say much, although I could just imagine what he thought of me.

"I suppose Sally won't be too pleased with me," I suggested as we waited for the doctors to report back on Richard's nose job.

"I don't know. I've told her what he's like, she knows." He

squeezed my knee without looking at me. "She's got to deal with this in her own way."

I took his hand in mine and held it. "I hope she deals with it better than me."

And then he lifted my hand to his lips and I thought he might be about to kiss it, but instead he squeezed it as he looked me in the eye.

"Thank you," I told him lamely.

"Anytime."

"I'm not really intending to serve up sherbet in lieu of cocaine anytime soon, you know." I smiled.

"No, probably for the best," he agreed, nodding his assent. "But you knew it was sherbet, though?" he asked.

"Well, yes, but I didn't know it would do *that* to him. I just wanted to, well, be horrible to him because…" The excuse hung there unspoken.

"I see." Charlie was looking at the linoleum floor. "He seemed to find it all pretty horrible, so objective achieved, I guess."

I nodded. "He told me he was in the Priory."

"I know, you said. Sally knows, too. He told her he was booking himself in there today."

"I'm sorry about Sally," I told him truthfully. "I feel really bad now."

"Well, if it's any comfort, she feels really bad too."

"About being taken in by Richard, and his lies. What did she say when he said he was booking himself into the Priory?"

Charlie looked sad as he shook his head and shrugged his shoulders. "She said, perhaps he will after this."

"Oh."

"No, she told him to piss off and hung up."

"Good on Sally, more sense than me then. Are you going to tell her about the sherbet?"

He smiled. "I think I'll find it difficult to resist."

I nodded, suppressing a smile of my own as the doctor came out and told us we could see Richard. I looked at Charlie and Charlie looked at me. Then I looked at my hand and saw it was still in his. I didn't want to let go of his hand and so I didn't, and so we went in to see Richard together—holding hands.

Richard looked truly buggered.

"Sorry about the, erm, you know, the sherbet. I meant for it to be a joke…obviously not a very funny one as it turned out."

Richard nodded feebly and closed his eyes, and after a while Charlie motioned with his head toward the door and we left. We were still holding hands and I was worrying about the part where we'd have to stop. Would it be in the lift? Would it be when we were getting into the car? I tried to imagine how we could manage to get into the car while holding hands. I pictured us struggling to shuffle over the seats, and the gear stick. It would be quite hard, and then, of course, reversing out of our parking space would be very tricky while holding hands. I pictured us driving up the Kings Road and around Hyde Park, Charlie negotiating all the turns and bends while still holding my hand.

It seemed unlikely, though.

In the lift he took both my hands and, ignoring the white-suited men with the cart, he kissed me on the lips and I kissed him back and my heart pounded so hard my tummy did a little flip. The white-suited men got out of the lift with their trolley and the doors closed, but we carried on kissing.

Charlie pulled away first. He was smiling. "Quite funny, though, the sherbet business. I mean, when we think of it later. Obviously not the blood, that was pretty nasty." Then he went back to kissing me.

"No, we shan't mention the blood," I agreed when the lift finally stopped and the doors opened out onto the car park.

Halfway toward the car he kissed me some more, which made up a bit for having to let go of his hand so we could climb into the car. And then he kissed me again at the traffic lights. I liked the way our mouths fitted over one another.

"I've wanted to do that for so long," he told me as we drove onto the Kings Road.

"You never mentioned it," I replied, placing my hand over his hand as it rested on the gear stick.

"You never seemed the type," he teased.

"The type for kissing, you mean?"

"Oh no, you always seemed the type for kissing. You just didn't seem the type to kiss me."

"What?"

"Well, you were always so professional. So calm, cool and collected. I never saw a chink."

"A chink?"

"A gap, you know, a chance to get my kiss in."

We were driving along the park now. "So you waited until I was an emotional mess, jobless with a boyfriend OD'd on sherbet before you made your move?"

"It was the first time I saw a chink," he said, a grin spreading across his face. He turned to me at the lights at Hyde Park Corner.

"A kiss-a-girl-when-she's-down strategy, then."

"I prefer to call it a damsel-in-distress strategy."

That night we stayed in with the bottle of champagne that Richard and I had never properly started. We called up Scotts and had oysters sent round. Convenience food, as Kitty would call it. Then Charles announced (right at the point where things were getting rather steamy), "The walls are closing in a bit here, what say we head back to the House?"

Slightly harassed that he was disentangling himself from me, right at the point I wanted him to entangle himself in me, I agreed. I watched from the sofa as he gathered up Jean's kit and popped her in her bag.

"Besides, I have to move the car," he remembered, referring to the draconian Westminster Council parking inspectors.

He pulled me up and, taking his hand, I submitted to his desire to be out of my flat and back at work, mollified by the way he stroked my leg on the drive there.

Carl smiled knowingly as we walked in hand in hand, giving the whole event a teenlike atmosphere. Then as we reached the door to the secret passage, Charlie went into the spy mode we'd been in the night I spotted Richard with Hamish and Jeremy.

"Quick, in here, no one's looking," he hissed, pushing me through the panel.

Scuttling up the narrow wooden staircase, I found it hard not to laugh. Charlie kept prodding me and talking like an agent on a mission. Then, just as I went to push through the secret passage into his office, he stopped me and pushed against the black brick wall…or rather what I thought was a black brick wall. The wall fell away easily. Charlie flicked a switch and we were standing at the entrance of an eighteenth-century bedroom.

I looked at Charlie quizzically. "Her Ladyship's private bedchamber," he explained as he lifted me in his arms and carried me to the finely carved oak four-poster.

"But I thought…" I began.

"My office? No, that was her public bedchamber, a mere front to the far more desirable secret chamber."

I giggled at the madness as well as the splendor of the room. "So this is where she brought her lover. What was his name?"

"Edward? No, this, my darling Lola, is where she brought her husband, Charles." He deposited me on the bed and looked at me. "Do you know I have had this mad idea of doing this, of bringing you here to this chamber and seeing you on this bed since the day you first walked into my office to apply for the job."

"You're a sick man, Lord Charles Mannox MacField Orbington," I told him, using his full title for the first time.

"Anyway, let me deposit Jean in front of the news in my office. I'll be back in a jiff," he promised, but I wasn't risking him out of sight just yet, so I grabbed him and pulled him down onto me for a long warm kiss I hoped would never end.

Jean would jolly well have to go without her headlines.

★ ★ ★ ★ ★

In all probability Edward died of natural causes, although no death certificate was ever issued. There is no formal record of his death, and there is no grave.

A letter to Elizabeth from Henrietta describes how she found him cold in her bed in the morning, Lady Posche having spent the night in her husband's chamber. To have called a doctor and attempted to hush up the incident could quite possibly have ruined the social standing of both Lord and Lady Posche and greatly disrupted the lives of their children. It appears that it was Lord Posche himself who came up with the macabre plan to brick Edward's corpse inside a cupboard within the secret staircase.

In this way the marriage of Charles and Henrietta was finally cemented in their grisly conspiracy to conceal her dead lover's remains. Edward had no family and had long since been cut by polite society. Archives and anecdotal evidence suggest that his disappearance was met with disinterest, the Countess of Harlow once remarking at a ball, "The man lived the life of a blaggard and no doubt died a blaggard!" little knowing that his remains were bricked into the very passageway of the house through which he had secretly come and gone unnoticed for so many years.

His name is never mentioned in correspondence again by either Charles or Henrietta.

The remains of Edward were exhumed after the death of Henrietta, who revealed their actions to her sister before she died.

Secret Passage to the Past:
A Biography of Lady Henrietta Posche
by Michael Carpendum

Join the authors of Red Dress Ink
this holiday season!

Scenes from a Holiday

On sale November 2005

Bestselling Red Dress Ink authors Laurie Graff,
Caren Lissner and Melanie Murray make the holiday season even merrier with three unforgettable
holiday stories starring three fabulous women.

**RED
DRESS
INK**
™

www.RedDressInk.com

RDIVA537TR

On sale November 2005

Hardly Working
by Betsy Burke

Lessons on how to catch a snooze, a fab deal on eBay and a new boyfriend— all on company time.

PR chick Dinah Nichols and the rest of the gang at Green World International have never taken themselves or their work too seriously—until now. When head office takes notice, Dinah has to spin her PR magic and work hard to make this "hardly working" crew shine.

RED DRESS INK™

Available wherever trade paperbacks are sold.

The Sex Was Great But...

by Tyne O'Connell

A novel about celebrities, sex and secrets

Holly Klein is an A-list celebrity with an army
of assistants. Leo Monroe is a smart-talking DJ
from the streets. She lives on Mulholland Drive;
he lives on...someone else's sofa. But when
Leo rescues Holly from a mugger, their
two worlds collide, literally.